matrix

an anthology of **new writing**

Huge thanks to the following for their help and guidance: Mike Oakes, Andy Vargo, Phoebe Phillips, Jon Cook, Terence Blacker, Anastacia Tohill and Vicky Winteringham.
We would also like to thank Anglia Television and The Esmee Fairbairn Trust for their generous support of this project.

Lines from T.S. Eliot's *The Waste Land* reproduced with permission
from Faber and Faber Ltd.
Lines from Brian Patten's "Her Song" and "Frogs in Woods" reproduced
with permission from Harper Collins Ltd.

Produced, designed and edited by Kaylois Henry and Alan Cowley
with assistance from Tracy Chevalier, Martyn Bedford, Cormac Mac Cárthaigh,
Bonnie Powell and Judith Rawnsley.
Preface by Matthew Humphreys

Cover Art by Caroline Davis.
Cover design by Kaylois Henry and Alan Cowley.

matrix

new writing **from the University of East Anglia Creative Writing MA Programme**

matrix

Published by the Centre for the Creative and Performing Arts
University of East Anglia

Typeset in Bembo.

Printed by The Ipswich Book Company Ltd., Ipswich, Suffolk.

1994. Copyright reserved by the individual writers.

All rights reserved. No part of this publication may be reproduced, stored in a retrieval system, or transmitted in any form by any means electronic, mechanical, photocopying, recording or otherwise, without prior permission of the authors.

British Library Cataloguing in Publication Data. A catalogue record for this book is available from the British Library.

ISBN 0 9515009 5 3

All stories are works of fiction. Any resemblance to persons living or dead is purely coincidental.

Contents

Preface   vii

Martyn Bedford
from *Acts of Revision*   13

Kaylois Henry
Skin Life   25

Matthew Humphreys
from *The Feeders*   41

B. Azab Powell
The Object at Rest   59

Alan Cowley
Danny Delight   77

Susan Elderkin
Letter from Earth   91

Martha Perkins
Scenes Without a Marriage   99

James Clatworthy
A Memory of Gating   117

Cormac Mac Cárthaigh
The Disappearance of Miss Effie Skinner — 125

Claire Ingham
Her Song — 141

Martin Aaron
from *Reptiles* — 153

Judith Rawnsley
from *Into the Light* — 163

Stephanie Newell
Circles and Stops — 179

Jeremy Page
Mise-En-Abyme — 189

Nicky Röhl
Celebration — 205

Ralph Goldswain
from *Natural Curriculum* — 219

Tracy Chevalier
You, She and Me — 235

Mark Radcliffe
Giving Head — 243

Preface

Dreaming in Public

Leaving aside the fact that we have no idea who you are, readers — that we don't know why you bought this book, or if you have bought any of the previous anthologies; leaving aside that these writers have as much in common as Mama Cass and Carpenter; that introductions are considered pointless unless they have the blessing of a famous name, a name for the cover, a name that in theory (or the lazy truisms of marketing that pass for theory) will attract you a damn sight more than a disparate group of nobodies dreaming in public (albeit in a more interesting and diverse way than is often found in the orgasmic dreams and nightmares of the somebodies) — we would like to say a few words about this anthology.

Collections dedicated to the launching of new writers have, almost by accident, created a literary genre known as "New Writing." Unlike most genres, from science fiction to metafiction, it is composed of texts with no common ground. This alone distinguishes it from "contemporary" writing, another umbrella referring to writing in keeping with the times, whatever they may be. The two are not mutually exclusive — the one thing that the writers in this anthology have in common is that none of them are dead. Contemporary writing is simply the framework that New Writing operates both within and against, which explains the practice of snaring an established author to write the introduction. A famous name is more than a marketing ploy, more than a few paragraphs before the stories: it is a pretext by which Rose Tremain or Malcolm Bradbury says to you, the reader, that we are to be taken seriously. It is a printed invitation allowing us to gate-crash the publishing party and contextualing New Writing within the contemporary.

New Writing is the most recent product of literature's ongoing search for innovation, and any attempt to define it merely illustrates our evolution from the 'schools' of the previous centuries and the beginning of this one. Whether or not the movements of Romanticism, Surrealism, et al, accurately represented historically their diversity of writers, accepted wisdom has it that they were all characterised by a common aesthetic goal, a similarity of purpose. But this is not the path we find ourselves following today. Now our only common feature is our difference: we can agree upon neither a shared history nor a future. But this eclectic labeling of writers threatens to turn New Writing into alchemy — having sold it as the great hope of literature, having passed its discoveries from critic to critic, it needs but one dissenter to point out that this new gold is in fact the same old lead, and for the search to be set in motion again.

There is the risk of new writers being picked up as novelties and then discarded like a pair of platform shoes. While the quest for newness focuses on the laudable project of discovering new voices, the question of what to do with that voice once it is up and shouting has yet to be addressed. We ask of the voice that it speak authentically, that it employ a distinctive accent in the sex-race-class chorus. But a nagging paranoia wonders whether the voices are being heard by only one ear — if the diversity of new writers is reflected in the somewhat homogeneous book-buying public. The crucial question, however, is if the voice will ever have the opportunity to address its own constituency. Will the new writers ever find their new readers?

A debate on audience is long overdue, though here it can be no more than an aside. But still we return to the opening question: Who are you? Who is it that reads new writing? Are you an aspiring writer, a relative or friend of a contributor, a reviewer, an agent, or just Malcolm Bradbury? You are being introduced to us, but will we ever meet you?

For many of us, *Matrix* represents our first move. The first gut-twisting time we step forward and open our mouths. Up until now, we have been living the nebulous existence of the writer-to-be. In the past, 'matrix' was a synonym for womb — something motherly, enclosed and protected. The environment that protects the new so that it can grow.

With this in mind, we would like to clear up a misunderstanding about the teaching of Creative Writing. A publisher at a "meet and greet" in Norwich asked one of us, "So you think you can be taught to write, do you?" A distrustful visiting writer seemed to think we had punctuation classes and dialogue workshops. To his credit, he at least listened when told otherwise; mind you, he was told otherwise over a bottle of scotch and a gun. You see, the voices in this anthology were not acquired on the MA course. Voice cannot be taught. It is a thing of the vocal cords, something inborn. It is all a matter of expression, the learning of the mouth and the tongue to clarify the speech. To make the voice something worth listening to.

In the final analysis, all that matters is the quality of the stories. The bars of the matrix may serve to contain as well as protect, and between them are eighteen stories desperate to escape into the world. Where they may eat free lunches. Where they may steal cigarettes from agents.

Where they may be read.

Martyn Bedford

From *Acts of Revision*

Martyn Bedford was born in Croydon, South London, in 1959. He has worked as a journalist on provincial newspapers since 1980 and has written two (unpublished) novels as well as a number of short stories. The following is the opening section of his third novel, *Acts of Revision*.

prologue: 1 *the preface or introduction to a literary work*
2 *(the actor delivering) a speech, often in verse, addressed to the audience at the beginning of a play*
3 *an introductory or preceding event or development*

They burned her.
It was a cold morning, January; twelve months ago. It was cold but the burning of her was not for warmth.

They gave me a small urn and we went outside where the sky was grey-white and our breaths hung in the air like visible whispers. We followed a gravel path to the flower beds. A rose bush, brown and spiky bare, was indicated and I knelt before it in the frost. Her name had been printed in black on a plastic label stuck in the hard soil. Marion Lyn. They'd misspelt the surname: one 'n' instead of two.

I removed the lid from the urn and took a handful of ashes. I uncurled my fingers. The ashes, distressed by the wind, made silver confetti in people's hair and left smudges on their dark coats as they brushed themselves down.

Lower, someone said. Hold them lower before you let go.

I took another handful, raised it to my mouth. The flakes were smooth and silky; they dissolved on my tongue and made my throat dry when I tried to swallow. Wafery fragments of her, and of coffin. They tasted of nothing.

Gregory, don't. Here.

Hands on my shoulders, and I was being made to stand up, to come away. Someone released my grip on the urn and it fell on to the whitened grass at the path's edge. An arm at my back, stiff scratchy hair against the side of my face, catching on the stubble where I hadn't shaved. A woman's bony hand wiping my lips with a handkerchief. Smell of perfume and of lipstick.

Cry, love. That's it. You cry as much as you want.

Martyn Bedford

I wasn't crying. The noise was not the noise my throat makes whenever I cry.

Sandwiches. Cheddar cheese and tomato, fish paste and cucumber, ham, sliced white bread. Packets of crisps tipped into glass bowls. Cups of tea. People mumbling between the silences. I sat watching them eat, waiting for them to go. Auntie, who'd seen to the food, was the last. She washed up and returned all the chairs to their proper places, she put on her coat and scarf and gloves and hat. She said things on the front doorstep, she said Marion would be with the Lord now. She pressed me to her, then she left and I closed the door. The house hushed.

Upstairs, in my room, I took the notepad and pencils from the locked drawer in my desk and turned to the first blank page. I wrote down the day and the date. I drew the boxes — six, in two sequences of three — then the scenes, then I did the colouring. No speech bubbles, no thought bubbles; that way you have to make the pictures tell the story. People dressed in black sitting in rows in a chapel; a coffin disappearing behind a curtain (hard, sketching the curtain to suggest motion); flames: oranges, yellows, reds, thick black spirals for smoke; people clustered round a rose bush in full bloom; a man kneeling, dispersing ashes at the base of the bush; the man crying, tears light blue against the pink of his face. On the facing page I sketched a beautiful dark-haired woman — upright, arms by her side, dressed in a summer frock; her head tilting upwards and feet pointing down sharply like a ballerina's. Her eyes were closed. She was ascending into heaven; only I didn't know how to draw heaven, so it became a picture of a woman floating in the air. Adrift.

*

My name is Gregory Lynn. I am 35 years old. I am an orphan, a bachelor, an only child from the age of four-and-a-half. I have one brown eye and one green.

I no longer have the notepad in which I recorded my mother's funeral. I don't have any of the books anymore. They've been confiscated for use in evidence, though it is unclear whether this will be of most benefit to the prosecution or the defence. My barrister is more preoccupied with their illustration of my 'personality' than in any question of artistic merit. Their significance is also lost on him: at least, he perceives a different significance. I am quite sane, but these cartoon strips, apparently, might enable him to suggest otherwise. Mitigation, he calls it. If this man is on my side then I am curious to hear the case for the Crown. I asked him if any of the drawings would appear in the newspapers during or after the trial and he assured me they wouldn't. But I remain hopeful. They found 57 of the books in my room, each containing 150 pages, spanning 23 years and six months of my life (the last 12 months being the most interesting from the court's point of view, I imagine). There were dozens of notepads and loose sheets besides these: sketches, paintings, collages, my collection of scrapbooks; in drawers or cupboards or boxes or under the bed or on top of the wardrobe or on the floor or pinned to the walls. And, of course, they discovered the maps, photographs and files, the accounts of each of the incidents; although a conviction would be inevitable with or without such incriminating exhibits. Motive and state-of-mind may be hard to establish, but the forensic evidence is incontestable. Fact: I did it. Me, Gregory Lynn (orphan, bachelor, only child from the age of four-and-a-half). I was there, the eye-witnesses confirm this, the tests prove it. I did it. The who what? where? when? and how? are matters of fact, the only unanswered question is: why? But, as far as the court is concerned, 'why?' is not relevant to the verdict, merely to the sentence. A mitigating factor. The irony will be of no consolation to him now, but Mr Boyle was right: it all comes down to facts, to logic, to science; everything, always. It is facts which eliminate doubt. Nevertheless I intend, against the advice of my barrister, to plead not guilty. This is not to deny the commission of the acts from which the charges arise, it is rather that I have no idea what they mean when they talk of guilt and innocence as if they were opposites, as if they were mutually exclusive. I have one brown eye and one green.

Miss McMahon would have approved of the above. The style is not too grandiose, and I have demonstrated a quick, firm grasp of the subject — the rudiments of the legal process — and its nomenclature. Long words, used appropriately and correctly spelt. She would most definitely approve. The point is, if something is important or interesting to me I immerse myself in it. I absorb. I learn. If it isn't, I don't. This doesn't make me unintelligent. Teachers (not Miss McMahon, but others — Mr Boyle, for instance) would tell me I ought to work at my weaker subjects, to knuckle down, to fulfil my potential. What they meant was: you can't switch intelligence on and off like a light. And I think: the fuck you can't. Look at the way I planned and carried out the series of acts. Originality and creativity which Miss McMahon and, it goes without saying, Mr Andrews would recognise and appreciate, harnessed with a precision, calculation and methodical thoroughness that Mr Boyle and all the other bastards wouldn't credit me with being capable of.

Mr Andrews.

He has seen the drawings, the cartoons. He sees their artistic merit, and he sees beyond it to their significance. He is closer to understanding the 'why?' than anyone, apart from me. He doesn't talk in terms of victim and perpetrator, guilt and innocence. He knows, as I do, that they seep into one another as the past seeps into the present. He knows, as I do, that the swathes of books and papers taken from my room contain the real evidence in this case, even though they are unadorned with hard facts. Mr Andrews, however, is to be a witness for the prosecution.

★

Alone in the house, in the hush. Drawings done and no need to lock the pad away in the drawer now. No need to keep to my room anymore. Even so, I stayed there all afternoon and evening with the door closed.

As if she was still there.

In the night I descended to the kitchen for toast and jam and a glass of milk. That was the last of the jam, and the loaf was nearly finished. Plenty of milk. Mum forgot to cancel it before she died. I would have to go out, to the shops. I would have to go outside. I drew a picture of outside. It was a blank box, a box filled with white. l drew the inside of a supermarket, Auntie carrying a wire basket heavy with tins and packets and jars. Sometimes by drawing something I can make it happen, I make it come true. Besides, Auntie had told me she'd pop round in a day or two, make sure I was all right. See if there was anything I needed. It was one of the things she'd said on the doorstep when she left. In my head, I told her I'd sooner fucking starve than have her lipstick here. Her perfume.

I drank my milk and went to Mum's bedroom. Not familiar. The bed was made, the thin yellow counterpane pulled up over the pillows and tucked in tight. The room was cold and smelled of stale smoke. On the dressing table I found her perfume in a glass bottle the shape and size of a cigarette lighter. She used to dab it behind her ears and on the inside of one wrist and then rub her wrists together. When it was in the bottle the perfume was the colour of whisky, but on her skin it had no colour at all. I removed the cap and fragranced my hands, my face, my neck.

In the morning, the day after the burning, the phone rang. I didn't answer it.

I made sure both doors were locked and bolted and checked the catches on all the windows. Then I went to Mum's room again. I went to every room in the house. All of them, except my bedroom, the kitchen and the bathroom, were unfamiliar. I wandered from room to room; at first not touching anything, just sitting on a chair, a sofa, a bed, or on the floor. On the floor was best because the room looked bigger, the ceiling would be higher and the windows would stretch and the furniture would become tall,

Acts of Revision

like when you are a child. Sitting on the floor you can make yourself smaller. In this way the rooms became like I remembered them. I stood up. I touched things: a china dog, a magazine of knitting patterns, a yellow vase (empty), a pair of pink slippers, a black-and-white photograph in a metal frame. I looked at the photograph. We were in swimming costumes, standing in an open-air paddling pool. Janice was holding Mum's right hand and I was holding her left. My head came up to her thigh. I was squinting because of the sun. Dad must've taken the picture, you could see his shadow on the water if you looked closely. 'Butlins, Bognor Regis, 1962', written in biro in the top left-hand corner, where the sky was. There were other photographs, on a shelf in Mum's bedroom. One of me on my own, in school uniform; Mum and Dad on their wedding day; Janice, skipping. She had one sock pulled up and the other round her ankle.

Janice went away when she was seven and came back as a baby. Then she went away again.

The phone rang a second time. It was Auntie.
Gregory?
Nn.
Hello, Gregory?
I don' t
I hung up. When the phone rang again I didn't answer it. I went up to my room and drew a picture of Auntie talking into the mouthpiece, saying my name over and over.

Auntie came. Uncle was with her, dressed as a bus driver. When they gave up thumping the door and calling my name and started peering through the windows, I let them in. He was angry but when he went to speak Auntie stopped him. She whispered, but I heard her.
Leave him. It's Marion.

*

Miss McMahon taught me the art of words. Mr Andrews taught me the art of meaning. He taught me about proportion and perspective. He used to say: never confuse proportion with quantity, or perspective with relativity. Art is not an exact science, Gregory. I've given this a great deal of thought recently and I'm not certain I agree with him. Art isn't a science at all. They are opposites, as Mr Andrews and Mr Boyle are opposites. Were.

When I try to discuss this with my barrister he says our time would be more usefully spent in focusing on the matter in hand.
What if this is the matter in hand?

He ignores this. He wants me to start at the beginning, and to speak slowly and clearly for the benefit of the solicitor, whose pen is poised over the notebook resting on her lap. I smile. She looks away. I wonder why the barrister and I get to sit across the desk from one another when the only person taking notes has nothing to lean on.

Can we begin, please?

I start to speak. The problem is that my idea of the beginning is not the same as his. He tells me to stop, to confine my contribution to what is relevant; to the specifics. He proposes a method: he will ask questions and I will answer them. This is called legal aid. He leans forward, elbows on the desk; he becomes avuncular.

Gregory, my only concern is with the issues which have a direct bearing on your case.

I think: I was involved in my case before you were and shall continue to be involved with it long after you've gone. What I say is: tell me, why do you fasten your bundles of casenotes with pink ribbon?

At the conclusion of the interview we shake hands and I am escorted to another room. In some respects it is similar to my room at home: private, secure. I'm assured that at a later stage in the legal process (post-trial, pre-sentence) I shall have the opportunity to co-operate in the preparation of a social inquiry report. It is then, assisted by a suitably qualified professional, that I can raise any 'peripheral matters'; to substantiate the mitigation. To begin at the real beginning, I take this to mean. I have spent time in the company of suitably qualified professionals. None would recognise a real beginning if it came up and bit them in the bollocks.

*

After the visit with Uncle, she came round every day for a while. She cleaned, she hoovered; she brought food. I gave her money out of Mum's purse. Which was my money. The money in the bank, the building society, the post office, that had become mine too. Not much, Auntie reckoned, but enough to cover the rent and bills and keep me for a good few months. The house belonged to the council. She wasn't sure what would happen now there was just one of us, but what they didn't know couldn't hurt them.

You stay here 'til someone tells you different.

That was me, the solitary tenant. If any of Mum's customers phoned I told them she couldn't do their hair because she was dead.

A week after the burning I started an inventory of the house. Every ornament, every vase, every book, every towel, every chair, every cushion, every dishcloth, every spoon, every clock, every plate, every photograph. I listed them in a scrapbook. I drew a picture of each item alongside its number and title. I drew grid maps of each room and gave every item a map reference. It took days. When I'd finished I could go where I liked — any room, any cupboard; even the unfriendly ones had become familiar.

On the last day I went into the loft (room H). The light didn't work. I fetched a torch (item D 17) from the cupboard under the stairs (grid ref. D-H5). The loft was the most unfriendly room of all. I pointed the torch. Cardboard boxes, old carpets, a suitcase, toys, a table-lamp, empty picture frames. Dust everywhere, and spiders' webs; a chink of light where one of the roof tiles was missing. A water tank so big I couldn't light it all up at once. Some of the toys looked familiar: an Action Man with no arms, a blue car and stacked sections of Scalextric track, a painting-by-numbers kit. I remembered to walk on the beams so my feet wouldn't go through the floor. Between the beams there were rolls of orangey-coloured glass-fibre matting that came away in candyfloss clumps when I picked at it. It felt scratchy and went on feeling scratchy even when I'd let go of it. I could see bits glinting when I shone the torch on the palm of my hand. I was never allowed in the loft on my own, but dad used to let me come up with him if he had to do anything to the tank or put away some junk. The light used to work then.

Now, the loft was too small. My head banged against the wooden rafters unless I stooped or kept to the middle, where the roof was highest. The dust made me sneeze and cough and made my eyes sting when I moved anything. I sat on a beam and went through the cases and boxes one at a time, took each item out in turn and held it in the torchlight before entering it on the inventory. The locks on the suitcase were rusted and I had to press hard to make them click open. Old bedding: a quilt made of knitted squares of wool, striped nylon sheets that smelled of damp. The first box split as I tried to drag it closer. It had 'Weetabix' printed on the sides. It was full of games and jigsaw puzzles: Totopoly, Chartbuster, Wembley, a ludo set, snakes and ladders. Some jigsaw pieces were loose in the bottom of the box, along with two dice, a plastic racehorse with a number 6 on its side, and a card saying Manchester United. There was a photograph of Tony Blackburn on the front of the Chartbuster box. Someone had given him a moustache and glasses and a speech bubble saying: "Hi, I'm a wanker."

I pushed the box to one side and pulled the other one in front of me. A pile of Woman's Own and Woman's Realm magazines, a mail order catalogue and glossy brochures full of photographs of women's hairstyles. Underneath all these was a plain plastic carrier bag. I lifted it out of the box and shone the torch inside. Exercise books. Some with pink covers, some with green. I thought they were my old school books, but when I pulled them out I found they were end-of-term reports. There were nine of them, winter and summer; the pink ones were from my primary school and the green ones from my senior school. I sorted them into date order: December 1966 to December 1974. Several were missing. The cover of each report bore the name of the school, the school badge, the name of the borough education committee, my name (in ink) and the words: 'This Book is the property of the School, and must be returned to the Head Master after each report has been signed.' Inside, the pages were thin, oniony, scrawled with handwritten biro in blue, black, red. I read them. I read them by torchlight. I read for so long the batteries started to go and the small circle of light dimmed from white to yellow to dull orange and I had to strain my eyes to make out the words. I read about me, and what the teachers said. And I remembered.

*

A beginning. Beginnings within a beginning, at least. Still not the start of it all, if such a moment can ever be isolated and identified, but a clue. Something which may be deciphered by those who do not care to be constrained by the terms 'irrelevant', 'specific'; by the science of facts.

Those reports were about me, Gregory Lynn (orphan, bachelor, only child from the age of four-and-a-half). They told of what I was and what I became, they contained the story of this transition. With my one brown eye and my one green eye, I read those reports; I read the names of those who had written them and I remembered their faces. I saw them, the teachers. I saw what they had done. My barrister has also read the reports. He fails, naturally, to perceive the connection between them and the incidents. That is, he perceives my making of a connection, but not the connection as such. I quibble with him, but he is insistent.

The court will not be persuaded to accept that these were 'legitimate acts of revenge', if I may borrow your description. Nor shall I attempt to persuade it of this on your behalf.

Acts of revision is what I said. Ask her, she wrote it down.

The solicitor looks at the barrister, then at me. Her face is flushed. She clears her throat before speaking.

Why don't you explain that subtle distinction to Mrs Boyle?

Mr Patrick, Mrs Davies-White, Miss McMahon, Mr Teja, Mr Hutchinson, Mr Andrews, Mr Boyle. Tracking them down was the most difficult aspect. Some were easy to find, others required a greater degree of ingenuity.

When I had finished in the loft, I took the reports to my bedroom. I made a large wallchart and wrote each name and subject on it in block capitals, leaving space for any additional information and photographs. There would have to be photographs. I opened files. I went to the newsagent and stationery shop on the corner; it wasn't far, I was only outside for twelve minutes. I bought maps — one of Greater London and one of the United Kingdom — and taped them to the wall. I bought felt-tip pens, pencils, folders, a 12in/30cm ruler, a pad of ruled A4 paper and a pad of unruled. I bought a packet of coloured pins and selected seven different colours, one for each of them. Then, I began.

Kaylois Henry

Skin Life

Kaylois Henry was born in Manchester, Jamaica, in 1967, but has spent most of her days running the streets of Miami. For the past five years, she has been a journalist for the St. Petersburg Times (Florida). Her fondest wish is for a full-page spread in *Esquire's* "Women We Love" section.

D︎ays of late have contained nothing. Heat and dust swell and ebb in a daily tide through town. Homes seem to move two steps to the right of reality in the rising haze of mirage. Bodies are cast in shiny brown and dripping clothes, heavy to movement, when they do move. Most folks have taken to sitting out in their back porches, trying to catch a bit of the breeze, fanning themselves. Language comes in languid lies and somnolent speaking, words laying round waiting for a nudge to move them, then only just a bit.

Yanahnome is on her front step alone, listening to the nothing. Her isolation is professional, her withdrawal personal. She watches dust swirl on a bit of breeze, rise up a foot or two, pause and settle back, still tethered. She wishes the day to hurry along, to bring on the cool night. That's when she flies.

There are songs then, lyrics of all the world, singing of secret selves, welcoming with cool open arms, promising fast-paced things. The songs are nearly too beautiful to hear, aren't meant for human ear. But when she flies she is beyond, she is spirit.

The bit of breeze brings a snippet of memory: swooping and diving with the songs, raised on their thermals, floating above the village where she is set apart and is part, looking down. And pity. How awful it must be for them, stuck in those weighted skin cages. Skin is poison, hindering the soul with its bars of bone and muscle and skin, the virus of humanity in the blood. The body means death, the wind tells her. She believes.

"Yanahnome..."

The knock and the voice at the back door are both tentative. The professional apartness has been broached. It is daylight and heat again and

Yanahnome is firmly entrenched in her skin. Time to go to work.

"Enter daughtah. What trouble brings thee?"

The girl is barely 15, tall, gangly, awkward. But the yellow glow from her soul nearly overwhelms the small home. Yanahnome hardly recognize s Iona before her in the halo. Nearly five years since the last seeing — when fever claimed a mother, and tragedy a daughter. Something else, half-remembered, hovers at the edge of knowing but flits away from a conscious grasp.

There is also something immediately familiar in her stance. The downward gaze, the jittery side-to-side steps, it's an all too familiar language.

"What man troubles you so?" she asks.

Iona's eyes open wide in surprise . You must be a seer, the look says. A smile plays on Yanahnome's lips. Belief is so easy.

"Loxley, the carpenter's son," she says, sitting. "Every time I see him, my body burns so." A pause. A swallow. "It hurts to see him. How can a man make a woman ache so?"

Yanahnome doesn't answer. Iona doesn't want an answer, not really. Yanahnome waits for the rest.

"But he don't see me!" Iona continues. "He teases me about being too long. Calls me 'giraffe legs' and 'tree'. He calls me 'little sistah.' 'How my little sistah, this day?' he say. I don't feel like his sistah."

Yanahnome waits for the inevitable request. She can almost mouth it.

"Make him love me."

Yanahnome grimaces inwardly. What a fool choice is this! Loxley is a known weyfadeau. Iona is the second woman in as many months to ask for such a love formula for he. Yanahnome wants to tell her how the tiny span of consummation will bring triple the pain, to nourish her bright light without that man. But skin makes you fiery, forgetful, foolish. She doesn't say anything.

Instead, Yanahnome gives her the nine bags of sugar and magnetic dust, soaked in jockey club cologne; tells her how to wrap them with thread, calling his name with each twist; shows her where to place the magic, behind an armoire, above a bedroom door, near her breasts and sex. It is a powerful draw.

And he will be drawn. And they will rut around in some overgrown field. After a few months, he will leave her for another woman, who has asked for the same spell. In six months, Iona will return asking for a potion to keep him or to get rid of his child. Such is the life of a skin girl.

"Why do you look so, Yanahnome?" Iona asks as she is handed the ready-prepared parcel.

She tells her. "I can see your future with this man. You won't be happy. No woman can be happy with what she gets like this."

Iona looks at her, then at the ground. She reaches in her pocket and hands over the coins. "I need him."

And I need your money, Yanahnome thinks, putting the coins in her bodice, remembering the dwindling pile. "Go then and be happy for a time."

The house, the yard, are bathed in a reddish glow, the brilliant hues of souls released to fly into the sky. Yanahnome feels the pull of joining. Age has brought slowness of body and fear. It peeks at me, she thinks, reminding me that soon I will be there, dead too. Painful suffering: like mother, like grandmother.

But not tonight. She goes to a large rocking chair, wood smoothed from decades of sitting. The weight of her body, her skin and bones, is heavier than she remembers. It gets harder and harder to deal with the nothing days. She lives for the nights and her flights.

The secret came a year ago, in a dream. A voice whispered a promise. "Freedom and forgetfulness."

Things had changed and gone: her magic had been revered and helpful, yet consigned always to the fringes of the village. To see the wise woman, they had to trudge through brush, cross water. But a new preacher called Symm made her sinful, her profession a crime. Then she too fell under the spell of a man. Yanahnome loved him passionately and deeply. But in the end, he too left and no amount of magicking could keep him. Yet he left her with a daughter, and Minah became the light of her life. Years later, he returned and took her too, drowned at the bottom of a pond near her home.

The whispers. Magicking had driven him mad. Abomination. Not natural. The will of God. Yanahnome knew the minister had begun them. They were worse when they got back to her. She doubted herself. The ministrations of the spirits of Ma-Iamfre and Ma-Mariah, mother and grandmother, failed to soothe. She eventually banished them and gave herself over to pain and isolation.

Then wind brought solace in a dream.

"How?" she asked.

Shed the body, with it humanity, and so too falls away pain, he said. A beautiful reality, better than dreams, escape from remembered things: A child. A minister. A death. A decline.

The Ma-spirits sang warnings. "Beware the easy way, daughtah," they said. "Open doors can trap you outside forever." But Yanahnome had long since stopped listening to them. She agreed and has agreed most nights since. She agrees tonight.

Yanahnome sits and rocks slowly, breath slow, slow-er, slo-w-ly. Her chin rests in the gizzard folds of neck skin. She listens to the scrape-creak, scrape-creak of the chair, concentrates until the sound fills her senses. Her heart slows to the rhythm. Blood meanders through veins, barely able to lift itself from the pooling in the feet and hands, joined in the scrape-creak of the chair.

She feels the opening begin in the small of her back. The split lets a draft in. She often forgets how cold it is when it first begins. The split travels the length of her back, up the neck, the head, and winds its way around front, face, chest, belly. It reaches her sex and stops. Yanahnome reaches her hands to the top of her head, yet the flesh doesn't move. Her spirit-hands knead the split at the top of the head and pull, pu-ull, PULL. It gives, peels away, falling. She wriggles and shrugs, steps out of it and kicks it aside, like a dirty heavy-suit. She hovers above.

She never fails to marvel at how beautiful she is like this, orange as the valencias that grow wild in the grove behind her house. No not her house, this house. Yanahnome doesn't own anything as a spirit. Her grey hair, normally pinned and plaited during skin life, stands wild and free like cotton plants waving in a field. Gnarled, aged hands, parchment wrinkles, have also gone. The spirit body has gotten younger since she let it free.

Yanahnome casts another glance at the body. It smells, a hefty unwashed funk. She needs to be out. It's time to fly.

Out the window, above...OH! The wind caresses her. She whirls and dips in the air, catching thermals from the potbelly stove chimneys from the village below. Leaves rise and mingle with her orange, sent from the trees in greeting. The wind brings tidings of joy, invitations.

"Come, come," he says. "There is much to see and not much time."

"Where, where?" she asks. The wind-lover's touch leads her over the housetops of the sleeping town. She dips lower, to see in the windows, to watch skin-life. She holds her nose. The smell! The dust swirls up to greet her. Dogs run from yards, yapping at the air, growling. Inside, the skins are going about their life, performing their routines. How odd they seem to her, like conjure dolls. Skins are the greatest conjure dolls of all. So easily manipulated by the slightest change of temperature or emotion. Not so in the spirit. Nothing for elements or hands to hold on to. Emotions can't grasp smoke. But still, the spirit is caught, attached to that nasty body by a silver thread. Yanahnome sighs and longs for greater freedom. She can only go so far.

The glow of the spirit is a barely discernible outline around the skins. It saddens her to see them in such a state. They are so majestic when they are young, babies in particular. She sneaks into the cribs sometimes, just to watch them glow. Occasionally she sings to them, when their sleep is troubled. Remember the one inside, she says. But they are doomed to forget. They start to forget once they are born.

Skin Life

Tonight, Yanahnome decides its time to comfort the old spirits, drying up in the skins bustling around at home. She breathes and sings:

> *Of air, of wind, of breath you are*
> *Of water, of brook, of sea;*
> *Tree and leaf, swirl and sway;*
> *Light–shine, rising dust, away;*
> *Free.*

It isn't a voice that comes. She no longer has one. Instead, a murmur like a rustle easing through a crevice, a primal sigh. Spirit ears hear what skin ones cannot. The dull outline shines brighter as the spirit begins to push. But the skin speaks.

"OOh, such a chill. Felt like somebody walked on my grave," the woman said. "Honey, you cold?"

"In this heat? 'oman please!"

"Well, summin's open. I got such chill bumps."

The moment is gone, the pushing subsides. The woman walks to the cook-stove to warm herself.

Yanahnome shimmies down an unlit chimney into another home. A fat skin, shiny from the heat, sets down food from an oven. As she does, she hums, patting pies, stroking the stew. Yanahnome watches her and wonders about the spirit inside. Probably been crushed 'neath the weight of the skin. This skin 'oman eats too much. Yanahnome hovers above the food and tries to tip it over. But spirit hands can't grasp skin objects, and she only succeeds in making it windy and denting one of the pies.

The old round skin looks around, wondering at the sudden breeze. She moves to cover the cooling food, but stops at the pie. Oh a little bit wouldn't hurt. No one at the church bake tomorrow would really fault her. After all, sweet potato is her favorite. She reaches for a knife.

Enough of this peering in windows, Yanahnome says. She flies up to the sky, swirls in the cloud. "Follow me," says the wind. He takes her on a fast-paced game of follow-the-leader. Out they fly over weed-dominated groves, skimming lightly over the tree tops. Branches bend furiously at their passing, leaves swish, scatter, and fall like confetti. Down they plunge, through branch and twig, into bramble and moss. She folds herself into a cone to squeeze through a small hole beneath a log, following the wind. Don't touch the sides, the voice urges. But she does.

Balance on the head of a toadstool, pirouetting on point, yet don't leave a dent. But she does.

Weave through a stand of small trees, baby limbs outstretched, to a clearing. She hovers in the center, above browned leaves, fallen orange husks, decaying fruit. She twirls, raising it all to her, above the ground, around her arms, over: a house of nature held together by air and will. She lets nothing fall until she wills it.

Kaylois Henry

Everywhere she flies, Yanahnome stirs and supplants, a creature bent on pollination, imbuing all with the idea of her passage, an idea that leaves a spot and change behind.

Further, the wind urges, and she follows still. Through cotton fields, over brooks made faster by her passage, she goes. Among the birds, around them, through them, she follows, free. Further.

Until she feels the pull at her ankle.

She looks down at the silver line around her ankle pulled taut. The skin has called, it is master still. Yanahnome howls in despair, the sound of the movement of a million leaves, brambles, thorns. She follows the cursed legchain through her roof, shudders in disgust at the still split body. Yet the spirit is weak and longs for rest that only the skin can provide. She steps back and in one quick motion rezips. She skin awakes. It is morning.

The body pays for the spirit's forgetfulness. Yanahnome feels an aching pain so deep no amount of eucalyptus ointment can ease. There's a knock on the back door. The day's business has begun.

Yanahnome's flights have ranged a little further each night. But still it isn't enough. Every time, the pull of the chain comes seemingly sooner, keeping her slave to the skin. The spirit loves and hates its master. But she doesn't know what it would be like to be completely free...and longs for it. She has seen shadows that accompany death. The shadows smell of nothing. But the wind assures her that there is only freedom.

It rolls up, through the grove, across the dust, up the step, nipping toes, swirling her skirt and finally to her nose. Yanahnome breathes fear. It comes from the village. A second breeze brings the reason. A constricting stench of hatred and loathing pains her nostrils. Her hands automatically go to the protection ward around her neck. What is happening there? she wonders. She begins to think potions.

There is a knock on her door.

"Come."

Three hoary-headed men come into her home. Highly unexpected visitors: Mayor Adu, Deacon Fisher and a dour-faced Preacher Symm. They have never come before and it would take nothing less than a disaster to send them. Indeed, for awhile it seemed that their job had been to ridicule her with rumblings of progress, to do away with "backwater beliefs holding us back," Adu had said in a rally.

Yet there they stand, hat in hand, the stench of evil, like their deflated pride, swelling around them.

"Yanahnome," Adu begins, "I suppose you know why we are here."

"Against my better judgement!" hisses Symm. "I still think folks are over-reactin'."

"Hush, Symm," says Adu. He continues to look at Yanahnome waiting.

She doesn't say anything at first. In another time, she would have enjoyed the discomfiture. But not now.

"I smell the reason," she said. "An evil reason."

The grey-haired men shuffle a bit, nervous. Symm widens his nostrils drawing in air almost visibly. He skins up his face in pious disbelief.

"There's not evil here," he says. "Just a plain run o'bad luck. Crop fail all the time. Animals die all the time. Women barren, chil'un die in the crib all the time."

"But never at the same time," says Fisher, tone hushed. "And there are zombies."

Yanahnome starts. She thought Ma-Mariah took care of this...she never thought...

"Who?"

"Fat Mathilde. She just walk around town, saying nothin'," he says. "Just shuffle and stare. She don't wash, don't sleep, don't even eat. She withering up and dying."

A memory flashes and floats into consciousness: Mathilde and Yanahnome in the kitchen looking at a lumpy yellow mess pulled from the oven. Cooking lesson number four was corn pone, and Yanahnome failed. Potions for sickness and the human condition she could prepare with delicate ease, but this corn-cake confection escaped her. There was Mathilde, round grease-shine face beaming, big body bumping with laughter. "Yanah, you don't know shit 'bout cooking. I'm surprised you so fat!" And promptly fed her from her own pan of perfect pone.

That was a years-ago them. They had both grown old and distant since.

Yanahnome reaches for her scarf and cane. "Show me." And walks past the men. They follow.

The smell is strong in the village. It's bright, Yanahnome hardly recognizes it like this, not having ventured in from the ground in what seems like years. Even without the smell, she can tell things are not quite right. Tin and wood strew the road from houses that no longer have roofs or walls. Leaves are withered, the trees they are born from spotted and wilted. Powdered ash anoints all.

She touches a tomato plant: its shrivelled husk emits only dust, all the life sucked out. The whole village appears drained, its life essence slipping away, turning sepia, fading.

Yanahnome smells her before she sees her shuffling up the road. Even then, she doesn't recognize her, not really. Fat Mathilde was her nemesis in youth and best friend in adulthood. Age had not been kind. She's lost so much weight, as the ugly brown dress hanging from her frame shows. Yanahnome gets closer and sees it isn't a dress, but her skin flapping as she shuffles.

"Mathilde..." she calls her, hands on shoulders. She feels the skin slide over the protruding bones. "It's me, honey."

Yanahnome looks in her eyes, her pupils are gone. She doesn't see or hear her. Mathilde's feet still shuffle as Yanahnome holds her. She lets go and she continues on.

"How long...?" she asks Adu, watching the retreating form.

"A week now, no more. It just happened one night during a storm." His face looks pained. "But there is more."

The group arrives at a front door just as a curtain falls back into place. A tall man with powerful hands and a tired, sweaty face opens the door before the knock. He beckons them inside.

"Frank," Adu begins. "I brung Yanah..."

"I just hope she can help we," he said.

The house is stifling hot on an already sweltering day. Yanahnome notices Frank is in his undergarments and even they are drenched. Preacher Symm kisses his teeth and mumbles something about being hot as the fiery pit. Frank leads them to a back room, even hotter. A woman sits shivering before a pot-bellied stove.

"Anabel," says Frank. "Yanahnome and the minister are here to see you. Can you talk?"

Anabel says nothing, just continues to stare at the flames.

Yanahnome places her hand on Anabel's shoulder and draws it back. She is ice cold. Anabel rocks back and forth, shivering.

"She can't eat nothing but the hottest uh food," Frank says. "Everything else turn to ice in she mouth. I have to heat it on the forge in the back."

Anabel speaks in a voice like icicles falling on wood. "I can feel the chill moving around inside, like it living. I can feel it stopping things. I can't feel my legs no more."

Preacher Symm lays hands on Anabel, a prayer to the Lord rising from his lips. He doesn't recoil, though his hands turn ashy and white. "Lord Jesus, if this is your will..."

Frank grabs him by the scruff of the neck, yanking him away from his wife.

"We prayed to God and church and look what it got us! She dying not from hellfire, but from ice." He looks at Yanahnome, the plea implicit.

Yanahnome doesn't know if she believes in her magic that much, doesn't know if she can stand the time, just doesn't know.

"How long has this gone on?" she asks Adu outside.

"Folks started noticin' changes about six months ago. But weren't nothing big. Here, a blighted plant. There, a messed up house..."

"The rest of this just up and happened," interrupts Fisher. "Seem like we just turned around one day and it was all like this."

Skin Life

"It's not all that unusual for phenomenon such as this," says Symm in his best seminary-school voice. "You got to expect some misfortune..."

"Come and take a good look around, Preacher," Adu hisses. "Then tell me it's not so unusual."

They travel further down the street. Everywhere are signs evil has taken root and grown. Here, a cow gives only sour milk. There, goats birth two-headed kids. Bananas are dust, cassavas husks, squash, pumpkin withered on the vine. Symm talks in a hushed rumble about Armageddon. Yanahnome believes him. She sees starvation peeking its head at the edges of the village, rubbing its hands in glee for the harvest. She will help.

She sees Iona on the road. The glow from her is brilliant still, out of sorts with this fading-away village. She stares at Yanahnome and then looks at her feet, caked in dust. Three months and three women have passed since she came to her for the request. She knows what has happened. Iona used the potion and it worked as she wished. Loxley saw her no longer as a giraffe, but a goddess. His hands roamed her body, stroking the lithe long lines. The cassava field behind the house made a place for the sex. He rutted around on top of her, possessed, words of lust whispered in her ear. It probably lasted a month.

Iona walks toward the group. "Iona, tell Yanahnome about your home," Adu says.

Iona looks past her, at something just beyond her shoulder, such is the guilt in her eye. Yanahnome sees the tracks left by tears in her eyes. "Nothin' has happened at my home."

Yanahnome looks at the mayor and back to Iona. "Nothing?"

"Nothin'."

"Show me."

The group walks to her home. Yanahnome looks at Iona's footprints. She's a month pregnant. Probably doesn't know it.

The constant companion stench ends at Iona's gate. Her and her father's house looks like the village should. Plants grow, house stays fixed, color perfect. How? Yanahnome asks.

"I don't know!" she screams and begins to shake. Tears well up in her eyes. "I don't know." She says more quietly. "I just do things like I always do. When things started to go bad, I tried to help people. I expect them to go bad for me too. But Pappa and I have nothing happen. Others' crop die, ours grow like it always do. Others' hog birth 'flicted chiles, ours don't. Others zombies, I like I always.

"People think I do it, but I didn't. I wish it would happen to me. But it don't."

Yanahnome touches Iona's hands instinctively. She looks in her eyes for some trace, some hint, sees nothing. "It isn't she that is causing this," she announces. "It is something far more powerful."

Yanahnome can do something, but it will mean recontact with the Ma-spirits. It will take time, something in short supply. A fortnight is all that is left before the plants turn to dust. A month before starvation comes reaping. "I can do something, I just don't know if there is time."

"And if there isn't," Symm says.

"Then you'd bettah hope you gotta direct line to God."

Iona grabs her hands. "You believe me?"

"Yes. I saw nothing in you."

Yanahnome pats her hand and feels a low grumble, like a hunger pang somewhere beyond her stomach, beyond the corporeal. She shakes her head to dislodge the thought. Concentration is needed for the weeks ahead. Memory too. She must gather, mix, breathe, beg. All of it will take time.

It will be weeks before she can fly again.

Days are filled with work and conjure. Yanahnome grinds stones and old bones, mortars flowers, boils herbs, grates root. She hollows fruit — lemon, orange, grapefruit, breadfruit, gourd — dries, pricks them with clove and cinnamon. Her home becomes a giant ward bag, filled with mountains of powdered magic, liquid conjure, baked power.

The Ma-spirits have returned invited, after years of silence and shunning. No need for explanation, they tell her. We know. They murmur things, how much to put in a poultice, how much to fill the hollowed fruits, where to find the best herbs in the blighted village, how much salt and string to recapture souls.

"Time, time daughtah," they sing in her ear. "Each passing day, it slips. Each passing day, you slide."

Dusks are filled with searching. Accompanied by the spirits, she looks for the right places to bury the wards. Few get the proper light or lack of it at the right times of the day. But the spirits guide as quickly as they can, singing directions in her ears. Prayers to God and guardians are made with each burial. Yet there are still many more to be placed...

"Time, time.."

Nights are filled with temptations. Wind-whispers float through the open window and swirl around as Yanahnome fills the wards. "Come out, come play...Just a minute, not long.." Ignored, they try another tack, caressing her body, filling her ears with sweet promises. "Only a second. We miss you so..."

Her soul aches to go. She can feel it scratching at the small of her back. But the skin her has things to do. Potions to fill and bury. She closes the windows, but the whispers squeeze through the cracks. She asks the Ma-spirits to keep them at bay. The Mas sing them out. But Yanahnome still feels them hovering, just outside, pressing, promising.

And still time slips. Day, dusk, night, she works, mashing, filling, burying. Songs fill the inside of the house, whispers surround outside it. The Ma-spirits encourage, caress, refresh. Still not enough. Two weeks have passed and half the wards are gone. Starvation is getting bold and has paid a visit to a cattle pen. Yanahnome needs help.

She knocks on the back door of Iona's house. Her father answers, scrutinizes, then looks over her shoulder to see if she was followed.

"Yeah, what you want?"

"Iona," she says.

She sees a lie, born of fear, form in his eyes and move to his mouth. Iona peers around him before he speaks.

"You need me?" she says.

"Yes," Yanahnome admits. "There isn't much time to do it alone."

Iona's hair is already in a scarf, her shoes already on. She looks at her father. "I will go." And passes him to Yanahnome.

The walk back home is quiet save the purposeful sound of shoes on gravel. Yanahnome's mind stretches to find the feelings that rise within her from the girl. "How did you know I was coming?" she finally asks.

Iona's gaze remains locked on the ground before her. She waits so long to answer, Yanahnome wonders if she has heard her. "My mother told me," she finally says. Pause.

Yanahnome nods. Her own mother speaks, she thinks but does not say. Mothers never really seem to let go when they go. She wishes daughters were the same.

At home, Yanahnome shows Iona how to hollow out the fruit to make a ward shell. Her fingers are nimble and she does it easily. Later, Yanahnome shows her how to fill them, spilling not a drop. At this she is equally deft.

As they work, the Ma-Spirits whisper instruction to Yanahnome. If they wonder about Iona or mind her, they haven't said. They fill the house with songs and warmth. Yanahnome sings along sometimes, careful not to let Iona see her. But sometimes she sees Iona's lips moving to an unheard tune.

Iona helps bury the wards. She has a gift of finding the right spots. The work goes faster, the time still singing in Yanahnome's ear.

The last night, after the last ward is buried, the women sit: Yanahnome in her chair, Iona at her feet. Iona begins to talk in a low singsong. It's about her mother.

"She come to me last year, I think," she begins. "I was putting up the washing, in the morning, and I hear her voice, clear as day. I wasn't scared, so much as surprised. Momma died when I was just a baby. But I still knew her. She said I ready for her to talk to me now."

Yanahnome only half hears the monologue. The wind has been whispering in her ear, competing with Iona. "Come..." it entreats. "Work is done. Nothing to do but wait."

"Momma said she needed to protect me...."

"Come play..."

Her eyelids, heavy as a lead shade, slide closed to the dual voices.

When she awakes, Yanahnome is above her body, floating. The skin lies sleep-like in the chair. How did she get out without realizing it? No matter. All her aches are gone. She stretches and marvels again at her beauty.

Below, Iona has stopped speaking and is looking at the body. She touches the arm, calling the name. Here I am, Yanahnome floats down to tell her. She touches the top of her head. Iona looks up alarmed, puzzled. Gently, Yanahnome strokes the back of her neck. Iona's hand flies there, rubbing it as if stung. Yanahnome touches her arm, Iona grabs it. Her eyes are wide now, her breathing shallow. Yanahnome wants her to see her. She floats into Iona's face, puts her spirit one before her real one. She opens her mouth and speaks.

"Here I am. See me. I am beauty."

Iona covers her nose and mouth and crumples to the ground. She pushes herself into a corner of the room. Her eyes are frightened, tears stream down. She wraps her arms around herself and rocks back and forth. Her lips move soundlessly.

Yanahnome reads them.

Momma. Oh Momma, help me.

Fear? Yanahnome is angry. How dare she not see, realize that she is witness to a miracle? Can't she see the joy, beauty, power?

Curled in the corner, Iona snivels and shakes. All she ever was and is, is a child, skin and bones and disgust. Yanahnome smells the stench of skin and writhes and spits in disgust. The house writhes with her, toppling Iona like a rag doll.

Up she flies from the house. No more time to bother with skin girls. Time to play!

"Follow me," she says to the wind.

They whip down the street, low to the ground, kicking up the dust. They leap over trees, spiral around homes, ripping off roof tiles, clothes on the line, and drop them in the middle of the road. Skins are coming out of houses looking up wondering. She and the wind laugh.

Trees jump to greet her, only to jump down again, sometimes on the road, sometimes on a house. Once on a dog. Poor thing. Shouldn't have gotten in the way, she says.

Doors rattle and fly from hinges, followed by flower boxes, more trees, plants, a few small dogs. All are gathered in the swirl in the middle of town,

Skin Life

a living dust cloud, Yanahnome has created, to expand and constrict at will.

She sees Iona's father stepping out of his house. She scoops him up and tosses him on the top of the whirlwind. His voice, getting hoarse from use, is a beautiful song. She whirls it faster, the music getting better.

Enough of this! The whirling comes to a stop, with all clattering down, the father last. Time for her to leave this land of skin and play elsewhere. She flies toward the woods. But at the border she finds her way blocked. She flies another way, and still is blocked. She flies up but still cannot escape.

Kept in? Who dares? As sudden as thought, she feels the pain.

A thousand tiny knives slide down her back. She screams, plants and people bend in response. She looks down to the silver leg-chain. It has blackened like a rotted umbilical cord.

Her body.

She rushes back to the house, cursing each new bout of knives sliding and slicing. Back at the house, Iona greets her. Rather, the skin her. Iona stands there, shaking. In her hands she lightly sprinkles white crystals on the sleeping form.

Yanahnome moves down, tries to reach inside herself to awake, rejuvenate. But she can't get in. The acrid taste of the crystals tells her why.

Salt. Iona has salted her skin.

She can't get back inside. Ever.

Her joy threatens to flatten the house and all its contents. Finally free! Forever a beautiful spirit. Yanahnome wants to sing from the roof tops, to the heavens, the stars!

She moves to hug Iona. To thank her for such a wondrous gift. Iona slaps at the attempted touches.

No matter, nothing matters anymore. Yanahnome rises above the home. A small crowd, lead by Preacher Symm, has gathered outside, pointing at the whirlwind above it. They kneel before it and pray. Iona walks outside, salt-box still in hand. The preacher takes her hands.

"Your father, baby...I'm so sorry..."

The stench of the skin is overwhelming. Smelly. Horrible. The preacher has gone inside and touched the body. He returns to announce the news.

"She gone."

Not gone, better! Yanahnome wants to shout, make them understand. She has beat the body. She has had death without a sting. She opens her mouth to announce the news, to laugh in the face of Symm and his pious God. Ma-Iamfre stops her. They are both there, looking at her with sadness and reproach.

"No daughtah," she says.

"Look at me Momma," Yanahnome says, twirling in air. "I am young

39

and beautiful and free. The body is gone. I am a slave no longer."

"No, missus," Ma-Mariah says. "Your slavery has just begun."

Yanahnome halts her cavorting. "I don't understand."

"Did you understand nothing." Ma-Mariah sucks her teeth. "If the spirit leaves before time, it's nothing."

"You are truly gone," says Ma-Iamfre. "And what is left is an abomination."

They don't understand, she thinks. They are jealous because they had to suffer and I did not. They had to die. I did not.

"No," says Ma-Iamfre, barely able to look at her, "even now, you are becoming nothing."

She looks at herself. The orange glow has become glassy and hollow, as if made of small marbles. Each breath of wind blows a few away. Her feet are already gone.

"Momma, make it stop!"

Ma-Iamfre says nothing. She and Ma-Mariah turn away.

"Nanny!"

But the Ma-spirits have gone.

As the marbles of herself roll away, Yanahnome cries for anyone to hear. And the wind answers back, mocking.

"Free, free, free."

Matthew Humphreys

From *The Feeders*

Matthew Humphreys was born in Liverpool in 1971. He has worked as an arts reviewer, barman and security guard. He also had a brief career as a stand-up comedian. *The Feeders* is his first novel. He is currently working on a second.

Still here?
All of you?

The day began with paranoia. I can't shake it. It's been following me around since I awoke. The way the city seems today, its rolling-eyed morning anxiety, the way it keeps turning from me, as if disturbed by something over its shoulder...the reluctance of its people...the anger of cars...is not something mysterious or new.

There are many people out today, pursuing whatever their day means to them, drifting along to their different rhythms and their different times...that man with his heavy eye over a cigarette is in his hung-over time...that commuter nervous at the bus stop is caught up in his busy time, forever in the now...but to be honest most of us are stepping to a dislocated time, the now and the then broken by the mind scrabbling away from the present, dreams becoming some kind of fingerhold on a sheer slope of glass...or a time meaningless in its aftermath to another...we can see that in the carnival dregs, their costumes becoming somehow worthless in the daylight, the right moments for them are long gone...such as that man dressed as a devil with a small boy on his back, the black horns on his head are in fact flutes which his son fingers, whistling some notes, the air blowing down through the horns, echoing in his skull and then out of his mouth...sounding weary tunes, the only ones worthy of this numb-eyed light. Of this head-down, hands-in-pockets kind of time. The city went to a party last night, got into a fight, lost, and it can't even phone in sick. Like all of us, it is condemned to work by the morning that hauls us out upon the streets. We try to get by any way we can. Buskers and dancers stand on the edge of the pavement, panning for gold in a river of shoppers.

A fat man with his vest stained and stretched holds out a tray. "Five for a pound of lighters, lighters five for a pound." His friend hawks elastoplast, and the devil buys one in the hope it will repair the ache in his head. If only I had a body to blame for the pain. Would you forgive me if I played the truant today? Suffering the pain of brittle pins of light in my eyes. "Get off my back," says the devil to his son, "and quit it with those horns. Can't you see your poor Dad is sufferin'." And the child manages two minutes of silence before he catches sight of Old Lord Mustard. The tramp is pattering away the slow-shoe shuffle in front of the Butchers and the child lets out a brief cry of joy at the sight. The devil winces. But you can't blame the Lord. There is nothing else for him to do but dress in his top-hat and tails and torn beard, dancing as he has danced all his life. For the pennies.

For the booze.

Admittedly, there is a fine line between dancing and just hitting the floor with your foot.

We wander along the pavement, duck our heads in doorways, looking for our quarry, finding only various shop wares...a wall of plump-roasted chickens pressed against the glass, the skin slowly greasing, cardboard crates of tomatoes and onions, the job centre selling queues of people...the pawn-shop with its jewellery...we don't need any of this...a café with amber and brown-striped wallpaper, yellow seats and waitresses to match. There they are...the ones you got me out of bed to find...if I can just muster the energy...Tumalooma Bravado and Aud Baggerley.

You still following me?
Led by the nose, we go in.

We are sitting on the toilet, our eyes to the keyhole, watching a blonde waitress. She plucks a plate of breakfast leftovers from the counter and clatters it down upon their table. Waxy lard solidifies along the edge of the sausages. They are forked, lifted, delivered to the mouth. Chewed and considered. Aud tries to speak while she eats but the sentences are all bitten off, mangled with the meat...Tumalooma leans toward understanding; we lean with her, a hundred thousand eyes to the keyhole to see

Buttocks in brown polyester. My god, we say, recoiling. The buttocks are aimed at a chair, the legs beneath them as uncertain as those of young deer. Tentatively Lil lowers herself away from us and into the plastic seat. She closes one eye for the smoke of her cigarette, rising in dragon's tails from the length of withering ash. Our view jumps around a little and then settles upon the stride of the waitress, who presents Lil with a cup of coffee. The muffled thank-you's are drowned out by the clack-chank-splash of the

The Feeders

cup and saucer. The old woman slides her emaciation painfully from the sleeves of a nicotine yellow overcoat. Her flesh is contracted, drawn miserly to the bone. Except for her mouth, where the features are abundant and loose.

Our ears lean the length of the cafe and we hear Aud say,

"I see they've put Lil on the Mogadon again. It's a shame. A damn shame what they do to her."

Aud speaks assertively. Quite the opposite to Tumalooma, who mumbles her words from beneath her hand, denying us even the slightest revelation. I would content myself with lip-reading if I could just see through her fingers. Or her thoughts. My god. What I would do for her thoughts. Everyone else is an open book to me. It's easy enough to flick from one mind to the other, like a man searching through files. So why her resistance, the hidden consciousness, the plain stubbornness of the real...like, she can trust me...if only she would give me her dreams, I'm up for some Freudian reconstruction...memories...fantasies...the bread and butter stuff, the raw loose matter of the now, I'd settle for just some basic sensory details...rather than this endless study of her exterior, just her body and her objects...

We watch Tumalooma. She pinches the bridge of her nose and closes her eyes. A slight shake of her head reminds us of her long auburn hair. The skin is gaunt. The eyes betray her previous evening, red with tears. Anger. But there is something in the way she moves today that goes beyond this...the shake of the head...silent womanish pity...some kind of empathy with Lil and all the other broken things around her.

Lil flounders at the sound of her name, she tries to act but becomes uncertain that it was spoken at all. Decides to concentrate upon her drink. Her lips effort toward the brow of the cup. They forget the cigarette. Cinders spin in the whirling coffee, the filter goes down like a frigate. Is this it, another wonder of the world, a kind of pitiful, useless tragi-comedy that makes a man just want to turn away...yes a few of us turn away...aren't I good enough for them?...weary of it, I finish and flush, slip myself out of the toilet, feeling you all on my shoulder...I abandon form and hang one bulbous eye over Aud and Tumalooma...get right in there, to the heart of things, no more distractions I promise. Time to take exploit our..what shall we call it...our ethorial presence?

"Look at him," says Aud, lips curled around a cigarette, the purveyor of smoke, "all gadded up with that packet in his jeans and begging me to watch. Boys like that make m'heart thrill, m'blood rush and m'mouth water...monkst other things. Hah." Her hand slaps the formica to the rhythm of her laugh: she can't stop, the insatiable twitching of a dog's hind leg when it is tickled.

"No, stop me, no don't. I'm serious. It would be good to have some young meat again. Of course, sexwise, Rag is finished, nothing but a beer belly on legs now, not even very nice legs at that...oh god, I'm awful today aren't I? No, don't tell me. Just nod. Isn't that the best bit of meat you've seen all week?"

The digger unpeels the T-shirt from his torso, gooseflesh raised in its wake. He wears boots with mud caked into the leather. He has hair weaves, the rainbow sown into his sandy-rough hair. The other diggers heave in the heat, heavy men shouting at one another over the machinery, offering a little street theatre for the traffic jam with their cynical shouts and playfighting. The young digger laughs with them and scoops the sheen from his chest...Aud's hands tighten around her cup...thighs meeting beneath the table...coming together in a conspiracy of flesh...I like youth; the frailty of a thin body between my thighs, the enthusiasm of novelty...all banging away at me like kids always do, eager to please, I push him over my body and congratulate the tickle of calloused hands...rough hair in my neck as his head ecstatically turns over and over in the grip of pleasure...and when he sleeps I will tell him how beautiful he looks whilst I fingerplay with his lips and twirl my nails in the hairs upon his thigh...motherly arms over little boys delight...fragile body and love, I could kiss it as he sleeps...

Aud fantasises. Desires sprawling all over me. We could know everything about her, I could dig out her soul for you, whatever you want...

So how much do you want to know?

She feels the sadness of her body. Under the pretence of smoothing her dress, Aud brushes the fat folded at her sides and thinks no he wouldn't take me, I cannot even dare to ask him. Languid desire becomes voyeurism; she says to Tumalooma,

"I know how you could get your revenge. (She twists a spoon in the air, stirring the mood.) You could take that digger back to your house. Have your way with him. It's your right. Revenge is a woman's prerogative."

Tumalooma's hand cups at her brow, concealing her face.

"Harry didn't fuck around." Tumaloom's voice is barely audible. The throat is reluctant to give up the words.

Aud reaches to remove the hand,

"You could have him, too, good-looking woman like you, I reckon he'd be up for it,"...and I watch the sandy rough hair now rocking in her slender neck, and it is Tumalooma's auburn hair that flicks backward as she rides him; is there some part of me with her as she fucks — my face?...no, I am inside and outside...stylised soft focus of a man's hard lips meeting a woman's yielding and

The smash of two plates against the floor, the face of the waitress is aghast and then apologetic.

Face barred by fingers. The two women turn to watch the diggers.

On Stanley Street, the cars are still snapping at one another, jammed up

The Feeders

behind traffic cones, slowly fuming as the digger walks nonchalantly by with his T-shirt wound about his fist. The upheaving of his pick-axe offers a study of his musculature: it is picked out smooth and round as pebbles beneath his ribs. It's rare to see such freedom in work.

From out of the jostling traffic, a truck leaps forward. A pedestrian is struck. The man stops his roll over the bonnet by gripping the hot metal and pressing his face against the windowscreen. A flurry of obscenity. And then he is running alongside the van, slamming his fists against the bonnet. The van is wedged behind an ambulance. The pedestrian begins kicking dents in the bodywork. At all times, the driver avoids looking at him.

Ceasing, the young digger swings down the axe to pose upon its handle. Time to watch the fight, plenty of time. While the city spits. Likewise the elder diggers drift from their work and stand behind him, their faces sheer and hard as cliffs. The pedestrian pulls the door of the van open and springs to headbutt the driver. Salmon leaping, twisting free from the earth.

The diggers point and laugh. Narrators of the street, nothing passes them by without a comment.

The diggers watch as the headbutt fails and the pedestrian resorts to punching a wing mirror. It shatters like their laughs...like Tumalooma's sudden wince at the violence, like Aud's concern at seeing her friend disturbed, like my head turning and words breaking at the awareness that I am watching all of them, in a chain beginning with Aud, rattling as the violence shudders through all of us...and then the digger goes back to work. His triceps elongate and contract with the swinging of the axe, the snake on his arm curls and flicks. The head strikes the road. After each blow, two diggers peel back the tarmac to unfurl tongues of stone...yes I could take a licking from him, as Audalooma...I want to grip his scalp and watch his head bobbing between her legs, my babe suckling...no, that doesn't work for me, I don't want any gunnysuckling child, I want to grip his head as it insatiably twists and turns with the fervour of a dog licking at salt...looking down at him between my legs, a curious distance, the tattoo upon his arm that coils and uncoils with the rising, falling of his arm...reaching out for me, for her. Yes I must remember him for later. His pavement slab pectorals, his gargoyle's tongue, his pillar prick.

Aud turns from the diggers, her buttocks searching the plasticky seat for a cool spot. The hand that reached for Tumalooma now settles reassuringly upon her wrist:

"I don't know. Maybe after Harry, you feel you've had your fill of men. After all, they've chatted us up and fucked us up all our lives. (Laying the spoon down, taking up the cup once again, designing a pause.) I don't know. We take a little pleasure from men. And they just take the piss."

Tumalooma drops the fingers barring her mouth,

"I could have killed Harry when I saw he had bought the piranha." (Fingers return to her mouth, forbidding revelation, finding only further confession.) "I never thought it would be this way, the two of us fighting over money."

"It's inevitable," says Aud, counselling.

"Yeh, well he had no right. It was the last of our cash. I mean, what kind of test is this? I have to fight Them and my husband? The last thing I need is a bastard in my house...no, that's unfair...Harry may be a bastard but he is not a bad bastard. As good a bastard as I am likely to find."

Tumalooma smiles ruefully. Her marriage turning over in her hands as if it were some strange object, and her husband some man who just wandered in from the street.

"Perhaps you could cope with the bastard if you had bastards," says Aud, advocating.

Tumalooma smooths the edge of her nails, idly contemplative.

"Maybe no bastards at all."

"You don't win the game by leaving the pitch."

"What's winning the game?"

"Victory is a rich old bastard with lots of virile young bastard servants."

"Oh, that's just bravado talking," says Tumalooma, off-hand and with a flick of her palm.

"What is victory then? A bastard who loves you? A new bastard? A reconstructed bastard? How about a pumpkin that turns into a bastard at weekends?"

"Well that's me sorted. I will go to the grocer's. Now you."

"Oh my ideal bastard is an idea. Men, like communism, are best in the abstract."

"I don't always follow you, Aud. It's like you are possessed."

"The Devil speaks through me, I know."

The fingers return, covering Tumalooma's mouth, her anger admonishing her frivolity. She says,

"I have to go."

"Go on and ask the digger. For me."

Tumalooma smiles as she stands. I reach out for her as she walks away...some hand of smoke...a hundred thousand fingers pointing...delay her...but I can't and she is gone. Aud sips her coffee. She smiles in support of Lil's dazed walk from seat to door. The waitress hastens to the arm of the old woman. She is led from the shop.

See. That's what they do to us, in the end.

Cautiously crossing the road, Tumalooma takes a second glance to check the way is clear. Whilst walking, she looks again. We suspect her eyes of lingering upon his tattoo.

The Feeders

2

Curiosity of an appetite aroused...belly still sour from that Winter Warmer...Rag fingered his pack lunch. Sandwiches of...bend back the bread...salami and cream cheese. Good. And there is an apple for like health and the heh doctor's absence. She's slipped in the low-cal orange. No! I'm a working man. Need my sugar. I mean, diet drinks at my age! Don't I get no chocolate neither; but I need my bar, can never get up after a meal without my bar. Yes here. No! She gave me wafer. S'meant to be a pack lunch not a bloody communion. Shouldn't really start eating it now but. One bite. Got to feed that hangover, I'll sit on the shitter later with a paper and a fag, feel it loosen, feel it fall from me.

With a thumb in his waistband, Rag relieved the pressure upon his belly. Next to him, Harry drove with a concentration divided between the one-handed steer and the instinct to make himself heard;

"Go ahead love, give us a smile. Might never happen."

The cars were trapped against one another. Packed and tense. Hearing Harry's leer, Susie Bickerstaff, assistant to the offices of Hyde and Sheik, a woman of blonde bob and nagging cellulite angst, fixed her eyes upon her knee and regretted her choice of a convertible car.

With my head out of the window, I could just reach over and touch her. But instead I shall play with patter whilst I give her my best come-to-bed-eyes. The songs on the radio this morning. Hey baby. Wontcha love me. Like do me. Like a woman and man should. So sue me Peggy Sue.

His body turned to follow his elbow as he thrust himself out of the window, his mouth chewing on some idea of coolness, a well-practised predatorial smile. He leant over her.

"What's your name? Wait a minute. S'Phillipa isn't it? I can tell. I know a Phillipa when I see one. Their passionate nature makes their hair go blonde. I can do Tarot and I can do etymologies like...heh, see I know a Phillipa because they are Philosophers of the Lips. D'ja hear that Rag?"

"Flipper?" asked Rag, ears confused by chewing.

Trapped in her car. Open for anyone to invade. There is never any peace. Little Susie is truly awake now.

"By the way, my name's Rex," said Harry Bravado. "I'm a musician."

Susie turned on the radio. Loud.

"No luck?" asked Rag. A neutral tone to the question. He restrained his grin.

I feel like I just stapled my tongue to my boot.

Harry wound the window up, cutting off the music.

"Aw she just didn't realise it was her lucky day." A flippant response. I can never get the day going on the good foot. Always in the middle of it before I figure out where I am. It is late and it is getting later. Will have to

49

sneak in to work for another whole day of Stanislaus on my back.

Oh Danny Boy...

Rag said, "I was speaking to Danny in the 'Alms' last night. We had an interesting talk about payback and sweetmeats and, as I said, I was interested and so I think maybe you'll be interested too."

Harry raised an eyebrow and settled both hands upon the wheel. Go on, I'm listening.

"Now you know me, I've always been a pretty honest man...a little rash when I was younger perhaps, but, you know, these days I regard myself as a bit of a pillar. But...like, a man can't live honestly every hour of the day. And, as Aud has always said, theft *is* the vote of a proletariat alienated from the political process. Maybe she's right. So I gave Danny his due and listened to what he had to say. Even though it was quite contrary to my normal ways of understanding the world, if u-seewarramean."

So what did Danny say?

A wasp battered itself against the passenger window. Insects ought to evolve an understanding of transparent objects. Save on aspirin. Rag continued.

"You see Harry, you and I are feeders and so we feed and this is our job. Nine hours a day holding spoons to the mouths of pigs. And that's fine. Danny was talking about us maybe expanding our scope, to feed more than just the pigs. Get it?"

Frankly, no.

The wasp flew toward the driver's window to begin its second lesson in transparent object as solid object.

Buzz. Bang.

"So Danny got me thinking about this and you know what I'm like when I get to thinking. Up all night I was. Thinking."

What?

Where?

Ah, there.

They took a quick left off Stanley Street. In the wing mirror Harry smiled to see himself smile back at him. Know a short cut I do. Leave the others behind sniffing at one another's arses. Like dogs.

What?

A hunchback walking the smallest dog I have ever seen. Stiff lead.

Doubletake.

An old man hunched as he brushes leaves from the pavement. I hate that. Those little gaps, the bizarre questions the world asks of you. Those spaces between question and answer that fill you with paranoia.

Morning rush hour became silent residential streets.

"Shit Harry, I got it all down my front now. Tell me next time willya if you are going to do like tank manoeuvres. This was a clean shirt too." Rag smeared at the cream cheese with his fingertips and plucked it from the cotton. Ate it.

Buzz. Bang. Ow.

The grinding, circular motion of a thumb ended the lesson in glass. The corpse of the wasp fell relieved upon the upholstery.

Rag continued,

"So where was I? Theft, yeh...it's not really theft so much as a sharing. A little bit for Them, a little bit for us. Danny first heard about it (what?) from Merph who is a bit of an expert at it (what?) now and you know what Merph's like with words, he calls it (what?) dipscoopliftdropeat. And that's it in a nutshell. I can say no more."

Rag held out his empty palms, offering Harry this revelation. His whole body said "well what do you think?"

"Rag," said Harry deliberately naming, "to be honest I don't know what the fuck you are talking about so wake me when you get to the fucking point."

There was a sudden tension between the two men. Rag lay down his sandwich as if it were a challenge;

"A word in your ear," Rag's skin had an oily sheen to it; it glistened as he squinted against the sunlight. When he spoke he waved a loose hand at Harry.

"The impatient man is ever the frustrated man..." The tension postured, the men shuffled at finding themselves confronting one another, "...but he is never as frustrated as his wife."

Punctured tension and the half-laugh in Rag's voice, "Aud again, she gets her turn of phrase from her mother. Not that she said that to me when we were in bed, after we...no, I'm no sheet sprinter. If u-seewarramean."

Getting there. The one-way street to revelation.

Two wasps rutted upon the dashboard with silent insectasoid determination. Where are they coming from? If only I had the ears to hear their sweet nothings. Right now, I would take anything that looked like an answer.

Buzz oh bang, Harry's palm slammed their coupling into smeared unification.

There. I pronounce you man and wife. You may kiss the bride.

"Tell me now. Exactly," said Harry with a grimace toward the wings in his lifeline.

"Danny said we are not fattening the pigs. We are drugging them. Bloody good drugs too. So as a little payback, a sweet bonus, we eat the slop, Harry, we eat the swill."

A wasp clutched at the underside of an apple, its sucking proboscis sticky with juice. Didn't I just? Buzz ouch, Harry ground the fruit against the window. The wasp didn't move, it was preoccupied with its guzzling to the point of failing to notice death. Maybe it was tongue-tied and trapped.

51

Insects, do they never learn? The car feels alive with them. Even though it's like they are not here at all. Wish I was not here. I have to get away...I remember running away to Cokey Park playground with Flanny, our kiddish delight at pushing our legs out so that we could swing higher and higher, the chains clack with their loosening then snap with their tightening, always the same autumn sunset, the same starched trees...the season that has never left me. When we swung to the highest point, Flanny shouted "Jump" and we leapt through the air to laugh and roll on the grass.

Where am I? First left at Treasure Island, up Matthew Street and then past the Old Butcher.

Arms waving in the air because we were birds; well there was always the chance that the wind may catch us, that we may never land. It's been so long since I remembered, in fact I can't remember the last time I remembered being that young. Swinging up to the height of the sky.

STOP. RED.

Rag swigged from his flask as the car idled at the traffic lights.

I want to go back to Cokey Park and hoards of kids running over the grass like they were falling off a cliff. Arms waving, up into the sky and wishing away the ground. But there is such a distance between then and now. Between here and there. There's no way for me except onward. Forward by frustrating inches.

Their car eased up to the rear of the convertible. So a man takes what he can when he can. A little light relief. It is her again, my little blonde bob. So maybe this time she will give me the green light.

GO. GREEN.

The engine of her convertible voiced its reluctance to go with a series of ratcheting chokes. "As if my morning wasn't bad enough," whispered Susie as she returned to the ignition. Just one spark of life please.

"Come on, come on, move. What the fuck she up to?" Harry drummed the steering wheel. He drove an inch closer to the convertible, trying to nudge it awake.

"She having some kind of problem?" inquired Rag, wiping coffee from his lips.

"I'll give her a problem if she doesn't get her arse in gear." Even my blonde bob relief turns to frustration. Just my fucking luck. The long road to revelation and I get stuck halfway. Trapped in this nothing of a time. A wooden fishing boat between converging ocean liners. Time to look for the impossible exit.

Harry hammered his palm against the horn; the streets glared as he screamed, "MOVE!"

But there is no where to go, so I am going to be late, time moves on and escapes me making me older and later and later for my appointment with Flanny at the swings. Late for the third time this week. Stanislaus will roast my arse. He can stick bread in my crack and use me for a toaster for all I care.

Again the horn demanded.

Susie coaxed the car. It acquiesced and sped off into the distance, her fingers flicked backwards in a V toward them.

Harry inclined over the pedals, his body hunched like a runner at the block. Get her. But the lights had run their course.

STOP. RED.

"No more, " spat Harry as he flung open the door and jumped out with a boiling scream in his throat. At the smell of fresh air, the wasps nosed their way from the backseat in a thick black stream. Their buzzing coiled its way around the door and then escaped into the sky.

Silent and bemused, Harry watched the sinuous wasp shape of a question mark ascend high, higher.

3

*you never let me down
and you never turn me away.*

A morning wink for you my dear pig, always so willing for what Harry can give and I will give gladly to cheer your sad eyes. There is something mournful behind them. A sadness because you can see beyond all this, a perspective far from me and my songs. You are almost human.

The pig was startled from its reverie by the clicking of Harry's spoon as he extended it along its telescopic length. The serene white air of the laboratory. Ceramic white tiles covered the walls, floor and ceiling; the strains of Bach's Harpsichord Concertos lilted slowly over the workmen, the only other sound was the schoolgirl giggles of the pigs as they were gently sponged. The pigs hung upon tentacles like over-ripe fruit.

So they strung you up to the ceiling and pulled you free from the earth, released you from gravity only to chain you to the air. Your helpless waving legs. I know how you feel believe me. (In my John Wayne voice) Why I oughtta wrench those goddamn pipes from your hide and take the tube outta your ass.

*In our endless time,
dancing on a beach to Bach,
Denying all reason and rhyme.*

The feeders began in unison; their spoons erected, their shambling bodies clad in white from head to toe.

Yet you are fortunate to have such an odd perspective to watch the world, all hauled up high so that you can apprehend the entire universe with its stars, planets and shit.

> *Oh, waiting to be fed,*
> *dreams in your brain*
> *like angels upon a pinhead.*

I envy your height. To be high again! I remember the ghostly fingers in my mind. I feel like a kid at Christmas. Rag better not be fucking me about on this one.

The feeders dipped their spoons into the pink swill. Stanislaus clapped. The day of work began.

First, I scoop (the sound of lips opening) and secondly I lift with the swill smooth and level. The artistry of feeding is the artistry of L.O.V.E. — Level Otherwise Very Expensive. I mean, Mothering Acronyms at My Age. Stanislaus treats us like kids. But I can remember things from before he was born.

The pig's snout unwrinkled with the effort to reach the spoon. Its eyes closed and its mouth opened in blissful expectation. Legs running.

Sorry to disappoint you my dear. Thirdly, I drop.

The pinkish mush fell to slap with a sunflower splat upon the tiles. Stanislaus wrinkled his nose with disdain, he spoke over the edge of his clipboard,

"Bravado! You are as clumsy as you are late. Very, and dangerously so." One click of his ballpoint to punctuate his warning, and then he continued his note.

> *One day, in an alleyway*
> *in a different time and place,*
> *we will meet and*
> *I'll be clumsy all over your face.*

I sing to you because I am so excited. Please close your eyes my dear whilst I transgress.

The spoon tremoured as Harry wavered between acts. I must begin by turning my back...memories gushing along adrenalin, the skin of my back was nervous as I turned it toward their eyes, when I was shoplifting with Kenna and the lads and the sweat that almost broke my back. I turned from the counter and walked away with their eyes on my shoulders (where is Stanislaus?)...for all their looking, you just have to trust your luck'...Tumalooma slapped my back as she hauled herself astride me, hair flying laughing, "Bravado, you are one lucky bastard," so young and like a dancer, she pledged herself to me. Finally, I did it. The joy of the threshold is as much the ring of the bell of the shop door as it closes behind you, sleeves stuffed with chocolate, as it is the chimes of wedding bells. When I kissed her on the stone steps. Bride in my arms.

Do it secretly, sly and foxily. Kenna said, "Always pick up two, look at one and put it back." It is a matter of deception, the magician's twirling fingers.

Keep your eye on the birdie Stanislaus.

There was the sudden pain of metal scraping and clattering against ceramic. Harry shrugged, apologised, and then bent to retrieve his spoon.

He rose, rubbing his cheek as if in thought.

Fourthly, I eat. Now I must hide my mastication. The swill tastes like mouthwash. It melts upon the tongue, as vaporous and satisfying as cigarette smoke. I had forgotten so much yet the body remembers. My back tingles and my mouth dries and my brain bounces and hugs its old friend, intoxication.

Now my dear I understand the depth of your eyes...oh, the excited spring of the spine, the bowing of a string, an elastic band of time yes I see clearly that all moments are sideways and stretched. There are some seconds which you can never escape.

I feel like my spine will burst from my body and bounce across the lab like a skull on a pogo stick. I want to be everywhere at once, the blood rushes along my arm, all my innards want to be out, I have no desire to be here any more.

And then out of this paranoia comes peace. Remembrance conceived, discarded. A yeastful rising of the flesh, high as a sun rising higher over the horizon and into the firmament. Regardless of earthly divisions and limitations. Like you my dear, I cannot trouble myself with gravity.

No keep a lid on it man.

Flanny's laugh as he swung in pendulous sunlit arcs...so high that the chains slackened. Jumping like baby birds. I will cut you free my dear, and once the tentacles are torn from you you will fly up into space to take up an orbit of the earth. I spend nine hours a day with you, and you alone. Would you be offended if I said that I love you, mon petit couchon, my giggle of pink love, may I pledge my trough to you...am I losing it?...toes edging over the cliff, my arms waving for balance, and below the rocks of hysteria...

Here's to you Stanislaus. Cheers.

Three little piggies,
Smoking ciggies...

A brief bursting snort. Harry went to blow his nose and laughed into his handkerchief. No, I have to contain this, I am too old. I need an anchor. Try to feed. The spoon flipped vertical, surprised. Harry dipped it into the swill (dip), measured intently the amount of swill in the small silver chalice (scoop), raised it to his arms length (lift), and let it tremor slightly beneath the searching snout (hold). Dipscooplifthold. Dipscoopliftdropeat. One for you and one for me.

> *I feed, you eat*
> *in this*
> *We are complete.*

I must be careful when I lift it up to you lest gravity lose sight of me. I feel empty, so light that I may drift away. I will levitate over that tube in your ass that sucks you dry. Of course to be empty we must first be filled. The transcendental enema. Clean me out with Holy Water, flush me clean of memories. I stand here, on the bank, watching the boiling, twisting flow of remembering. You teach me so much with your silent PigZen wisdom. I must tell Rag. Yes, he has to know of all the things you saw when your soul rocketed through space, perched upon a meteor, howling its melancholic hog hymns.

Harry turned away from the pig just as its mouth opened over the spoon. Again, it had been denied. Its flanks trembled angrily.

So here I go again. Close your eyes my dear, for I am about to cross the threshold. Harry strolled away from his feeding zone and into Rag's. His friend looked at him bemused, the two men dressed head-to-toe in white, their bellies pressing against the midriff of their suits, Harry's palms slowly rising toward Rag's face; with astronaut grace, Harry lovingly scrunched Rag's cheeks and smeared them like dough.

"You were right. Good drugs. Bloody good drugs. I feel twenty-one again."

Not a flicker upon Rag's face. I won't speak to Harry. Once he gets started...and Harry felt the reluctance of his friend. A guillotine of paranoia fell at his back. They are all looking at me. A hundred feeders have laid down their spoons, a hundred pigs are cocking an eyebrow in my direction. Can they all read it on my face, the sheer waste of myself, where once time was a party for me, bouncing on into the night and never settling, now it is over. The best guests are long departed. I see my time as a man as fat and slumberous as a settee, and I lie upon it waiting to die from the obesity of my moments.

What? I see melancholy has decided to pay a visit.

Harry trudged back to his pig. He felt the euphoria subside.

The setting of the sun. The descent back into the body with all its agonies and its thousand nagging voices; the mucus sticky in my nostrils; the

The Feeders

anus weak and unable to prevent the bowel; the roaring blood of the ear overwhelming; the lips with their aubergine clumsiness; the penis a mere absence of sensation; yes, I am thrust back into the body where every orifice craves.

The spoon curved from the hold to the dip. Upon its concavity, there was a bulbous face. It peered out at Harry.

Who is this man who follows me everywhere, eyeing my eye, who exists only to drag me down?

The dreaded heels of Stanislaus pounded up to Harry. With slow eyes, Harry turned to face his superior. A lean, tanned young man with very expensive cheekbones. Stanislaus simply pointed, and Harry shambled back to work. The snowman of despair.

B. Azab Powell

The Object at Rest

Bonnie Powell, 22, American Sagittarius, seeks tall, self-aware (not self-absorbed) Fire Sign, 25-35, who appreciates bad action films, midnight feasts, grand gestures, and clumsiness. No owners of small dogs, hairy shoulders, or Melanie Griffith videos. Must be willing to move to New Orleans.

You don't know where to look. The fluorescent lights are bright streaks across the ceiling and there is a scratchy purr from the machines next to each bed. There are no curtains between beds. There is a black family on your left kneeling on the floor beside a man with a gun wound in his leg. Only the old woman stands. Her hair is grey, cropped close to her head like tapped ashes, and she is not touching the man. Instead she is systematically shredding a pink kleenex on to the floor. The white linoleum has little footprint-shaped piles of mud on top of faint brown stains.

Out of all the people who have heard, you are the only one who has come here, to Charity Hospital. You followed the signs to the ICU and had to look at the charts to find him. Because you didn't recognise him. Dan is asleep. You know this because his machine beeps at the top of each red peak. There is nothing on his swinging tray except the book of openings and the National Enquirer that you placed there a few minutes ago. You are surprised to see no traces of any teachers, or any family, having been here before you. Looking at him, you realise that they knew better, that the night after it happened was too soon to come.

Dan's eyebrows and hair have gone white. Yesterday morning when you saw him they were bushy brown. Now his eyebrows vanish against his face and his hair is a white shock like Andy Warhol's. His head is swollen to twice its usual size. His eyes bulge strangely beneath the closed lids. You realise you have never seen him without glasses. A clear tube runs from each nostril and from both arms, which are laid out flat on his stomach palms up. The bare skin of his forearm and wrist has the faint yellow tinge of cheese, but his face is the gray-white of the floor.

You do not want to look at the bandage, but it is like trying not to think of elephants, and you finally cannot look anywhere else. It is as wide as his wide face and completely hides his neck. Blood has crept to the surface in an inky smile under his chin. A loud whistling grunt comes from the next bed and a fetid smell covers the copper one coming from Dan's. You turn your head — the old woman is holding the crumpled tissue to her mouth — and when you look back Dan's eyes are open. His irises are barely visible over the crest of his cheeks.

"It's Gabriel."

You feel odd standing there and so you too crouch by the bed, watching his eye revolve slowly to the corner like a searchlight pointing above you.

"I heard and I wanted to see if you were okay. If I could do anything for you."

The eyelid lowers, widens again, and his hand curls and uncurls on top of the sheet.

"Can you understand me?"

Fine wrinkles on the side of his grey lips spider into a lift; one eyebrow twitches in the lop-sided sneer that is Dan's smile. He raises the hand nearest you an inch, then lets it drop. You take it. You have never touched him before. His hand is cold and smooth as a shell and you hold it in yours, careful not to stare at where the tube goes into his arm or at the brown crusts under his fingernails.

"I didn't know you'd be this bad off or I wouldn't have brought you those."

His eye swivels at his tray and you hold the book and the Enquirer in front of his face in turn. You replace them, chess book on the near end, tabloid on the other corner. You are glad you did not bring flowers. No one in the ICU has flowers or cards. They are all too busy dying quickly or else have just arrived.

Without releasing your hand he drags his to the edge of the book and pulls it, then the paper. Castling them so that the paper is closest to him. His arm drops and he squeezes your hand tightly, briefly, then his eyes close. You have never seen a dead body, never been to a funeral, but you think nothing could look worse than he does.

You are wondering if you should let go and leave, if that might wake him, and if he is even asleep, when a woman arrives stirring a plastic cup of coffee with a fork. She is surprised to see you and sets the coffee on the tray.

"Hi, I'm Ellen. Dan's sister." She looks at least fifteen years older than he used to and too normal in her flowered shirt and blue cardigan.

You mumble your name and, because you are not a 'patient' or a 'client' or even a friend, nothing else. You slide your hand from Dan's, embarrassed that she has seen you holding it, and shake hers.

"I was going. I just wanted to make sure he was okay."

"I'll walk you out."

The Object at Rest

You nod, touch Dan's finger, see that his eyes do not open and turn away. You do not want to talk to her. You did not know that Dan had a sister and you do not want to admit how little you actually know about Dan's life. You did what you came to do and now you want to go home and think about why you did it.

"I didn't know they told all you kids."

"They didn't. They told us he had an accident. I got it out of the secretary."

"You must care about him a lot." She pats your shoulder and you jump as a bell shrills and a red light comes on over a bed at the far end of the room. She steers you to the elevator around nurses bumping from all directions.

"Have they caught the guys who did it yet?"

She studies you, guessing how much you know. "No. Dan isn't going to press charges."

You knew Dan lived in the Quarter and had assumed a mugging had gone out of control, that he had tried to talk them out of it. Now you wonder if a patient from his private practice cut him. It would be like Dan to refuse charges.

"Is he going to be all right?"

"It looks like it. He should have died. The doctor told me when they brought him in his blood pressure was zero. Somehow they stabilized him in time. Now the question is whether he...they have to do a CAT scan for..."

She presses the down button. "I'm sure he will tell you all about it when he recovers. I'll hold on to your things for him."

You ride down in the elevator with an orderly and an empty stretcher, the sheets tangled red and yellow, and walk through the hospital out into downtown. The bus stop for the lakeshore is quite far away on streets piled with uncollected garbage. Every other streetlight is broken, but flames from the oil refineries on the river light the air with a red haze. You watch the shadows of doorways, checking for movement as you always do without thinking.

You live with your mother. She is on call at nights. Often you wake up to the sound of the phone and then you hear her car gasping down the driveway. In the morning she is tired and snaps at you if you refuse breakfast, if you are wearing a shirt with a hole in it, if your hair is over your eyes. Aside from that she leaves you alone. She was notified about Justine; she knew all of you were required to see Dan once a week, but she did not ask about it. She believes that the two of you are close and that if you need to talk to her, you will.

Your parents split up when you were four and she decided charity did not begin at home. You spend every other Christmas with your father in

B. Azab Powell

Lake Charles. He is training to be a paralegal to be more effective against Dow Chemicals, who are dumping into the river upstate. Baths in Lake Charles are brown and gritty. Last year he delivered medical supplies; the year before he was in Hawaii, learning to scuba dive so he could start a wreck salvaging operation. The years you do not spend Christmas with him, you spend the weekend of your birthday instead. You are uncomfortable with each other. He wears black reeboks and a prophet's beard, and shares a house with a twenty-eight-year-old redhead named Corinne. He says it is a crime to have no ideals at your age. The last summer you spent with him, you were eleven and he was living in Santa Cruz. You came back with lice and a sprained wrist that was never seen to and healed stiff. Your mother went to court to get summers removed from the visitation agreement. You were relieved.

The night after you visited Dan is Friday night and you have been invited to the group's party by Sarah. You used to be one of them, but they have been avoiding you and you them since Justine. In art they were talking about Dan and Sarah said that he had died, but the principal didn't want anyone to know yet. You said from behind your easel in the corner, "No, I saw him last night," and there was a silence and then Michael, who is growing his hair like Morrison's and has a lizard tattoo around his wrist, said "You went to Charity?"
"Yeah."
"Did your mom go?"
"No."
The Chopin from the art teacher's tape deck floated over the respectful scratching of charcoal. You were sketching a crumpled paper bag. From your angle the bag had a face, a lot of wrinkles spiralling around a ragged mouth. Then Sarah asked you if you wanted to come to the party tonight, Michael said he would pick you up, and you shrugged. Why not.

Now you are at the party and everything is as it was five months ago. Shine On You Crazy Diamond is playing. Karen is making chocolate chip cookies in the kitchen by herself, except when someone comes in to steal dough. She eats by feeding. The video camera has already been pointed at the TV monitor so that infinity can be experienced. Jeremy, prize guest because he is a senior and gay, is rolling on the cover of Sticky Fingers. He only comes around when Michael has pot, now that Justine is gone. Khan is crying in the corner of the hall over Dan and Michael has his arm around her and is kissing the tears off her chin. The appropriate level of melodrama can still be achieved even without Justine, you think. You slip outside to lie on the slide. It is December, it is cold, and you are the only one by the pool, which is covered with a tarp and piled with dead leaves. In August the

The Object at Rest

parties were swimming parties and the girls wore t-shirts over their swimsuits so no one would think they were showing off. Except Justine. Justine has big breasts and no hips and always looked unbalanced in her blue one-piece.

Sarah slides open the door and walks over to you, her arms folded on her chest, shivering.

"They've got the Ouija board out. I should have burned that fucking thing."

"Why?"

"Because it's evil. Because Jeremy says Asteroth is living here in my house since we invited him. I can never sleep after we play."

"So burn it. It's your party."

"It was Michael's idea." She stands over you on the slide and lets her fingers rest briefly on your neck. They are cold and a little damp.

"Tell me about Dan."

"Why don't you go and see him. In a few days."

"I can't. I would feel weird. I wouldn't know what to talk about."

"He can't talk anyway."

"Is he really bad off?"

"What do you expect? He had his throat cut." You know that you sound superior, nasty, but the only reason they invited you back is for the gossip, and if you give it you will belong again and you do not want to belong again.

"I guess not." Reading your mind, she says, "Gabe, we have missed you, you know. Everything's falling apart. Now we don't even have Dan."

"You don't need Dan."

"Maybe I don't, maybe you don't. But —" she flicks at the glass doors, "they do."

"They don't need anything except some real problems."

"What's happened to you?" There is hurt in her voice.

"Nothing," you say. "Just being bitchy, that's all."

You did like Sarah: she was the one that could be counted on to organize cram sessions, to hold Karen's head when she puked, to talk to parents when everyone else was stoned. She is down to earth and unembarrassed about it. But she cannot see out, you think. She cannot see outside those glass doors.

Justine was the nucleus. She did not believe in small talk. She collected people based on their ability to ask the right questions. If someone brought up the last exam she stared through them until they stuttered. She lived a few blocks away from you out by the lake and stopped by for the first time at eleven o'clock on a school night. Your mother showed her into your room without comment.

B. Azab Powell

You had nodded at each other at the bus stop. You did not know she even knew your name. The first thing she said to you was, "What are you so afraid of?"

You were lying on your bed reading under a green sleeping bag. All of your furniture was arranged to make a cave around the bed: bookcase in front of the window at the head, desk at the foot, a bureau on one side that left a doorway.

"I don't like a lot of space."

"Or light? Why not?" She sat on the desk cross-legged, on top of the papers and record albums.

"I don't know. I like to wake up and not be able to see anything but the ceiling. As if I'm underwater."

She stayed until one, looking through your record collection, reading aloud her favorite passages from *The Fountainhead*, glancing at you for confirmation. You guessed she was giving you signals, but you did not know why.

After she left your mother came out, to see if the front door was locked. Her hair was flat on one side and she looked tired. You told her to go to bed. She said, "I want you to have friends, but wasn't that a little late to be over?"

"She's not a friend. I don't know why she came. I'm sorry to keep you up."

"That's okay, honey. I wake you enough nights. She's a pretty girl, isn't she?"

"I guess. Good night."

Later you wished you had asked Justine what she was doing, had yawned and said you always went to bed early on school nights. Avoided everything. You knew that she wanted your secret. She never got it.

When you were referred to Dan you were annoyed. Justine was in the hospital. The problem was gone as far as you were concerned. Katie should go, her palms burlap from picking them with a safety pin, words scratched on each wrist. Or Karen, ballet dancer built wrong, like a Valkyrie; her instructor slapped her ass with his walking stick and called her crisco butt. 5'10" and 105 pounds soon after that. Her collarbones and ribs showed through like lace. But not you. You had nothing to say.

You sat in the orange plastic chair by Dan's window and watched people jumping across the tracks in front of the streetcar, going to the Lotus or Camellia Grill for lunch. The high school was uptown, in the middle of the city, in a courthouse condemned yearly for inadequate facilities. There was no cafeteria and no gym: you went to the supermarket or a restaurant for lunch and you ran laps on the sidewalk around the school for phys. ed. Dan was new then. There were already three guidance counselors, but finally someone realised this was not a normal school and they hired him. They

The Object at Rest

thought academic pressure was pushing people over the edge. What they did not realize was that requiring an IQ test and an entrance exam only screened out dumb kids with problems. Smart kids invented them faster.

His office was an old storage closet, just large enough for a desk and two chairs. There was a big window that looked down over Carrollton Avenue and you had often seen the back of his head from the street, or else him smoking in the open window.

"Do you know why you're supposed to talk to me?"

"Because we have been exposed to a traumatic incident."

"Well, true, but mostly because the vice-principal is concerned about this clique you're in. She thinks that as a group you are self-destructive and that you are trying to deal with problems no teenager should be responsible for."

"So if we tell them to you, you'll fix them."

"No...I don't have a magic wand. But I would like for you to consider me a pressure valve. You can come in here whenever you want and let off steam. Confidentially."

"Are you a psychiatrist or a psychologist?"

"Why?"

"Do you prescribe drugs?"

"Why? To who?"

"Anybody."

"Does someone you know need a prescription?"

"If they did, I could get my mom to write one. She's a doctor. Just wanted to know which kind you were."

Dan laughed and sat back in his chair. He was one of the ugliest men you had ever seen. He had two fat moles like ticks on his face, one above his left eyebrow and one over his lip. His glasses were thick and square as factory safety glasses. From your side his thin white shirt showed a nipple and its corona of hair. You classified him as a middle-aged nerd who chose social work to jazz up his existence. No possibilities, but no threat.

Then Justine returned to school. Briefly. She was tanked on halidol and hopelessly behind in classes. Justine with her blond bob cut so high her neck required shaving, her too-small men's undershirts. Leg twitching, words slurring, she told them that you needed help, that she was showing you the way to get it. She sat next to you on your bench and clawed at your hand, her voice keening in your ear. Asking why you wouldn't talk to her. Everyone hovering in a loose scared ring like kids when their parents argue. You shoved her off the bench, harder than you intended. A matter of mechanics gone wrong. Force equals (inertial) mass times acceleration. She scraped her leg bloody on the cement. Didn't come back to school. They all avoided you after that. You started talking to Dan.

B. Azab Powell

You spent your last birthday in Lake Charles.

Your father had bought no present for you. He had stir-fried some vegetables and served them with rice turned beige by the water. You sat on the carpet with him and Corinne, getting stoned for the first time. You did not know how to so you drew on the bong until you could not stand it and swallowed all the smoke in one acrid gulp. A cake from Gambino's was melting in the corner by the radiator.

"You're wasting it." He took the bong from you, peered at the red coal glowing on the stem, and drew until the water bubbled and the smoke clouded the glass. He passed it to Corinne and she cleared it.

"He doesn't know how to inhale, Marty." She scratched your knee with long salmon nails. "I'll fill it for you. Just take it in your mouth, don't try to inhale it straight. Breathe a little air in at the same time."

She did and you couldn't. You coughed until you almost retched, then you burped and a tiny fillip of smoke floated out. They finished the rest of the hit alone.

Their living room was empty except for a plant in each corner, and a black and white television on a cardboard box. Your father believed in traveling light. Corinne had left her things at her ex-husband's and was afraid to get them back. You liked her better than your dad. She was pretty but blue eye-shadow made her brown eyes look punched. She tried to make things normal for you when you visited: cooked scrambled eggs in the morning and fried bacon while your father muttered about poisoned flesh. She told you if you ever wanted to bring a friend with you that would be great. She made little finger quotes around friend when she said it.

"Did you know my mother was Jewish?" he asked you, lying on the floor with his feet on the box.

"No." You never met his parents.

"Yep. I had a Bar Mitzvah when I turned thirteen. That's when you become a man, you know. You're a year into adulthood now, Gabriel."

"Goody."

"Are we going to eat that cake or not?" Corinne lit the candles and turned out the light. She sang happy birthday while your father played the plastic of the TV like a bongo. They both kissed you and Corinne fed you cake with the tips of her fingers in the dark. It was white cake with bits of cherries in it; the icing was hard and waxy. You were feeling sick, but the two of them scooped at it until it was gone.

"Did you make a wish?" your father asked.

"I forgot." You had wished you were going home tomorrow instead of Sunday.

Then he gave you Corinne. He found her hand in the shady black and put it in yours. He said good night and stumbled out. They had separate rooms. Hers had a double bed and his a small flat futon. You sat there on the floor with icing on your face holding Corinne's hand. Your heart was beating very fast and there were two pinches of ache behind your eyes.

Corinne pulled you up and led you into her room. She lit a candle. In the light the purple carpet was black and gleamed with fallen strands of long red hair. You watched her in the oval mirror of the dressing table as she began unbuttoning your shirt.

"I don't understand."

"No? It doesn't matter. You don't need to."

Through the thin walls you could already hear your father snoring. Corinne sat you on her bed, and then pulled off her t-shirt. Her breasts were big and bulged out of the sides of her bra. There was a little pouch of fat between each strap and armpit. She leaned down to kiss you and cupped your hand around a breast.

"Not like that. Kiss me back. Pretend there's a strawberry in my mouth and you've got to find it." She tasted like cake and bitter leaves.

You could not sleep. The candle burnt out and dropped into the wine bottle with a hiss. Twice she woke up and went down on you. She rubbed your penis between her breasts and over her nipples but it refused to be anything but soft. She took your fingers and put them inside of her, moaning so loud you were afraid and took them out. You heard your father blowing his nose in the bathroom just as the curtainless windows were turning pink and you were falling asleep.

In the early afternoon you lay in the middle of the bed listening to see who was in the house. There was no noise so you dressed and opened the door to see your father reading the newspaper flat on his stomach on the living room rug.

"Sleep okay?" Impossible to tell if underneath his beard his mouth smiled.

You nodded and ducked into the kitchen. There was a plate of cold pancakes on the counter and a note that said "O.J. and syrup in fridge. Gone shopping for dinner."

Your father turned on the television and you watched soap operas and talk shows together until Corinne came home and the spaghetti was ready. You were unsure if last night was Corinne's idea or his. You thought if you initiated nothing, if you just let it happen to you, it would be all right. You tried again to get stoned and managed to inhale two burning lungfuls but felt no different. Again your father went to his room. This time she succeeded in getting you inside her and made a lot of gasping noises while she scratched at the soft fat on your back. You did not come. Your penis slipped out of her and lay against her leg like a shrimp. When she slept her hair was over your face, a mask of red moss.

The next morning they walked you to the Greyhound station. You were looking at your father's black tennis shoes. You could see an orange dime of sock through a hole in the toe. Corinne hugged you and told you to remember about bringing a friend. He asked you if you liked your birthday present. You looked away mutely and boarded the bus. You sat on the side where they could not see you and rubbed at the brown streaks on your palms with the edge of your sweater. No action. No reaction.

Justine put her arm through the door during a party at Karen's house. You had been upstairs with her while she got drunk.

She took your hand and put it to her lips. "All I want is for you to touch me. No one will touch me. My father can't even look at me. Do I disgust you?"

"No."

"Then why won't you?"

"I can't. I don't want to. I'm sorry."

She took the bottle and fell down the stairs. You followed her. When she went into the living room everyone shut up. In a low voice, she said, "What. What are you looking at. Why is everyone so afraid of me."

She pushed at the door to the back yard but it would not open. Then she smacked it. The glass rattled and shivered but held. When she used the hand with the vodka bottle in it her fist went through. She was not usually very strong. There was glass in her fingers, long shards stuck in her wrist and forearm. Blood everywhere. Without pulling her arm in she began removing the pieces while everyone watched in shock. It was only when she passed out and her arm came crashing back through the remains of the glass that Katie screamed and Sarah called 911 before trying to make a tourniquet out of a headband. You stood shaking quietly with anger in a corner. You left before the ambulance came.

The last conversation you had with Dan was about your secret. He said nothing for a few minutes. His eyes blinked behind his glasses and he rubbed his bare forearms. He had a lot of veins on the top of his arms: they stood out and crossed and recrossed like rivers running into his hands. A man's arms.

"Why didn't you tell me about this before?"

"I don't know. It didn't seem relevant." What you were wondering was why you told him in the first place. You had never thought you would. You had been talking about how Christmas was coming and how it was his year and you didn't want to go. You felt mildly tricked into telling, but you didn't see how it could make any difference.

The Object at Rest

"Did you ever tell Justine?"

"No. Not anyone." The bell rang, meaning your study hall was over. Next period was English. He did not tell you to go.

"Did you want to have sex?"

"I had thought about it. Not like that."

"How did you feel?"

"When?"

"Whenever. About it."

"You mean while she was fucking me or afterwards?"

"Both."

"I felt stupid. I felt like I was not there. When I think about it I can see me with her. I am in the picture. I can see my facial expressions and everything."

"That's not unusual for that type of situation. It can be useful. Do you think you were taken advantage of?"

"Not by her. Maybe by Marty."

"Marty is your dad? Okay. Why not by her?"

"I don't think it was her idea."

"He wasn't standing over her telling her to blow you, was he?"

You laughed at the mental image and he laughed with you. Once you would never have believed he could be so crude. At first you had played chess while you talked. You knew he was listening whenever he got distracted and you beat him.

"No, I guess not. I didn't do anything to stop her. I could have stopped her, I think. I don't know."

"How do you feel now about Corinne?"

"I don't think about her much."

"Do you think it affected what happened with Justine?"

"Of course it did. But I don't see how telling her would have helped me. Or her."

"Maybe. Probably not. What I mean is, do you think it has affected you in regard to women?"

"Dan, I'm fourteen. I don't know any women except Corinne. And my mother."

He leaned forward then smoothed his hair over his balding forehead. His foot started to tap against the leg of your chair.

"How do you feel about telling me?"

"The same, I guess. It doesn't seem like that big a deal. So I had a crappy first time. You've got to hear about those every day. At least."

"I could be wrong, but I think it's more than that. We can talk about it in a few days, if you want. You should go to class. If I keep excusing you Ms. Jergen is going to have my balls in a rubber sling."

71

B. Azab Powell

"One question." There was a tentative tap at the door. His next appointment.

"Yes?"

"Do you still respect me?" You said this in a sultry voice and looked wide-eyed at him.

"Did I ever say I did?" He plucked at the hair over your eyes, then handed you a signed pass and stretched. "Tell whoever it is I need five minutes. Stop by in a few days?"

When you opened the door Katie was standing in the hall picking at her hands. You hated meeting them coming in and out of Dan's office. You did not want to be lumped with them. You imagined that telling him about Corinne would be like sound in a vacuum, go nowhere. You told Katie to wait and before she could say a word walked off.

You lied to Dan. You felt different. Something was moving, shifting. Breaking up like ice under hot water.

A month after that, after he was hurt, you see Dan standing at the main office in between classes. His hair is still white but it is short now. He is wearing a turtleneck and leaning on a cane. He looks like the hostages did when they were released: blinking and afraid.

You look away but he sees you and says your name.

"Hi."

"I just wanted to tell you I'm leaving."

"Bummer." You stand there fiddling with the straps of your backpack and wondering who will see you.

"Can you come up for a few minutes and say goodbye?"

"I've got French. I'm failing."

"Okay." He puts out his hand and you take it. It is warm now, the fingernails clean. "Thank you for coming to see me. It was brave. It did mean a lot to me."

You want to say "me too" but the words are only in your head. Instead you shake his hand and do not think of what might have happened if he had not been hurt. The tardy bell rings and you say goodbye, leaving him leaning in the door of the main office.

You cut class anyway, wait a few minutes, then stand in front looking up at his window. You can see him putting his few things into a cardboard box on his desk. You have heard that a man he picked up in the Back Pocket on Royal street, near his apartment, was the one who cut him. That is why the school is asking him to leave. You do not know if it is true but it comforts you to think that it is. Even random violence has a catalyst. Still, you did not want to know. You thought there was nothing to know so he was safe. If you had gone to talk to him the scar would be in the way, even under his collar. Instead you stand there watching until he appears at the window. He must see you but you do not acknowledge each other. He moves away and the light goes off.

Once Justine called on your line and woke you up. She was across the river and wanted you to meet her downtown. She said she was upset and did not like changing buses on Canal Street alone. You locked the bedroom door then dressed in your cave. You sweated to move the bookcase away from the window so you could climb out. There was no reason you could not go out the front but it seemed like the thing to do.

You were interested in her interest in you. You had gone to their parties and watched her build them into a house of cards that collapsed when she went to the bathroom. If she was absent they might talk about her — "Justine is so domineering"..."Justine makes me believe that there's no point but it's not true." And yet when she was there they were molecules in her wake. She tried her questions on you and you countered with more questions because you didn't need to answer hers. She said your passivity was your best defense. Most people would tell you everything if you asked and were prepared to listen.

When you arrived on Canal you had half an hour to kill. The streetlights were reflected in puddles of oil like bruised stars. Fog rolled in off the river, swallowing the hookers' legs up to their knees. A man came over to where you were standing in a doorway with a view of the bus stop and asked you for money. You shook your head and stepped around him. He was so close you could smell the vinegar stench of his clothes. You spent the rest of the time in Mardi Gras Games, the arcade on Canal known for dealing. It was crowded and dense with smoke; people jostled you and you felt fingers once in your back pocket. You could not play Afterburner because climbing inside the cockpit meant you would not be able to get out quickly.

Outside Justine was already at the bus stop. Hugging her arms to herself with her head lowered into them like a bird trying to sleep. You touched her back and her eyes flung open.

"Fuck. You scared me. I didn't think you would come."

"I said I was."

"I know. Thanks. Not many people would."

You could think of several who would jump at the chance but instead you stood silently until the Lakeshore bus came. No one bothered the two of you. You sat next to her while she shivered in the plastic yellow light and touched her again when it was your stop. You offered to walk her to her street.

"I don't want to go home. Can you get me in your house?"

You both climbed in the window and into your bed. She was tired and

B. Azab Powell

shaking; you wrapped her in your sleeping bag. It was strange to see her like this, not acting. You felt almost tender towards her and told her to be calm, to sleep.

"Has anyone told you what happened to me last year?"

You remember Katie being snotty about something when Justine was not there and them shutting her up. Looking at you.

"No."

"I was raped." She sat up and leaned on one elbow, sharp edge of her jaw obscured by blond hair.

"Someone you knew?"

"No. I was walking on the river front. Around those buildings from the World's Fair they haven't torn down. He pulled me into one of the loading bays and did it right there. In the open. He had a gun. I don't know if it was loaded."

You felt she had played her trump card and you did not want to play. "Why are you telling me?"

"I thought you would understand. I see how you are with people. We're opposite but we both need to control. That was the first time I was not in control. Now it's worse. I wondered if you had felt that."

"I don't think I am that way. Besides, that was something you couldn't possibly have stopped. It was not a question of you being in or out of control."

"So it shouldn't have affected me that he left me tied to a railing with come on my face until a kid walking her dog found me?"

Her questions were too rhetorical. It occurred to you she had told this story many times before, waiting for the right reaction. Equal and opposite. Someone to solve it for her. "Well, you have been affected. It's given you the power, hasn't it? None of them can top that."

"Fuck you." She turned over and buried her face in the pillow. Her shoulders shook and shook and you heard her say fuck you many more times before you gathered her into the curve of your arm and stomach. Whispered her hair to sleep. Be still. Nothing can hurt you if you don't move. Be still.

Four days after Dan collected his things is January 28, your fifteenth birthday. You are sitting in biology alone at your lab table. You are failing biology and French and possibly even geometry, which you like. Your mother has been called in for a conference on your academic probation. The teachers are perplexed and willing to attribute your apathy to Justine and Dan, but you tell them that none of that matters, that school itself matters least. At the end of this semester you will be kicked out and sent to Catholic school, since your mother thinks the other public schools are too dangerous. Once the only thing you would have missed was Dan. Now you are sorry you will be unable to take physics. You wanted to learn all of the rules.

The lab tables are black, vulcanized rubber eroded by carved initials and song titles, including "Blasphamous Rumors" on Justine's old side. That 'a' has bothered you for months and you have tried to make it into an 'e' but without success. The teacher is late and comes empty-handed: you were supposed to be taking a test on taxonomy. He announces that a bomb threat has been phoned in and that everyone must line up and file out as quickly as possible. Several people cheer — bomb threats and fire alarms are frequent and kill three hours at least. At first you are glad because all you know is King Philip Came Over From Germany Singing and that would not have gone very far. You stand outside among the kids smoking and laughing and flirting. You watch the fire truck and the police cars with their flashing lights wasting their time on someone's idea of how to duck an exam. It occurs to you that you would rather be in school, taking the consequences. After lunch the all-clear bell rings and people trickle back in from the daiquiri shop and the pancake house. No one remembers to sing you happy birthday in any of your classes, but the year is over.

Alan Cowley

Danny Delight

Alan Cowley is Sussex born and did his first degree at Bretton Hall College of the University of Leeds. The following is an extract from an untitled novel in progress.

Arthur, Alvin and me

"I don't understand," I said.
Luscious Maria's fluorescent dentistry beamed as her enamelled lips peeled away into a smile that was dazzling. Rory Calhoun said so. Luscious Maria leapt up and down, waving her arms above her head in an ecstasy of fulfilment; her body was pneumatic. Rory Calhoun had told me.
The music died, and with it the audience's whoops of pleasure found bliss. Pleasure...Found...Bliss. Bliss. Bliss.
Caught in the excitement of the crowded, brightly lit and happy studio, the King Charles Spaniel yapped on into the silence, causing Rory to miss his cue. Rory took this in his stride; Rory was a pro. His body straightened and his face widened as he snapped into his Cary Grant routine. "Madam, Madam. Kindly control your dog!"
The audience howled (I can think of no better word) with approval. TV audiences often do. A man seated in the front row spread his hands across a corpulent belly and shook with laughter, eyes twisted tight into crow's feet that reached across his face to join with his mouth and for a moment, a dust particle of time, he looked more alien than human, a Klingon extra wandered into the wrong studio by mistake. Members of TV audiences often can.
Rory's voice was good, you had to admit it, but at five one — five four in his elevated shoes — it would have taken a great deal of straightening to give him the physical presence of the movie star, and as for the face-widening! Someone should have told him about physiology, someone should have shown him a mirror, what were agents and managers for? Rory winked to the camera, Rory swaggered while standing still, Rory called himself pint-sized. The pint-sized king of comedy, your pint-sized host. I laughed. How

had such an absurd analogy become a cliché?

Rory read from the autocue with a letter-box smile, his voice rose and the audience roared again. It was time for the grand final of Doggy Do or Die.

"What could possibly cause you to put your dog's life at stake for a game show?" I asked.

Alvin's eyes were fixed on the screen, his cheeks and nose lightly flushed by his excitement. It must be quite an embarrassment to have a nose that blushes, that turns into the proverbial beetroot, especially with a nose as prominent a feature on a face as Alvin's was: bulbous-tipped, like it was full of air and could be pumped up. I thought of reaching forward and bending back each of his ears to see if I could find a little pump hidden behind one of them, or perhaps his earlobes themselves were pumps! If you squeezed them and pulled them, kind of like milking a cow, his nose would inflate and become redder and if you put a finger in his ear, kind of like deflating a tyre, it would shrink his nose. Perhaps he deflated it before he went to bed, like taking out your false teeth and putting them in a pot. Perhaps he really had a nose like post-op Michael Jackson and was too ashamed to show it to anyone. I am cruel, and this worries me sometimes.

On the TV, the audience sang in unison, following the movement of Luscious Maria's crimson-tipped hands which moved like an orchestra conductor's, only without the baton, only without the orchestra.

"Doggies do, doggies do, doggies do or die!"

"Doggies do, doggies do, doggies do or die!"

For the briefest of moments Alvin took his gaze from the screen to look at me, his mouth holding a close-lipped enigmatic smile. Great word enigmatic, I could get addicted to it. Enigmatic. Enigmatic. But I don't use it self-indulgently, he definitely had a genuine enigmatic smile and he used it frequently.

"The financial aspect is crucial," he said, "Don't you think?"

An air horn started the grand final; there was another vocal eruption from the audience as the dogs leapt from their traps, urged on with desperate enthusiasm by their owners. Alvin sat forward in his squashy sofa chair, his smile unchanged. Cynical? You could suggest his lips possessed the sneer of a cynic, it would hold validity among a group of watching strangers, but when you knew him — and you'll have to take my word on it for now — you found he didn't have a cynical bone in his body. Shall we say a bashful, modest smile with a trace of the dark unknown. That sets it up nicely for later on.

The grand final of the small pedigree class of Doggy Do or Die was between the previously mentioned yap-happy spaniel and an albino dachshund called Arthur. Things were looking pretty grim for Arthur. He trailed by eight points and as he nosed his star-spangled yellow ball through the obstacle course his little white legs pushed him forward with a casual ease that pronounced him pitifully unaware of the consequences of failure. Coco the spaniel exited the plastic tunnel before Arthur had reached it. The owners ran alongside the track, leaning as near to their animals as they dared — the rules preventing physical contact. Arthur's owner urged him on with pained eyes.

"Look at that face, think of the emotions involved, the implications of winning and losing, it's such an experience! Awesome!"

I liked Alvin, he had zest. He also had a view of the world that made you think. Perhaps he had belief. I'm not sure if I've got belief or not, that's another thing that worries me.

The second time I visited Alvin he was doing the washing up, and afterwards he did what he called the washing down. This involved holding every piece of cutlery, every plate, every cup, every pan, individually under the running hot water tap, just turning it under the stream in his pink marigolds before arranging each item meticulously on the draining rack.

"Why do you do that, Alvin." I asked.

"*The Pulse of the Nation* advises people to do it. Did you know that the detergent suds left after washing up dry on the cutlery and crockery and then come off on the food when you next eat. It can give you stomach and intestinal complications, and can even cause the dreaded Big C. Why take the risk!"

I momentarily saw the inside of my stomach, with 26 years worth of accumulated soap suds fizzing and bubbling around my spaghetti bolognese. No wonder I belched so much.

The owner of Arthur, a pale baggy-faced woman with a limp bob, an ochre cardigan with bulging pockets and a shiny name-tag that flashed in the light so you couldn't read it, was wailing hysterically into Arthur's ear. This turned out to be a successful change of strategy, Arthur skipped up a gear, or perhaps bounced up a gear would be a better choice of words, synchronizing his speed with his control of the ball; his rear legs thrust up as his nose went down and he looked like a cross between a floppy-eared rocking horse and those nodding dogs people used to put in their car windows until they were banned because other drivers mistook them for the driver's hand waving them on, causing them to pull out in front of oncoming vehicles.

"I've got this theory," Alvin said, "that all humans have a need to experience the full range of emotions which they are capable of feeling and that modern society suppresses this. For instance, we don't fear for our lives on a daily basis, we don't have fights to the death any longer, and that's why we need shows like this. They're a substitute for the life and death experiences nature has prepared us for and which unconsciously we still need, only this

way it's safe because nothing will really happen to us or the contestants!"
"The dog!" I protested.
"Precisely. The dog and not us. You can't get closer than man's best friend."

I pondered on this for a while and decided to say no more; I didn't want to upset Alvin.

"Look at him go. Look...at...him...go!" He slammed his hand into the soft pillow of his chair arm. Arthur was gaining on Coco, going clean through the chicane where the spaniel had bounced his ball clumsily off both side walls. "Stamina is the key to the race."

Now, I had better come clean. No fudging. Coco was the kind of dog I hate, the kind that yaps 23 hours a day, runs incessantly across your feet and I have no doubt he would have liked to luncheon on my cotton/acrylic-mix socks, with my ankles still in them, given the smidgen of a chance. Arthur, however, had a character for which I couldn't help but feel affection, and I say that as a fully paid-up member of the anti-dog league. He might have been a dirty, smelly, portable crap-dispenser, but he had a charm of sorts. I wanted to sit on the edge of my seat, like Alvin, my fingers biting the chair arms, I wanted Arthur to win and live. Why?

Fraud.

Sucker.

Gullibility.

It didn't matter if Arthur won or lost, either way a dog would be killed.

Having to accept that you're not as fucking great as you think you are is a foul medicine to taste. A frequent if irregular dose is dispensed my way and it's no good, no good at all. I have an image to live up to, for myself if no-one else. I am cool, the unaffected observer who controls the distance between himself and what he observes. But the truth will out at times and there's nothing that can be done about it. Method acting is for actors and not for freelance forklift drivers and part-time mysterious mystical investigators, but we must try.

So for a few moments, milli-minutes in the mega-hours of life, I am forced to confront my own fallibility, question my autonomy, for a few moments, milli-minutes.

"Argh, yeeessss!" Orgasmic glee, feverish fulfilment, the kind that makes TV executives' eyes sparkle with malevolent satisfaction. What tongue touch, what kiss, what liquid, jet-propelled moment had brought Alvin to that point? Disaster had befallen Coco. Through the watersplash, just a ten-metre sprint from the finishing line, the spaniel had lost the ball. It bobbled enthusiastically in the blue tinted water, ducking and diving with new found freedom as Coco spun about yapping and panting in equal measure. Arthur nosed his ball past the confused spaniel, pausing briefly to blink pale eyelids over pink eyes in Coco's direction.

"Go, Arthur, go!"

I want to mention milli-minute manipulation, the crown jewel of TV. For milli-minutes Alvin's whole passionate heart (I dare not speak for you, I dare not even speak for myself; let Alvin stand proudly as the representative of the manipulated masses while we watch, perhaps bemused, perhaps smug, and I prattle my pedantic philosophy to my heart's content) yes, Alvin's whole heart and mind were committed to Arthur's unwitting battle to save himself and condemn a less charming dog to death. For those milli-minutes the world had shrunk to the size of a T.V set and Arthur's fate had become the central concern of Alvin's life. Nothing mattered but that Arthur triumphed, elation or depression, contentedness and discontentedness; the poles of emotional well-being were tested by the milli-minute moment. If the phone had rung it would have been left unanswered, if the building had caught fire it would have burnt down around him.

Alvin's surround-sound four-speaker TV system brought the crescendo of audience noise to my eardrums: I felt them vibrate like wobble boards. Arthur was through the watersplash. With sleepy-eyed dignity he shook the droplets off his coat, pushed his ball forwards and trotted on towards the glittering finishing tape. As he did so a digital clock flashed up into the top right-hand corner of the TV screen, counting down seconds.

"The final countdown!" declared Alvin. "They both have 60 seconds to finish the course!"

Blink-and-you-miss-it editing.

Arthur, audience, owners. Coco, audience, Arthur.

Coco, Arthur, Coco, Arthur, Doggy Delicious Delights.

Doggy Delicious Delights?

"The ultimate test of dogability!" boomed Rory. "Can they resist the taste of the dog's favourite treat!"

Maria ran down the course scattering Delights all about.

Mega crescendo, Coco out of the water, with ball and 30 seconds to go.

One metre from the tape and Arthur stopped, he sniffed, he turned about, his nose to the ground and Coco was gaining, Coco was gaining, Coco was...

Arthur had a poise that I would aspire to — if only we could all pass through life so unaware and unruffled by trauma. He kicked his ball over the winning line, he trotted through the tape to be scooped into the arms of his owner, and Coco was...

Tucking into the delicious delights, as if telepathically aware that the audience, caught in its milli-minute moment, wanted him to do so more than any other thing in the world. To Maria's cheerleading the audience

83

Alan Cowley

counted down the last ten seconds, and Coco wolfed down his delights like there was no tomorrow.

Bells, horns, sirens.

Wails.

The end.

Coco's owner, her face paling to a monochrome grey, lifted the spaniel and held him to her breast. Her eyes were two bruises, dark and painful. Turning from the camera she bolted off the set.

"She's done a runner," said Alvin, smiling unenigmatically. "Want another lager?"

Now the milli-minute moment was over. They finish just like that. What was central to your desire became irrelevant in the blink of an eye. Milli-minutes are to be condemned. Milli-minute moments are to be avoided.

"I'm fine, thanks." I lifted my half-empty can and shook it lightly.

"Help yourself when you're ready." Alvin went to his kitchenette, peering at the TV from over the counter as he ripped another Purple Heart from the six-pack in the fridge.

Arthur had been put on a pedestal, he had a garland around his neck and was surrounded by cans of dogfood. He had won a lifetime's supply of Rovermeat with added breath-freshener, a doggy make-over at the Dogetiquette Grooming Parlour and a gold-studded collar.

His owner had won £50,000.

In the corner of the studio, monitored by two members of the security staff, Coco was hidden behind the huddled, bent form of his owner. The audience had started another chant, they threw out their arms as they sang, pointing, pointing, pointing.

"Your dog must DIE!"

"Your dog must DIE!"

Meanwhile

    Black, blue and red.
    Black night.
    Black city.
    Black feet.
    Black blue.
    Blue black
    Blue black uniform, static cackle.
    Blue lights on rooftops, dance floor flash but here's no party.
    Red Blood, blood red, not roses, most definitely not roses.

Danny Delight

Five blue bodies, black clad, tainted red.
Now the story can really begin.

Just Me

Montpellier sounds a great place to live, doesn't it? If you tell people from outside the city that you live in Montpellier their eyebrows raise, they crack jokes about living in the South of France. Behind knowing smiles you see their minds weaving images of tree-lined avenues, summer parks and Georgian architecture, immaculate streets used as locations in BBC costume dramas. It's a good idea to fantasize that you are seeing these things; I do it sometimes when I walk home at night, it takes my mind away from worrying if a mugger's about to spill my guts out for my wallet or the local pusher's going to grab me from behind and inject an illegal substance into my arse to get me hooked as part of his latest sales drive. We've got bars on our windows and a steel plate screwed to our door, most people have around here. Safety is the box of brick and plaster called home, a mini castle in the feudal land of Montpellier, a mini olde England with concepts like honour removed; if they ever existed, and the reinstatement of trial by combat.

We have a mini castle, a box on the second floor of a Victorian terrace, a flat with a bedroom, a lounge, a kitchen and a bathroom. Four little boxes inside the bigger one. And outside is Montpellier, which is a box itself, squeezed between the Central Business District (remember your schoolkid geography, we might not know Birmingham from Manchester on a map but at least we all know about CBDs), the new retail business park to the east, the canal and ring-road to the north, and to the west, the Asian community that takes a street out of Montpellier on average every two years, operating its own rule of apartheid.

Boxes need walls and there are walls aplenty round here; there's even a Wall Street, which I walked down that night on my way back from Alvin's. It runs the length of an old factory that's been closed forever by the looks of it. Wall Street is the red-light district (have you ever wondered why it's called a district when it's always just one street or one half of a street?) I always use Wall Street at night because I feel safe in it, there are so many people around, loads of traffic, the cops patrol it regularly and if you walk on the side with the houses you get hardly any hassle from the women. That particular night business must have been bad because a girl crossed the road to speak to me.

"Company, mate?" Eyes rimmed with crusted mascara, blusher that looked like a bruise, perhaps it was.

85

One of the first times I walked up Wall Street with Cally, just after we'd moved to Wellington Road, there had been a kid standing on the corner of Kettle Street; she was on her own and had the shakes real bad. Cal had given her 15 quid, all the notes we had on us, and then we'd walked her back to her bedsit.

"It wont do any good," I said afterwards, "she'll be back on the corner in an hour."

"I know, I know."

I don't know what's worse, just walking on by or trying to buy off your conscience.

"Another time!" the girl called after me. I waved.

Wall Street seems better lit than the other streets, though that's probably a psychological trick played by my own mind. Whatever, my walking pace always picks up in the final two streets before Wellie. I have to confess that I've never been attacked in Montpellier, my height serves me well in that respect, but I feel it's only a matter of time before, statistically, I must become a statistic, as our home, our mini castle, has twice joined the police list of unsolved burglaries and I guess it's still there unless they've beaten some misanthrope into confessing to a backlist of crimes in order to clear their books.

Cally walking through Montpellier alone worries me very much, but what can you do? I've no right to stop her. She has some statistics of her own, and she throws them at me whenever my chauvinism so much as peeks from beneath the foot that I have tried so hard and so unsuccessfully to squash it under, where it will remain squirming for as long as I live.

Cally, Cally, Cally.

I'm toying with the idea of changing the chapter title from Just Me to Cally and Me, but Cally's not a central character to this story so can it be justified? Arthur isn't a central character either and he got his name into the titles, so why not!

Mmmmmmmmmmmmmmmmmmmmmmmmmmmmmmmmmmmmmmmmmm mmmmmmmmmmmmmmmmmmmmmmmmmmmmmmmmmm

Decision.

Cally is mega-hour material, Cally is the passion of my life and she shall have a chapter all to herself and damn the indulgence of it.

I guess I should tell you about mega-hours. Life is made up of mega-hours and it is not made up of milli-minutes. Whether Arthur lives or dies, whether England win at football, whether Hollywood Hunk has got in the knickers of Supermodel matters nothing to your life beyond that milli-minute; but who you share your life with matters, loving and being loved matters, things that reach to your core and stay there matter, even why you live in Montpellier while Mr and Mrs Rich-Winker live across town matters.

Danny Delight

These things are important, aren't they?
 I should campaign to highlight the mega-hour quality in people's lives, it is the way to happiness, it really is. It's truth above fraud, a new way of seeing, and it's not about BIG hours it's about different hours. I'll start a mega-hour party and stand for Parliament! I'll break the mould of British Politics!
 Perhaps.
 Or perhaps not.
 Perhaps I'll just write about Cally, about why she's so beautiful, why she's so special, why I love her and how she makes my life so mega-hour brilliant! And you might get the idea just the same.
 But you'll have to wait for that.
 Now where was I?
 Right, hurrying between Wall Street and Wellie, slightly in fear for my life and nothing unusual in any of that. Down Godolphin Road and cut through Pink Street, which has three houses that were refurbished as stage one of the gentrification of Montpellier; was that ever a daft idea! Trees in raised beds, brass door fixtures, pseudo-Georgian windows and now spray-can prole artwork; plus the fading image of power-dressed guys an' gals sprinting out of the street with their tarnished Beamers tucked between their legs and their potential capital investment returns stuffed up their arses. I guess they win some and lose some.
 Wellie has council-built bumps, raised strips of bitumen that reach across the road every 30 yards to stop the street being used as a racetrack; whoever thought it sounded like a great idea forgot to consider it might be even more fun to use the humps to experiment in the possibilities of wingless flight. I mention this only as an explanation for why the noise of an approaching police siren and the crash of a car's suspension system succeeded in drowning out my thoughts as I fumbled for my house keys in my jacket pocket while I stood outside number 87 Wellington Road.
 Number 87, with its windows like shiny bright eyes and its door a cheerful smile of contentment in a grey neighbourhood. The roof a perky hat to lend it that cheeky-chappy look, and I kid you not when I tell you that there are fairies living in the back yard. Number 87 in a line of happy houses and this is where we live. There are two keys for the two locks on the outer door and three keys for the three locks on the door of flat four, two of which have to be fitted and turned at the same time to get it to open (insurance company demand) and the single third lock has to be opened last. Follow me? I have no idea how we will ever get into our flat should we ever lose our keys — hire Harry the Housebreaker I guess.
 Entrance gained, I found the flat dark and empty and I'll be completely honest with you here because I'm not one of those guys on some macho ego trip; I don't want to hide the truth, I have a deep fear of returning to an

Alan Cowley

empty house. I suppose it's a selfish characteristic, the need for me to come home to life signs — the jacket hanging on the coathook, boots kicked in the corner, the hum of something electric and the anticipation of touching and sharing with another — a kind of validation of myself, and when it's not there the eggshell fragility of my life and my happiness flashes into my consciousness, my gut knots with dread. I think there are few things more painful than loneliness, it's a hurt that cuts through the physical and while there is a limit to physical pain, a point where it becomes so great you pass out, the capacity for emotional hurt is infinite and it is a terrifying prospect.

So.
Door unlocked.
Darkness.
Stillness.
Emptiness and other things like that.

And me in my morbid moment, thinking of that twist of fate, that act of God that could happen, that might happen to unbalance my egg cart, unbalance me. Myself. Selfish thoughts make me feel guilty, can you understand that? Do you feel that too? Perhaps you should cross out this paragraph, strike it from the book, who wants to dwell on such things, who wants to be pummelled by the seepage from the darker corners of my mind?

There was a note from Cally stuck on the phone with Blu-Tak.

Vicki rang
Dinks want you tomorrow
be back when I fucking want to
         Kiss Kiss

Bugger.
Six-thirty start tomorrow to be at Dinkins 'We pine to do business with you' Timber Merchants to clock on for eight.

Let me ask you, how do you feel about work? How do you feel about being an exploited cog in the capitalist machine, or the drop of oil that keeps the cog turning, depending on your luck of the draw? I try to make the best of it as I await the day of mega-hour fulfilment for all, and you know, for my own needs, I think I've got it pretty sussed. Getting up at six-thirty is a bugger but once I'm there it's fun if I want it to be. I reckon I've tweaked the system to suit me.

How? How have you successfully tweaked and sussed capitalist exploitation, I hear you cry, or is that just wishful thinking on my part?

Well, the answer is to become a freelance forklift driver, but don't tell everyone or there won't be any work left for me. You see, it has no responsibility beyond making sure you don't run somebody down or impale them through their eyeball socket with one of your forks; you get paid the same for a three-day week as a full-timer gets for five days, and you have control over when you work, you fit it around your life, not vice versa.

So I can devote most of my life to the things that make it great, and for a break, for just two or three days a week, I whizz around warehouses playing at cars, and I get paid for it! I have to admit though, lying in bed until lunchtime is slightly more fun, and when the truth be told, I don't really believe I'm bucking the system because the system can't be bucked, can it? Bravado, wish fulfilment, call it whatever you want and dress it up in bold words but I'm just a dog turd on the pavement of life like everyone else, what do I really know? What do you really know? We've got to eat. We've got to work.

I screwed the note up and threw for the waste paper bin and missed, turned to put on the radio but thought better of leaving a paper bomb on the floor after past experience.

"Rubbish...bin. Bin...rubbish." Cally had an example of each in her hands. "See how it's done!"

Then she hit me around the head with the bin, which was made of metal, but only thin stuff, like biscuit-tin lids are made of, and it didn't really hurt and she didn't really mean anything by it because it was a gentle blow and she hit me with its softest part.

I put the paper bomb into the bin then put on the radio because I hate the silence when I'm alone. I have a game I play with the radio, an ambition I want to fulfil. I want to skip across the dial listening to each station in turn just long enough to hear what they are playing. ZZZZZZZZBlahZZZ ZZZZZBlahZZZZZBlahZZZZZZZZZZZBlah. I want to catch all the stations playing the same record at the same time (excluding, of course, talk radio, sports radio, news radio, classical radio and easy listening). The best I've had so far is five stations playing a cover version with one station playing the original and I haven't made up my mind if that counts or not. That night I was again thwarted, a couple of records could be heard twice and that was all. I've found it's best to try during the day, the shows are less specialized then. ZZZZZZZZBlahZZZZZZBlahZZZZZZZBlahZZZZ Cool Groove. Cool was an 'in' word again, I had noticed that. It runs in a cycle, at this moment in time it is simply the 'cool' thing to use, but by the time you read this it could well be the 'uncoolest' word to use, once again taking its place as the cardinal sin of street credibility, guaranteed to produce ignobly dire consequences should you miscalculate and drop it into your conversation. Social ostracism will be the end result.

I decided to settle the dial on talk radio. ZZZZZZzzZZzzZzWhat people do in the privacy of their own home is their business, but it is unnatural and perverted and we don't want it shoved down ourzzZZZZZZ. Then I changed my mind and tried news radio. ZZZZBlahZZZZZZzzZzDeath penalty is the only way to stop these kind of crimes. The death penalty. The death penaltyZZZZZ. News is talk, talk is news; my mistake. I tuned back in to Mr Cool Groove and grabbed an apple from the fruit bowl, then let myself fall over the back of the sofa so that my head and back rested on the seat cushions and my legs dangled over the top. As I bit into the Golden Delicious I reflected on how my mother would have told me not to lie like that, I would get indigestion if I ate that way, and then I thought she would be right, I probably would get indigestion eating that way, but it didn't stop me doing it.

I ought to warn you about my passion for sofas. I LOVE them. You can flop on to them any old how and be comfortable, feel the soft foam bulging against its fabric casing, push it in and watch it pop back out into shape. That's why I'm particularly enamoured of puffed-up squashy settees with back cushions that wrap over the top and are fixed behind with wide buttons covered in matching fabric that make dents in the shape. I like soft arms but I hate hard arms. I hate bare wood on a sofa and most especially I hate vinyl coverings. We have two sofas in our flat, one a sofa-bed for when we have visitors, which is coloured in blue-and-red checks and has round arms that can be pulled off to be used for pillows, and a big three-seater which is green and yellow with red flowers on it and has a high squashability rating, plenty of fabric-covered buttons and gently sloping arms that you can snuggle your head and neck into. Sinking into its baggy cushions is like pulling on your favourite old jumper.

I lay there with my feet over the back until they began to tingle with pins and needles, remembering making love with Cally in that position last week, first with me in —

Stop.

At that moment the phone rang.

Susan Elderkin

Letter from Earth

Susan Elderkin was born in 1968. Since graduating from Cambridge University, she has worked in book and magazine publishing and as a journalist. She was awarded the Curtis Brown Scholarship to study Creative Writing at UEA.

When I met Rosa, writes my father, nothing could have stopped us.
The world was tugging at our fingers. She was as eager as a cat.

The day my mother turned 35, she took the long swathe of thick brown hair that hung around her shoulders, twisted it tight like a corkscrew up to the nape of her neck, and fixed it to the back of her head with a metal clasp. "That," she said, "is that." Her husband stared at her from across the other side of the breakfast table, looking as if he had just landed heavily and on the wrong foot after an effortless pirouette that had lasted 12 years. He raised a folded napkin to his mouth to hide his twitching lips. They looked at each other for a moment, he from over the white wall of his napkin, she from under the blank and dewy cover of her eyelids. Then, with a magician's determination, he drew the napkin across his mouth from one corner to the other, and presented the world with a pair of lips newly cast in a seal of bitter composure. He never saw my mother with her hair down again: from that day on her face loomed large and pale around the house, her temples and jaws squared off by their home-made wimple; and he took to spending weekends away from home.

That, in any case, is how the story looks to me. My father gives me one side, and I fill in the rest. There are, of course, unequivocal things like the rain falling hard and fast like nuts on to the corrugated iron roof or the blare of ships' horns in fairytales about sailors returning from sea, but as far as I'm concerned, the rest is up for grabs. Jerry's hands, for example, are a matter of opinion. Huge black hands with veins crisscrossed like mountain ranges on one side and on the other a network of dark rivers scouring out the creases; but are they good hands or bad hands? Sometimes, in the night, I wake up to find myself staring down into the two great bottomless caverns of his nostrils, bored out by God's two fingers to act as my windows on eternity, each one edged with a muscle that flexes in and out as I watch, as strong and vig-

Susan Elderkin

orous as the invisible pulsing energy on the very limits of the universe that holds the stars and the planets in place.

I am 19, and I am not interested in my father. Up until now he has left me more or less to myself. This is thanks to Rosa. It is also thanks to Rosa that he has started to write to me, or so I suspect. He writes long, feverish letters. I only take in the bits about Rosa. I am using them to build an image of her. I do not believe everything he says; I build her more or less to my own specifications, and now Rosa squats in a shoe box under my bed, and keeps an eye on me. I like having her there.

When my father met Rosa, she was working as a waitress in a café in the city. My father was one of the men in suits who came for their business lunch, enormously pleased with their buttoned-up paunches, which they carried before them like presents in striped boxes. They waggled great wads of gold-tethered fingers to attract her attention, and over she came, watching them as they rocked back and forth on their rounded backsides, hissing through clenched teeth at their own waggish jokes. One by one they became aware of her, looking up at her with sidelong glances, and then quickly coughing into their fists to hide the spittle on their lips. One by one they raised their eyebrows at one another over their coughs and knuckles. She moved round the table pouring out the wine, and as she went, each in turn squeezed his buttocks together and inched himself to the edge of his chair in the hope that she might brush against his arm, or his ear. When she had been round the table, they watched her walk back into the kitchen and began to murmur amongst themselves. My father brushed the breadcrumbs off his lap, and thought: Her thighs move like brandy rocking in a glass.

> *But things are never as good as they look, writes my father. It's all temptations and promises, and then you fall down the trapdoor in the floor and find yourself stuck there for another ten years.*

Sometimes at night, if we're not quite ready to go to sleep, Jerry and I get up to dance our 'hokey'. We don't put on any music, but Jerry sings in soft, inky notes, the rim of his teeth just showing behind his bruised lips, and we dance slowly round and round each other's bodies, seeing how close we can get without touching. Sometimes it's so dark that the air is full of black and white dots like newspaper print and we could even be in space, floating in the vacuum, like two uncreated people waiting to be born. Jerry leans backwards, bending at the waist like a lean brown sapling, and I lean over him, balancing on the tips of my toes. Jerry says we mustn't touch: if we do we break the spell.

> *Angels, having no bodies, are free to concentrate on the abstract*

Letter from Earth

> *things in life. I, however, have been tangled up in the physical turmoil of legs and arms and hair and teeth, quite helplessly, and without an inkling of how to get out, for the past 50 years.*

Afterwards we get back into bed and our bodies are warm and we lie side by side, still without touching, and talk about anything we can think of. Jerry's face glows with a warm, sweaty film, and his eyes shine out like moons. If you could go into space, I ask Jerry, what do you think you would find? He tells me that he would find a planet, dry and crusty with the empty shells of long-dead creatures left behind when the seas dried up — starfish, shrimp and scorpion shells, and the brittle grey skins of snakes — all crackling underfoot like a million splintering fingers. This planet does not have its own place in the cosmos, but is whipped up by the winds, and sent spinning from one corner of the vacuum to another, the empty shells sizzling every time the planet passes too close to the sun.

> *It would be nice to see you, Sylvie. Maybe I could come and stay with you and Jerry in your little shack by the sea? Just to see how you are getting on.*

And what about you? asks Jerry. What would you find? I tell him I would go out to the garage and put on my spacesuit: my motorbike helmet, rubber gloves and painting overalls with the zip up the front. Then I would float out through the skylight and up over the sea, buoyed up by an enormous breath that comes from somewhere under the ground, as if gravity, holed up down there, has filled its lungs to capacity after a billion years of breathing in and has decided that it's time to breathe out. And when I'm up there in the blackness, with the meteors and satellites and bits of debris from the universe drifting past, I'll reach out my hand and pluck things from their orbits until my pockets are full; and then, weighed down by my souvenirs, gravity will suck me back through a gap between its teeth, back down through the skylight, and grip me firmly by the ankles. And then I will show you what I have found: a piece of granite stuck with bright quartz like cut glass, so sharp that it pierces my hands through the rubber gloves, and three translucent stones, smooth and perfectly rounded, in blue and red and green, so bright that they hurt our eyes.

> *I can't help thinking that the fundamental contract was unacceptable. It should never have been signed. "Allotment per being: one life. Average life span: 70 years, but no guarantee thereof. Each life to be cut off at any point in time without the being's consent and without prior warning; or, alternatively, with ample warning, in which case*

the cut-off time may be long and drawn out. Deal." There it is, the piece of paper slapped on the table, and within all the rush and restlessness of the unknown time span, you're supposed to find happiness. On your marks, get set, go. You may laugh, Sylvie, but the day I think about most was spent not with your mother, or Rosa, but driving through France with you to see your grandparents. We were doing 95 and the trees flicked past one after the other and we had the sunroof down and you were singing one of your interminable, wordless, tuneless songs. I thought you would drive me mad, but I have never been happier than that.

Then, when we've listened each other out, we lie back on the bed, and feel the firmness of the mattress beneath us, and the wooden bed legs beneath that, and then the floor, and the ground going all the way down to the centre of the earth, and we listen to the earth itself. And out of the silence, if we listen really hard, we start to hear the soft babble of all the people living around us, scraping back their chairs, stacking their plates one on top of the other, turning their keys in the locks for the night, whispering to each other in their sleep; and then, country by country, all the people from around the world join in, some in low-pitched murmurs, some in jangles and torrents, but all softly and slowly and coming from far away; and then we hear the animals join in, the booming of the whales under water, the rattle of snakes, the screech of monkeys and the drumming of buffalo hooves over the African plains; and then, if we listen harder still, we hear the shiftings of the continents as the earth's plates slide up against each other, and the lapping of the oceans and the seas as the water swells up and reaches for the moon and the tides turn in succession; and all of this luminous together under the moon, pounding and breathless together with long, deep sighs escaping from the centre of the earth.

And then, finding ourselves lying side by side in the middle of all this, Jerry and I turn to each other, and, for the first time, touch.

I bet it's a fine life down there, Sylvie, by the sea. Listening to the waves at night and the seagulls early in the morning.

Rosa's eyes are getting bigger every day. She watches everything that Jerry and I do together. She encourages me: go on, you're old enough to judge for yourself. Her eyes dance towards the kitchen, goading me in. Jerry's hands are on the table. Rosa watches, to see what I will do. I sit down opposite him. The hands are enormous, lying there with their palms facing up and fingers curling in. The strong nails with perfect white trimmings cut to match the curves of his fingertips. I think about the fingers,

Letter from Earth

what he uses each of them for. The two middle fingers that wipe the sleep from the corners of his eyes in the morning. The little finger that tugs at his lower lip, just for the fun of it, and lets it spring back on itself. The fourth finger that he dips in the hot wax around the candle wick to make a finger-cap. And now, as I watch him, and he watches me, the index finger that he takes and places in the dark hollow between his eyes, and then draws down the length of his nose, over the broken joint with the skin stretched tightly across, over the hump of vein that scrambles down the slope to one side, and along the main drag, worn smooth and shiny as burnt tarmac by the weeks and weeks spent just looking at me and thinking about things like this. I smile at Rosa, and Rosa smiles back. We have decided, between us, that they are good hands.

So that's decided, writes my father. I shall come and visit. Jerry and I can go to a pub on the pier and chat over a couple of pints. And there's a good steak house down there I used to know — I'll take you both out, for a treat. We may not know each other very well, Sylvie, but I have a feeling that the three of us will get along fine.

Martha Perkins

Scenes Without a Marriage

Martha Perkins was born in 1971 in Maine. This is an extract from her first novel.

It staggered by the water, feet splashing and spindle legs sent into a skewed frenzy, the shot rippling through the hills. The initial punch of sound dropped an octave for each hill it encountered.

The body, crumpled, lay almost motionless on the ground. It started to get dark in the early afternoon, his brain falling into an eclipse, shadowed by the air that was once pointedly thin and now so thick that it wouldn't pass through his lips. He let the eclipse cover him, let it drag his body so heavy with every muscle screaming to the edge of the woods where his childhood friends had come to pick him up and take him home to his mother, her face soft and gentle and young, why are you so young he wanted to say, but she was quiet, her hands smoothing out the worry on his face, the only thing he could feel was her hands.

It smelt its own blood before it felt the pain in its shoulder, its blood swirling into the water and ice of the pond. The once velvety shoulder felt cold, numb with the flesh exposed to the air.

The lips opened and closed, a fish out of water, gasping but not breathing. Spittle stretched from his mouth and found its way to the patch of exposed orange needles that carpeted the woods beneath the blanket of snow, the needles that smell of husky thick pine when burned at the end of summer, but these needles, damp and cold and near frozen, didn't. They don't smell like a thing. His face was almost in the needles, a foot pressing his head to the ground. He heard it before he felt it, the scuffled swing of a thick-soled boot bringing the needles to the air to scatter against his face, the boot headed in a different direction, to his stomach where the muscles tried not to clench again against the blow, but they did anyway and the boot sank into the leather ache of his stomach as a ball smacks into a glove. The needles stuck to his lips, he had one in his mouth and it tasted of nothing, the sap long gone out of it. He couldn't remember the last time he'd breathed, yesterday it seemed, so the sounds had become the air and he tried to soak them in, to hear what the argument was between the wielder of this boot and the other boys, but the foot stayed on his head and he thought about how eventually they'd leave him alone and how he'd lie here in the quiet for a while, maybe until it got dark when the breeze began to rustle dead branches against one another. The lips opened and closed but nothing came in or went out, except the needle which had found its way out of his mouth and hung suspended halfway to the ground, and he thought about the air, how it was going to hurt when it seeped into his body again, the February air that illuminated the edges of his lungs.

Another shot rang out, this one closer, more pressing, and this time the feeling, if it was feeling at all, came first, with more than just the thought of running lodged in its brain, more than just the thought, if thought at all.

The first kick didn't feel like it should have, there was supposed to be some reward in this, and this kick gave none of it. They stood and watched him heaving, the only sound between the three of them being the hacking of air, bending on their knees, everyone trying to catch their breath. The stockier boy decided: he's going to get it anyway. The other two stood and watched, felt the need to object but couldn't find the words to stop him, something like He's had enough. But he hadn't had any yet. He stood over the body, used his foot to prod it, the silence of breathing broken only by the most hesitant of the three, the boy who stayed back and felt more doubtful by the second while sniffling repeatedly, only to have the clear mucus stream down his face. He circled further away from the scene, sniffling, and pulled his arm across his nose but it kept on coming, until finally he blew hard into his hand and wiped it off on a crusted bit of snow. The determined one took his foot back, withdrew a couple of yards and in a few quick steps landed his smooth leather boot into the bared stomach — I'll show you your fucking heart — he muttered to the gagging body.

The ice came hard on to its knees, the staggering turned to falling. Its legs sunk into the thin water of the barely running stream, a trickle which fed the pond in the summer but now only kept a spot open in the ice. When it finally fell its sides still heaved, involuntarily, steam and drops of blood escaping from its nose. With the steps getting closer, heavier, an almost delicate motion of metal sliding against leather exposed a blade into the air.

The body ran through the woods, others chased it. One followed by three. Deadened branches scratched against their faces, blood welled to the surface, but no one noticed. The woods had become a blur, everything lost except for the running and the pounding inside each skull . Their boots all fell heavily on the ground, the ground giving nothing, frozen solid. But it ran and they followed. This was the chase, everything disappeared except intention, to get away, to catch. The pressure of their veins increased as though all four boys were swelling to the bursting point, their necks hurt and their ears hurt even more, the air cutting through them and freezing their noses and fingers and the thin skin over their cheekbones as well. Sweat came through their skin, inside their parkas and through the t-shirt that each of them wore, the sweat turning cold at the touch of air that leapt up their stomachs every time they had to jump a log or avoid the rambling end of a long-forgotten stone wall, when in the movement the parka pulled up slightly and the air slipped forward. The sweat mixed with the chill, a chill that made their bodies feel hard, and the air whipped at their eyes, worse than the branches because at least with the branches there was something to avoid, but the air came at them and there was nothing to be done except keep their eyes open, to let the air pull water out of them, streaming down their faces.

A heap of its intestines, lungs and stomach lay in its place. The marks of its pawing the ground were obscured by the thick-smelling blood, with the snow now creased in a trail by the drag of its body through the woods, like the stream of a plane left in the sky.

2.

In the locker room there is a hole in the wall by the coach's office, a triangle-shaped hole that goes right through to the yellow insulation, fiberglass which fluffs chick-like out into the room. Everybody tries to ignore this hole when they're suiting up for the game because Jason made this hole, and he won't be in the game tonight. Dipshit, some of them think, when they pass by it; others wonder what it must have felt like. The only one who saw it was the janitor, Neena, who came in when she heard all the banging. Jason lay on the floor in convulsions, kicking and flopping about, the hole already made, the bits of paper on his tongue soaked and torn, chalky plaster dusted on his face. People knew he liked acid, did it once and a while. Until the doctors sedated him and did a cat scan, nobody knew he had epilepsy, or took five hits at once. Doesn't matter, he's suspended for two weeks anyway, epilepsy or not. The sheriff came to the school and interviewed every boy on the basketball team to see if he could find out where Jason got it. Nobody knew. The principal talked to them as well, held a little private pep rally in his office, threatened them with expulsion if somebody didn't come forward. They laughed in the hallway when he let them go. Expulsion, what bullshit. What absolute bullshit. They didn't have anything to do with it anyway. Jesus christ, what an asshole.

With their sweats zipped the boys saunter out on to the court, take some shots. The other team still hasn't arrived, and the coach is having his own talk with the principal. The yelling can be heard all the way from the principal's office to the gym. The boys slow their rotations, pass fake shoot, pass fake shoot, trying to catch the words that come garbled and intermittent.

Probably aren't going to let us play, someone says.

Yeah, well my dad's going to kick some ass then because he's cutting work just to come to this game.

Everybody stops, even the dribbling stops, to listen to the noises coming from the office. A door slams.

Someone laughs. Jesus, coach probably got fired.

A few others laugh before a boy says, Here he comes.

They get in their lines and go through the lay-up routines, running hard as though they've been working all the time. The coach's clipboard slaps on the parquet and the sound of his whistle, not the one hanging around his neck but the one of his fingers between his teeth, brings the boys to a halt.

Everyone go sit down on the bleachers, we've got some shit to shoot.

His voice is hoarse and he doesn't look very happy to anyone. They run to the bleachers with enthusiasm as if this will make things better. He paces a few minutes, goes back and gets his clipboard, and walks over to the boys, slapping the board stuffed with papers softly against his thigh.

You guys know what's going on, the coach booms, so let's get to it. Jason's gone at least two weeks, and Montgomery probably isn't going to let him back on the team when he does come back to school. Besides, he'll be lucky if I don't break his neck next time I see him. Now, you guys are here to play ball, and that's it. Montgomery thinks this is a team thing, that all of you guys are in on this somehow — lower and closer to the boys — *like a fucking drug cartel, and I don't know how the birdbrain got that idea*, but, he did, and that's what all the screaming was about. He wants to suspend the lot of you as an example, but I said no way. From now on there will be no excuses, and for christ's sake, if I hear about any one of you messing around with drugs during the season, I'll put your head through the wall. Better yet, I'll have Jason show you how he did it, then I won't have to mess with you. Let me tell you guys something — the coach threw his clipboard down again, this time with real anger — No matter how much time each of you sits on the bench, whether it's only two minutes a game or the whole friggin' game, you are a member of this team, and you are a representative of this school. If you want to spend your time off in La-La Land, then go ahead, but you'd better quit this team first. You know what? I bet Jason's parents are just crying their eyes out right now, because you should see how old Jay looks, and I'll tell you, because I went into the hospital last night, he doesn't look too good. Maybe some of you have seen him too, and he's not looking so hot now, is he? Nope. You know what really pisses me off? Do you?

The boys all stare at the floor. In their silence the visiting team filters in through the double doorway and heads to the locker room. Some of them have their uniforms hung on coathangers and draped over one arm. Most of the boys have school-colored duffel bags, orange and black with the picture of an open-mouthed tiger. Everyone has a tie on, and their hair combed. The coach turns and says to the other team's coach: Gene, I'll be with ya in a minute.

The man waves in response and heads into the locker room with the boys.

On the bleachers the boys' faces have changed visibly. With the other team here he won't keep them much longer. They jostle about, one boy's knee hopping in a high-speed rhythm.

The coach changes to a calm tone, quieter.

Look, I just argued with Montgomery for half an hour, trying to convince him that he should let Jason play when he comes back. I don't even know if Jason will want to play, or if his parents will let him. But, I am going to give him a second chance if I'm allowed to, and I'm going to give the rest of you the same chance right now. You want to play, then good, but if you want — and his voice went whisper-like — to fuck around, then I want you to take off your uniform right now and leave.

All the boys look him in the face and stay quiet. The knee stops. Some of the parents and kids start coming in from the hallway with their tickets in hand. Montgomery stands in the doorway leaning against the frame, arms folded. Nobody knows how long he's been standing there.

Good, he says, stooping over to pick up the clipboard once more. Let's get warmed up.

By the time the game starts there are barely 30 people in the bleachers, and some of them are there for the other team.

Christ, why doesn't anyone come to our games, a boy says on the bench.
Because we suck.
Because you suck, maybe.
Hey, I don't see you out there, Kareem Abdul Jabbar the Hut. The first boy looks up, hurt slightly because he is the only fat boy on the team. He

narrows his eyes and stares:
   Fuck you, dickhead.

   They run up and down, up and down, scuffling feet as it drags on, not exactly a passing game, one would say. At the end of the third quarter it looks hopeless, especially without Jason. He was easily their top scorer, usually more than 15 points a game. True, they're only ten points behind, but everyone is winded and feeling the backs of their calves, squeezing their sides as though searching for the stitch that won't go away. Jason's parents are in the bleachers, waiting to watch their older son, Jon, come out and lead the team in the next game. Jon is top scorer and captain for the varsity team, but he's nothing like Jason, not reckless and hot-tempered. Jon watches the game dully from the stands, slightly angry that his brother has made a fool of himself, and a fool of Jon too. When the third quarter ends Jon escapes into the locker room to change and stretch out. His father tells him, Play Hard, and adds a wink.

   The JV game is already over but the cheerleaders have yet to move. They only cheer for the varsity team, but their coach makes them watch the younger boys play. The girls sit on the first row of the pulled-out wooden bleachers, uniforms slightly too small around the breasts, a little too much distance between the knees and the hem, and hair pulled back except for a little bit of fluff protruding from each forehead. Gum snaps and they pull up their panty hose at appropriate intervals to avoid the embarrassment of it slipping down at some unforeseen crucial moment, and a boy sits beside his girl on this chorus line, his arm hanging over her shoulder, over her chest, the hand dangling dangerously near, so near he can feel the warmth coming off her breasts and he hasn't asked yet, but he's going to, he's going to give her a ride home if she'll let him and god, the way she smells and looks right now, if he could he'd take her out to his car in a second so that he could touch her with no one looking, let those panty hose fall all they want in the front seat of his brother's old Camaro, the heater blowing hard on their skin to drive out the cold, her soft inner thighs, god, he'd have to stop thinking about it if he was going to get through this game without a hard-on. He shoves his free hand between his knees.

   The varsity manager, a frumpy girl who wears sweaters that hang halfway down to her knees, knocks on the locker-room door to ask if they're almost ready, and since they are, she turns on the tapedeck that's hooked up to the school speakers, the big box ones that are used for dances as well as these basketball games. The sound is much too loud, and as if on cue, the cheerleaders get up from the bleachers and start clapping in front of the crowd, which has grown considerably more dense since the JV game. One of the cheerleaders turns and gives her boyfriend a kiss before getting up, pushing her tasteless gum into his mouth. He smiles and chews with abandon. The music suddenly skips to a different song, like it does every game because this is the same tape always used, and "The Eye of the Tiger" comes screaming through the velvety boxes, breaking on the high range of the sounds. The locker-room door opens and older boys come jogging through, prancing around the court in a line to the whoops and cheers from the crowd. The boys start their drills, running, passing, shooting, taking off layers of their sweats as they warm up. The buzzer goes off, only a test, and they halt for a moment, but then continue. The whoops burst out and smuggled air horns go off intermittently; the crowd enjoys their solidarity. They love their home team, this crowd.

The other team also comes out, walking and watching this display, slightly embarrassed that they don't get anything like this at home. They slump into their own routines at the opposite end of the court.

The varsity boys have a feeling of maturity about them when the game starts, something more than body hair, mustaches, attitudes. Their muscles show definition but have no bulk; these boys are lean, cautious with displays of embarrassing emotions. They snap the ball at each other and catch it without the slightest surprise. Tempers flare when one boy catches an elbow on the rebound, the elbow sinking deep into his stomach and knocking the wind out of him. He gasps, gapes and stays hunched over on the floor while his teammates shove the other boys around, pulling at their orange and black uniforms, making the weight of their fists known. The crowd groans while individual men yell their opinions out onto the floor, and the ref ejects the offending boy to keep the home team happy. Air horns call out, mocking, as the boy walks back to the bench. He slaps hands with his teammates as he sits down, they murmur to each other but resist the urge to flip off the crowd. The away team is outnumbered.

There aren't enough girls to form two squads, varsity and junior varsity, so while the girls sit talking to each other, the older ones avoid the younger ones, the girls who are only on the cheering squad because there aren't enough older ones to make up all the routines, all the jump/flip/falls that they'd want to do. The younger ones become beasts of burden in these routines, catching the older ones, supporting them on the squat-squared knee, forming the outlying ends of triangles, and this grows into a resentment that they will carry within until they are the older girls on the team, and they can impose the same sort of burdens on the fresh girls coming up.

During half-time the teams retreat to the locker rooms, the home team leading on the scoreboard. The music comes back on again, this time something dancy, and the girls clap their way out into the center of the court to go through their routine. Much of the crowd gets up to stretch and get something to eat, but the girls continue forward. A little boy, not much older than four, runs out on to the floor in the midst of their pyramid, and they have to halt the routine, balancing for much too long, until his mother comes out to get him. He is in awe at this stack of girls.

When the game ends it is no surprise that the home team has won. The teams line up and slap hands going through, but the ejected boy won't touch them, the hands of the home team, and this doesn't go unnoticed by anyone.

The away coach grabs the boy by the shoulder and makes him go through and shake their hands, embarrassing the boys on both teams. They were happier with his defiance.

In the emptying parking lot the boy sits in his brother's Camaro and lights up another cigarette while waiting for his girlfriend to change into something warmer. He laughed, said, Wear this, while feeling the hem of her cheering skirt, touching the warmth of her thighs through her tights, but she said, No, it will only take a minute, and she disappeared into the girl's locker room. The cigarette clouds the car so he opens the window a little further, and in turn pushes the slide on the heater up to full to fight off the draft from the outside. He doesn't enjoy the cigarette much because of how stale it is, a half-used pack found under the front seat of his dad's car, but he draws on it heavily anyway because of his mood. It's taking her a long time and he doesn't want to have to go back in to see if she's waiting at the other doors, or if she's just talking to her fucking friends, none of whom he's too fond of, mostly because they treat him like he's not good enough for them, though he doesn't see any of them getting dates. They're probably just jealous cows, he thinks.

The cigarette gets flicked out into the lot, and he rolls the window back up. He'd listen to the radio if he could, but his brother decided last week that he wanted it for his truck, and just took it out. The hole in the dash gapes, wide-mouthed and toothless. In front of him he can see the away team sitting on their running bus, the shadows throwing things at each other, the engine laboring on into the darkness. Somebody must be jerking off in the showers, the boy thinks, for them to take so long. Finally the coach comes out of the building with a net-full of practice balls and heads for the middle of the bus. The engine revs for a minute, slides into gear and the bus wanders off to the roadway. The coach seems to be lecturing them, or at least holding everyone's attention.

Scenes Without a Marriage

The boy shifts in the bucket seat, and begins to feel like he's going to have to take a piss before he gets home. The parking lot's empty now except for a few cars which always seem to be at the school, but he doesn't want to piss outside. Too damn cold to be introducing the air into his pants. With reluctance the boy turns the engine off, leans across the seat to lock the other door, then gets out and zips his jacket. Just from touching the outside door-handle his hands are cold, so he shoves them deep into his jeans and walks like a quick penguin, body closed and tight, to the doors.

They're locked from the outside, so he bangs on the glass, hoping someone will hear him. In a couple of minutes one of the janitors comes up to the door with some headphones dangling around his neck and asks him what he wants.

I'm looking for my girlfriend, he says.

Everybody's out of the building, he yells through the door, making no movement towards opening it.

She's in the locker room changing.

Nope, just locked it up.

They stare at each other through the glass, the boy stepping back and looking around the parking lot as though she might have snuck up behind him, played a trick on him.

You gotta use the phone or something? The janitor obviously isn't interested and wants to go back to his floor polisher.

Uh, phuuu...No, thanks anyway.

In the parking lot one of the sodium lights flickers and dies as the boy walks back to his car. It makes a strange humming noise while attempting to come back on again. Before leaving he drives around to the front, thinking maybe she just misunderstood him, or maybe he misunderstood her, but there's no one at the front of the school either. He lights another stale cigarette before spinning out of the lot. The bottles of MD 20/20 chime under the seat as the car rights itself violently on to the road. Smoke from the tires floats up to the sodium lights long after the car has disappeared.

This dog licks his face, leaves its drooling hanging from his chin. They look alike, smile slap-happy fools, and this mad dog comes back, licks his face again and forces its tongue down his throat, smells of muzzle furriness rank dog-food dust, its tongue trickles warm drooling down his throat but it doesn't stay, this kiss lasting too long and he gags it back up, this kiss, to the sand by the tire of the now silent Camaro. The pit echoes with the sounds of his throat, the sand steams with his effort. The dog sits and waits, watches, wants to come to him again but he talks the dog out of it, sit, stay, good boy. Fetch. Doggy runs to the steep side of the pit and yelps when he hits, empty and shattered against the sand and rocks. This dog went blind.

109

He brings the puppy out of the car, full of happiness, bubbling over, running around his legs until he catches it and brings it up for a kiss. They kiss long and slow, the sweet muzzle new to him now, but the pup grows older as the kiss lasts and lasts, until middle age makes him set it down. It's no longer exciting. It's just a dog now, doing the same old doggy things. But he loves it all the same because it still sees 20-20. So they climb into the car and he lets his doggy dog sit between his legs while he drives, and it sits quiet despite the slobbering that spills on to his leg. Bad pup, sit up straight, put your shoulders back, look me in the face when you talk to me, mister.

They drive slow and careful because they don't want any trouble from the county mounties, nosireebob we don't, thinks the boy, and it's really a lot easier than they say, concentrating on the way the headlights catch the underbelly leaves, the way it seems one headlight is aimed cockeyed and the other on the road.

The wind whistles as he wrenches it open, the handle sticking at every half turn. A shrieking almost. He can hear it reverberate. Where have you been, pal, don't think we didn't know you weren't home yet. Your breath stinks. A shove to the shoulder, slap on the face. Look at your mother crying, mister. Think that's funny?

With the window down it's hard to keep the hair out of his face, driving a bit too fast maybe, but the dog's gotta go, yup, gotta go cause it's making a mess on his jeans, red cherry-flavored slobbering soaking through these jeans, shit, probably staining the seat and smelling up the car and the way the old dog grumbles unhappy in his stomach, gotta go heave-ho seeee yaaaaah.

The bottle smashes in the roadway in a spray, shooting down the street, framed in the rear-view mirror by brake lights. The car stops, the door heaving open on to the quiet, and vomit splatters to double yellow lines.

3.

My brother has the beauty of a yearling that has broken its leg in the race. He is pale and thin and has the face of a woman on a magazine cover, unblemished and smooth. There are photographs of him in which the only thing you can see is his eyes, those eyes which on late summer days tracked the movements of every cloud in the breathing sky. There is a gravity that only my brother could feel, and it worried him. When the world moved he felt it, the breeze pulled not against his face or his body or his soul but against his time. My brother felt the world move because he had to. He read the flecks in his spittle as one might read the arrangements of tea leaves: they told a future in terms of a lack of it. Nobody could have read it differently.

When she brought my brother home from the hospital he breathed in a frown, his little worm tongue stuck out of his mouth, moving in the effort of his rasping. They knew when he was born that something was wrong: my mother says that when the doctor slapped his bum, he only stared back, as though he were hurt by the lack of a formal introduction. His lungs are weak, they said, and left it at that. By the time he was three he'd had pneumonia four times. The crib, nestled against the heater in my room, began to inhabit a sound of its own, a presence which seemed inseparable from him; he and the crib were the same. He didn't walk until he was three because he didn't have the strength to, all his body went to breathing. By the time he was five he was a boy, not a baby anymore, and the crib was put away in favor of my bed, and I moved to the sofa. The next year school started for him but he didn't go. She took him in to register and they made him take a test. Can you jump on one foot? Can you turn completely around without stepping outside this circle? What is your full name? He tried and he came home and he waited another year. He's only slow because he's been so sick, and my mother nodded. He needs some time to develop. If he started now he'd be left behind by the other children; he'd feel out of place. Francis came home and stared out the window by the table with his crayons in an old cigar box and the coloring book open. The sapling swayed against the late summer storm, the sky gaining the darker shade of autumn.

I remember our father, Francis does not. He came to see us only twice after Francis was born, once on my birthday and once on Francis'. My father didn't want him to be named Francis. He wanted Frank, but my mother said no. Frank sounds like a hot dog, she said, Francis sounds like a name. Francis sounds like a girl, and he stormed out of the trailer. It rocked slightly in the wake. My mother didn't care what he thought, except that it didn't bother her to displease him. They were divorced before my first birthday, although he lived with us until I was three. For two years he didn't work. Instead he chopped wood out in the yard and sold it by the cord, delivering it in the truck that my grandfather let him use. When the truck broke down he chopped wood in the yard and great rows of split beech, maple and birch began to surround the trailer. He lowered the price and people came with their own trucks. When people had enough for the season and the snow settled in, the rows sat there, guarding us in the moonlight. The chainsaw and the maul and the axe stood outside the door, barely lumps underneath the drifts that skirted the trailer.

During the winter my father didn't move from the sofa, his eyes never left the TV. I stayed in the playpen and watched through the bars. He gave me bottles of too warm milk and graham crackers to gnaw on, only for me to leave them soggy and disintegrating on the plastic floor of my cell. His hands had the musk of motor oil and wood chips, with every crevice darkened by the remnants of both. When I cried he changed my diaper, when I

Martha Perkins

cried again he gave me a bottle and a cracker, when I continued he brought me up out of the pen and laid me across his knees, gently thumping my back until I fell asleep, the sounds of jungle warfare and statistics murmuring into my subconscious.

(You and three classmates meet after the end of school, purposely missing the bus so you can walk home by the orchard with your empty bookbags, and, stealing into the orchard with a quick glance behind you, everyone runs to the stone wall on the far side — *miles from the main road it seems: you imagine yourself a marathon runner, sprinting the final leg in the boycotted Olympics through the slalom of gnarled trees, winning it for a thousand families eating tinned television dinners, all of them vaguely watching you in some foreign country coming up on the victory lap, gumming their toughened sweetcorn* — where an old pesticide shed stands, just big enough for the four of you to sprawl out, leaning and tar-papered and empty with the exception of a calendar that has the yellowed, crinkled months of 1973. Someone produces a near-empty pack of stolen cigarettes, a soft pack that's been twisted and mangled at the bottom of the book bag so that the papers have the bends, and out comes a brand new plastic lighter, the flame rocketing three inches high to the first snaky cigarette. Trembling hands scorch the paper far beyond the tip, and the draw leaves you coughing before handing it on, the choking shakes off the ash. They're stale as hell. Someone else says "bebackinaminute" and darts out among the squatting trees, throwing good-looking apples from the ground into their bag, hiding behind the trunks in case someone comes out into the fields and spots you. No one ever does though, sees you, that is, and this is why you've come here.

The cigarette is passed between you, along with the gathered apples, bruised dark macintosh and granny smith green-skinned, everybody eats and smokes and acts like this is normal even though the smoke is starting to mix sour with the apples and the pigs-in-a-blanket served for lunch at the school — *and you think that pinkish baloney baked and curling up around the creamy scoop of potatoes, a moat of orange baloney grease afloat around the potato mound, is "pigs-in-a-blanket" until you discover that it's something quite different*. Everyone feels sick to their stomach but they're afraid to say something, be the wimp, but he says he's got to go pee so he runs out beyond the rock-pile wall into the woods and pukes behind a tree, a lanky birch stretching to the top of the canopy. Everyone hears it in the stillness of the cool afternoon, retching, and feels the idea of it coming up in themselves too, the sound preceding the action like time running backwards, until two of your friends say they've got to get home before dinner, thinking that the further they get away themselves the less likely it is to happen to them, but you, you know this won't help, so you sit leaning against the front of the shed by yourself,

Scenes Without a Marriage

listening to the dry heaves 30 feet behind you, waiting for it to come surging, your mistake.)

He was 19 when they married, 22 when he left. There is a room in town above the McCregor's which was pointed out to me once as the place where he lived when he left us. It wasn't his apartment but the place of a woman he'd met at his new job in the mill. He went from us to her and then Francis came to take his place. Francis filled the trailer with his breathing; everything else seemed silent.

On that birthday, my birthday, he arrived with whiskey on his breath and a blue stuffed penguin that he'd won out of a machine. His girlfriend dropped him off, and he jumped out of the black Nova as if a plague had been discovered inside of it. She barely waited long enough for him to get out before reversing haphazardly out of the yard: he nearly had to run back to shut the door, chasing the side-sliding car as it edged its way to the road. She came back two hours later and honked, the engine running rough against the sounds of dusk, the tail-lights illuminating the exhaust. He apologized to me while grabbing his coat but I had my mouth full of birthday cake, said nothing. The penguin sat in the middle of the kitchen table for a week until it found its way into the crib where Francis covered it with loving spit every night. It turned matted and dark and the fur became rough, and when she washed it, it fell apart. Francis cried the only way he has ever cried, in a choking, snotty rasp.

(He arrived late. You came before you were supposed to, and they had no choice but to let you arrive feet first, the cord around your neck. The operation room stood ready to carve a crescent in her belly, but no one came. You were bluer than most, and you didn't cry. He stood in the waiting room on one leg, the other propped up against the wall; his parents had been called and were staying home. They didn't like this girl, nor this marriage. They barely liked their son anymore. When they placed you in the nursery it was three hours later, and she was heavily sedated. He went to see her before you, and she lay there, face swollen, breathing heavily into the room, asleep. You were one of those babies that opened their eyes immediately, so you sat in your heated plastic cubicle with your eyes open and saw nothing. You couldn't focus. When he came to see you the nurse had left the station in the nursery, so he peered through the window and tried to place his daughter. His forehead pressed the glass, left a grease mark. He couldn't tell. He went home having talked to nobody and cried in the darkness of the empty trailer. This wasn't how he thought it would be.)

Both horses snorted out into the frosted orange morning, their legs pawing as a person might jump up and down to keep warm. They felt the quiet broken when a flock of geese, late in the leaving, honked overhead. The poles running along their sides, the blinds and the straps, had become familiar, but it was not something that they were completely comfortable with yet. Perhaps it took a few seasons, although some horses took to it immediately. Blankets covered all of this, pressing the gear against their flanks.

    The men came out of the barn laughing and carrying cups of coffee. They had other jobs, so training had to be early. The first lap was slow, as was the second, the men letting their legs dangle off the sulky harness, but the horses became eager as they kept pace with each other: this felt too much like the start of a race, the sounds of their synchronicity. The men agreed: by the post. When the horses got there the whips snapped against the poles and they knew they were racing now, this wasn't just training, although the emptiness of the air felt odd, they had become used to the sounds of a pace car and a loudspeaker which droned their names over the track surface, the sounds of other horses straining against their gear, and the turns felt too soon, the track being smaller than what they were used to. When they finished the first lap they were still neck and neck, and the men shouted insults at each other, laughing. One of them had to win, so they went around again, this time more serious, and the horses felt it. When they came around the third bend Jolly Rodger was in front, Whipper Snapper behind by half a length. The whip came hard against the pole, and then against his side, but he couldn't seem to catch up. He broke stride once but the other driver didn't notice, they were whipping the horses on in a frenzy that pulled at their attention too much, the reins slipping and giving mixed messages. The wheel caught his hoof, or his hoof caught spokes of the wheel, and the misstep put him off his stride into a panic that sent him straight into the sulky. The driver was thrown, rolling down the track, but the cart upended and slammed into Snapper after he fell to the raked surface. The horse screamed as it tried to get up, tangled in the mess on the ground, but the driver had seen what had happened, and quickly ran over, pulled the bit out of its mouth and blew into its nose, trying to calm it down. The pain ran from the leg to the body to its brain where something clicked, something very simple and dark and intrinsic and the horse knew that this blowing meant something, the words cascaded over him, his name again and again, this blowing, this quiet, meant something and it stopped trying so hard to stand up, the other horse now standing by itself down the track, nerved and jumpy by the sounds Snapper had made. The driver held on to its head smoothing behind its ears and said its name, and said Fuck, and said Jesus, and said its name, the blinds still on its head blocking out the world, what it didn't want to see was the connection between sights and sounds, the sounds between intention and end, and the horse had the feelings of the races before, the depth of its own breathing, the pull between muscle, tendon and bone, the sounds of cracking in the air. In its head it kept on running.

4.

On the way home the air rushes up its nose and runs to its throat where it empties out into the open carcass. It watches the whole ride, roped to the front bumper of the man's car, the fur pushed up and ruffled by the force of the wind. At the tagging station the man gets out and unties the body, letting it drop into the slush of the parking lot. He grabs on to the horns and pulls the body over to the scale. A few men come out of the store and watch, because this is the last day and the pool's getting tighter by the minute. This one's pretty big but nobody wants to make a guess about how big it is. Could be two hundred, someone says, pushing back the rest of his beer. A biologist checks the tag around the antler, then loops the scale rope around its front legs and pulls it tight. Two men heave the body up, their fingers turning white under the pressure of the rope, and secure it. The needle hops higher, lower, higher, lower, and settles. Two-o'-three, one of the men says, and crumples his beer can. Fuck. His is only one-ninety-three.

Some of the men laugh and clap the man on the back.

S'alright Pete, you'll getter next year.

They all help string the deer back on the car while the biologist writes down the weight and sex of the deer on a master sheet. The biologist forgets until after they have it back on the car, asks the man if he can have a tooth. They hold the head up from the bumper, pry the mouth open and wrench out a molar with a pair of pliers. One of the men stands back and winces at this process, his tongue sliding over his new dentures. Slowly the men filter back into the store and wait. There are a few hours of daylight left; it might not be over yet.

James Clatworthy

A Memory of Gating

James Clatworthy was born in 1966. *A Memory of Gating* is a drawing together of some strands in the short novel he is working on.

Pulling out the touch poles with Daddy once the game is over and it's getting dark, a nip in the air but it's nice because of the warm clubhouse to come. You can already smell the sweet and sour fug of beer and cigar smoke, the cheese and onion crisps on your fingers. Charging with a corner flag in each hand like the American cavalry while Daddy tucks the rest under one arm, through the players' entrance scattered with patties of mud with holes in them from the studs and tossing the poles in the store cupboard. Then passing by the huge baths with players already lying back in one of them, joking with each other through the steam, pints of bitter balanced on the edge. "Well done, Humph," Daddy says to the hooker, who has a big hairy stomach and, as if to keep it all in, a little towel pulled tight underneath; in one hand is a cigarette sending up a stalk of blue-black smoke and in the other he has a comb, a bottle of shampoo and a sachet of conditioner. "Good result," Daddy says. Humph starts to say something but coughs instead. Daddy smiles, tuts, and shakes his head with admiration.

When Humph has stopped coughing Daddy says, "It was actually won in the forwards in the first half," as always, as Daddy was a forward and never gives the backs any credit unless he's talking to Peter Mailins or one of the other backs that are thinkers. After talking with some other players you stop to spend pennies in the stand-up loos; on tiptoes, you pee in an arc to reach the bowl, while Daddy windypops and makes a lot of froth and milks out the last drops. Then it's to the main bar, where Daddy buys a bottle of Coke and whichever flavour of crisps you want, and a pint and a watering can of bitter for himself.

Daddy talks to a few players who come to the main bar for something other than the beer provided in the baths — usually for something soft, to

James Clatworthy

quench their thirsts — like Daddy did when he was a player. But they don't stay long. You soon go through to the President's Bar, so called because Daddy donated the carpet which the rules say you have to take your wellies or boots off to stand on. Daddy talks with other spectators and then with players as well as they trickle in, hair wet and cuts on their faces. Daddy refills from the watering can all pints more than a third down.

Everyone always agrees with Daddy's reading of the game, and sometimes Daddy chats up the referee and tops up his Harry-sippers — the half-pint favoured by old men and referees! Daddy tells the ref how when he played for Gating they had just one side, shared a pitch with Shale Old Boys, one playing at home while the other was away. They changed in the back of the King's Head, where they then did the early part of their drinking, before going on to meet the girlfriends and wives at the Trusthouse Forte, a more...gentle place. Whereas now...! And the ref will agree with Daddy that Gating has the best facilities around for its size, that it's a friendly club for guys who enjoy their rugby without wanting to be showy or...*important* in any way. Unlike your Seven Hills and Leatherhams, who'll spend eight hours on a coach so they can put St Ives on their fixture list and get caned in the process!

When Daddy has emptied the watering can you take it to the bar, people joking about how you drank all that. Then you can hold Daddy's hand, which is dry and ridgy and *hot*, like the outside of a hot-water bottle, while Daddy holds his pint in his other hand, elbow tucked into his ribs so it won't get nudged and spill: the drinking movement — Daddy once explained — being all in the forearm, a straightup arc to the mouth. Taking similar precautions with your Coke, crisps lodged securely in the hammock created by turning up the hem of your jumper.

Going around with a notebook once the players are bathed and in the bar, getting all the 1st XV and the referee's autographs and writing under them in brackets their positions. Another time you ask the spectator Daddy is talking to if he has a double chin and everyone in the circle laughs and Daddy says, "*Sau-cy*," and introduces them all to his son Karl —

"For those who hadn't already guessed!" one of the others puts in. He reaches to slap Double Chin's back — except at that moment Double Chin turns to the man on his other side and takes the slap on the elbow, which he hasn't tucked in, thus releasing much of his pint down three pairs of trousers.

There's even more laughter now, people shouting, "Careless bugger!" "Pissed again!" and "Gordon's wet her knickers!" Wills — who Daddy once got in an argument with on the touchline and called a cunt and when you later asked what that was, Daddy said it was like a runt and not to tell Mummy — has turned from his circle of Shale Oldboys and is watching

A Memory of Gating

everything. The way his tiny dry eyes fix on each of the men in turn as they brush down their trousers, how the collar of his sheepskin coat is turned up so it fans out behind his ears — he looks like a cobra about to strike...

"Gordon's wet her knick-knicks!" someone is repeating.

Wills' eyes swivel onto Daddy. He watches Daddy for a moment without moving, then draws himself up and back and says, "Saucy's about right!" in a loud voice but without having to shout. Out of the corner of your eye you can see Daddy's face: he's smiling at Double Chin and it seems like he hasn't heard but he has really. "Like father like son!" Wills says.

Daddy turns to the Shale Oldboys, pretends to look for who was speaking, and finally sees Wills. Hopefully Daddy won't say anything to annoy Wills now, he looks even younger than he did on the touchline, whereas Daddy! You don't need to look at his fat stomach or hanging cheeks or watery eyes — neither does Wills — to know how much older he is: leaning against an inwardsloping bony thigh, you can *feel* it!

"Gordon's been a naughty girl!"

All of Wills' friends look a lot younger than Daddy's.

"I've been a naughty girl." The man who nudged Double Chin's elbow sees no one is listening so he forgets his wet patch and joins the others in looking at Wills with mild curiosity. Suddenly you go cold, feel a bit dizzy. Move behind Daddy's leg. Step away, sliding your hand out of his. There won't be a fight, there can't be a fight, not here, in the President's Bar, in *Daddy's* bar...can there? Need to wee, hard to stand up. Reach for Daddy's hand, pull back. Then — to warn him — give the hand a squeeze.

Daddy squeezes back. He raises his pint at Wills. "Afternoon, Wills!" he says. He smiles at Wills in a way Wills must surely see is friendly, not a dare...

Wills turns back to his circle.

Daddy drops your hand. You continue to look at the back of the turned-up collar of Wills' sheepskin coat, wanting to be sure Wills isn't about to spring, ready to raise the alarm...Daddy's hand rests on your neck. You turn to look up at him. Daddy is looking at his friends, his pint on an upward arc and his mouth opening like a trapdoor.

Before long the President's Bar begins to drag. You get money from Daddy to buy more crisps and Coke and go into the dining area, where players shovel in beans, fat-fried eggs, sausages and chips with their forks, and mop up with white bread and butter. It's different in here from the President's Bar, less friendly, but more relaxed too. The players don't talk that much, mainly they watch the football results come up on the TV, perched on a shelf in one corner so high up a player has to stand on a chair if he wants to get at the controls.

"Sheffield Wednesday, *one*, Wolverhampton Wanderers...nil. Leeds

United, two —" and some cheers gurgle up through the beans, because you know by the level delivery of 'two' that whoever was playing Leeds has won, and a popular response probably means it's Liverpool — "Rotten Scouse ponces..." someone else chokes, spits and coughs over the announcer — "*Six!*" all retort, including you this time, to your surprise and pleasure — no one turning round — as the result comes up on the chart. Eventually Doctor Who comes on, and you sit up and become alert for the next half hour, knowing that at any moment Daddy could come along and say it's time to go, which he's done before but usually he turns up as it finishes.

It's dark and cold as you walk to the car. Daddy opens the boot. You each take out your own shoes, put them on the gravel and resting a hand on the edge of the boot, hook, pull and shake off a welly and wiggle the foot into the correct shoe, then do the same for the other leg. In the car, the first thing Daddy does is switch the heating on full blast. Then you nudge or graze any thoughtlessly parked cars on the way out, and if it's bad enough leave a note under a wiper. Soon it's really warm in the car and your ears begin to burn and you might feel sick if you weren't so happy talking with Daddy about the match. Daddy says what the forwards need most is a leader, like we had with Kiwi Tucker.

"But what about Micky Denis," you put in, the flanker often being praised by Daddy for his aggression, as well as being your own favourite forward.

"Denis is a thug," Daddy says. "He's too excitable. He's not a thinker, he leads but in the wrong direction."

"But what about his...aggression, his commitment?"

"Micky Denis is..." Daddy creases up his face and shuts his eyes, "*vay* strong." He opens them again and eases the car back onto the right side of the road. "But he won't tolerate opinions other than his own. For some reason he believes himself to be more...important, more...*entitled*, perhaps?"

You don't feel like talking about Micky Denis any more so you begin, "What about dropping..." it feels good to let that hang there, while you pick your victim, "Sandy Calloway," who Daddy has said he thinks is too fat, "and replacing him with Nigel Warwick from the 'A's?"

Daddy is quick to respond. "Sandy's got his problems. He's slow about the pitch —"

"He's grossly overweight!"

"He is not grossly overweight, Karl." Daddy seems annoyed, which makes you wish you hadn't said it. "Don't exaggerate. It's prop's privilege to be...stocky."

It's passed! He isn't angry any more!

"But more important," Daddy says, "Sandy can *play both sides*. Whereas Warwick, or the other 'A' prop, another Nigel I think. Nigel..." Daddy

A Memory of Gating

clucks his tongue. "I forget. But both are strictly one side only — if that in Warwick's case, from what I hear of his disgraceful performance last week."

"Why — what happened?"

"He punched the ref, apparently."

You let out a shriek of delight. "He punched the *ref!*"

"Apparently. Though of course he says the ref punched him first, which I think is unlikely.

"But it's always been my philosophy," Daddy goes on, "that the meat and potatoes of propping is the set scrum. So your Warwicks of this world have the odd flashy run, usually from loafing outside the mauls, but what good's that if he's weak in the set? Whereas Sandy's a grafter — his heart's in the right place," Daddy says.

Which will you turn out to be, a Warwick or a Sandy Calloway? Warwick's chicken, no doubt, but none of the players seem to hold it against him, he's always got a group around him, telling stories, laughing. Whereas Sandy stays for one pint and goes home. It wouldn't be nice being called chicken though, even if it's only behind your back, you'd be bound to find out sometime. Maybe you'll be the best of both, a grafter and a mate, or not play at all, the spectators have it easiest of everyone! But they all played in their time, or say they did. They all earned their right to comment.

"Sandy just needs...fine tuning," Daddy says.

"Whereas Warwick needs brain surgery!"

Daddy dips the lights for some oncoming traffic and concentrates on the road.

When you get home Daddy stays outside to rearrange the cars so Mummy's is outside the front door for her early hair appointment tomorrow, while you go into the lounge. "Who won?" asks Mummy.

You try to think. Who *did* win? You look at the fire popping and flaming up from new logs, at Mummy kneeling on the floor before a tray with the china tea set on it and a sponge cake with jam in the middle and icing sugar on top, no doubt made by Granny. Granny still here from lunch, sitting in the armchair Grandpa used to love, with Shauna curled up against her shins; the two of them angled to watch Mummy and the tea things out of one eye, and the TV with Bruce Forsyth and his contestants out of the other. It's so nice in here, so warm and cosy, like being laid in a jewellery box with cotton wool all around. But there's also the feeling, perhaps from the seeming completeness of the scene, that you're not meant to have seen this: it's for those who don't go to the rugger. The situation not being helped by your complete inability to remember who Gating played this afternoon, let alone who won. But you have to say something, so you say, "Gating."

"Phew," Mummy says. She pours out some tea. "What was the score?"

123

James Clatworthy

Suddenly you remember: Gating won 17-9! In the end it was a trounce, the real match being won by the Gating forwards in the first half. You start telling Mummy all about the match, how in the end it came down to the front five in the set pieces, adding that Pete Mailins — who Mummy once sat next to at a dinner party and found most charming — had a good game at full back. But Mummy is concentrating on pouring cups of tea and cutting cake and isn't really listening, so you're pleased to cut short the match report in order to take a cup and a biscuit to Granny. Then you get some cake for yourself and go to your room to watch Bruce and his embarrassing contestants in peace.

Cormac Mac Cárthaigh

*The Disappearance of
Miss Effie Skinner*

Cormac Mac Cárthaigh was born in
Ireland in 1971.

My father knows nothing about writing. He doesn't even read the newspapers. But he's always trying to show an interest in what I do. He goes on about one particular story he thinks I should write. He believes in local history. It's got to do with a murder that happened — is "happen" the right word? — more than a century ago, in Dripsey, a rural district very near to where I grew up. When I returned home a few days ago my father solemnly produced a file he's compiled over many years, of anything that might be relevant to the incident, and much that is not. To keep the old man happy I took a look through it. Here are whatever of the basic facts of the case I could make sense of.

Bringing his own troop of horse, a man called Cross came to Ireland with Cromwell's army in 1649. Like many of the other soldiers after the "war", this man was granted a portion of the conquered territory — in Dripsey, in the county of Cork.[1] His son Epinetus — who later also came by land in the county — was to become a Justice of the Peace in Cork City. This Epinetus' son, Capt. Epinetus Cross, in turn, became High Sheriff there in 1680, not, however, being survived by any son of his own. My father, never one to be bettered by such inconsideration, has traced the pedigree of the younger Epinetus' brother, to a certain Philip Henry Eustace Cross, born in the family home, "Shandy Hall" in Dripsey, in 1834. (In the meantime the lack of Protestants in the area had ensured a high rate of intermarriage between the families of the local gentry.[2] For some, it was too troublesome

---

1. *Book of Survey and Distribution of the Kingdom of Ireland*, (1641), p. 163.
2. In the parish in question, for those whose interest lies in the direction of statistics, in 1844 there were some 126 Protestants, as against 2,383 Catholics.

to travel to another part of the countryside to socialise, court women, etc., I suppose.) A historian named H.W. Gillman recounts a story about this Philip Cross:

> A gate near the entrance to the deer park still bears the name of Geata-na-Sciursachta, [pronounced "Gata-na-Shcur-shocta"] which is Irish-English[3] for 'the scourging gate'. This seems to have been used for the benefit of trespassers on the land. And thereof a story is told: once upon a time a servant of Crowdy of Cloghroe [an adjacent district] came to the place with a mare on business, for as will be presently noted the Cloghroe folk fostered the breeding of good horses. Crowdy's man trespassed in some unauthorised way on the deer park, and was promptly tied up and received an allotted number of lashes. His master, to whom he reported the tale on his return home, did not relish this treatment of his servant, and the next day, dressing himself in the latter's clothes, he presented himself with the same mare again to the then Cross of Shandy Hall. Cross bade him go away, but Crowdy said Cross should be off first, and so on, and soon a stiff, honest fight with fists ensued, and Crowdy, who was a powerful man, scored heavily over his antagonist. It is said that Geata-na-Sciursachta fell somewhat into disuse after this episode in its history.[4]

The records of the Cork Winter Assizes report that on 27-9-1896, Philip Cross, a magistrate of the county of Cork, was tried at the Quarter Sessions Court for falsely imprisoning Timothy MacCarthy, and, being found guilty, was sentenced to imprisonment for one calendar month, and fined £10. The judge's sentence describes him as

> ...an eccentric, litigious and dominating squireen [sic] who seems to derive more pleasure from browbeating his tenants than from combining with them to increase the property's viability.

In August of the next year he was tried for assault on one of his grooms. A few days later he was up before the courts again, the case being brought by a brother-in-law, for having diverting a stream. But the best bit of background I found in the file reads as follows:

> An incident in 1892, when he seized the chattels of an impoverished widowed tenant to compensate for rent unpaid, completely alienated him with [sic] his neighbours. Following that his family was boycotted and the Hussars of Blarney[5] fearing the wrath of the farmers, forbad him to hunt with them.[6]

---

3. There is no such language.
4. *Journal of the Cork Historical and Archaeological Society*, (1905), pp. 225-6.
5. The military town where I grew up.
6. *Henchion's Cork Centenary Remembrancer*, (1992), p. 174.

The Disappearance of Miss Effie Skinner

Whatever social life he and his family had must have been reduced to nothing then.

Cross had served "*with credit*" in the Crimea, in India, and in Canada, rising to the rank of Surgeon-Major in the course of 20 years' service. While visiting London in 1879, he met a Laura Mary Marriott, 16 years his younger, who, after a very short courtship, he took as his wife. On retirement they returned to his family estate, a stud farm, where he lived on his pension and her inheritance, dutifully surrendered to him. The surrounding countryside provided Cross with much opportunity for hunting, shooting, and fishing. (I have a friend who lives out that direction, who even today makes the same use of the surrounding lands. He recently bought a gun–dog called "*Trigger*", a name neither of us could take seriously, so I suggested he rechristen her "*Lia*", which is Gaelic for "grey", which she is, which he did.) What it was that occupied his wife's days I wouldn't even hazard a guess. After 8 years of marriage Cross became "involved" with his children's governess, Miss Euphemia Skinner. Mrs Cross soon heard the rumours of this being circulated by the neighbours and insisted to her husband that the young woman be dismissed from her post, a wish with which he immediately complied. But Cross followed Miss Skinner to a hotel in Dublin, where she had been instructed to wait for him. They shared a room there for several nights, signing themselves "*Mr and Mrs Osborne*". When Cross returned to Shandy Hall, he discovered that his wife had fallen ill on the day of the governess' departure. The melodrama of life. To the neighbours who inquired about his wife's illness, Dr Cross persisted in describing its symptoms as "trivial". Nevertheless he asked Dr Godfrey, a friend, to take a second look at her. My father — the grammar is his own — writes that this man

> ...had not been told the full symptoms by Dr Cross, thought that Laura was suffering from a bilious attack, and he could see no symptoms of Thypoid [sic] Fever. He reassured [sic] his friend that nothing more than a strong purge was called for.

Cross' wife died on 2-6-1898 and was buried in the local Protestant graveyard two days later. (The family vault, in the city cathedral, was full.) James Cross, a close relative and an undertaker, took care of the funeral arrangements. Dr Cross visited the grave very early each morning — my father says "*...to check if the grave had been interfered with*", though I can find no confession of such an intention in any of the court records he has. Cross told one inquiring neighbour that his wife had died of an attack of *angina pectoris*, another that she had died of typhoid, and so on. A fortnight later, he made the journey to London, where he and Miss Skinner were married. Couldn't wait, I suppose. By any account it might have been a happy ending for all concerned, were it not for public disquiet, which soon put an anonymous letter into the hands of the local constabulary, accusing Dr Cross of murder. The body was exhumed, and the autopsy, finding traces of arsenic in the viscera, declared "death by poisoning". Philip Cross was tried between 14th and 18th of December, in Cork, and hanged there on 10-1-1899. His last will and testament left his two daughters, described as *"being of weak intellect"*, to the special care of his brother. One son, not yet baptised, was to be named John. Miss Skinner was bequeathed £60 per annum. There is no further account of her.[7]

To be fair, maybe I should add one or two more details. For instance, a year before her death Mrs Cross took a long holiday in Britain, depressed at her isolation in the large country house — *"alienated from her neighbours"* the phrase my father uses — complaining there of repeated fainting fits and dizziness. Her return to Shandy Hall found her preoccupied with a fear of death by heart failure. The month before she did die, she was constantly vomiting, had diarrhoea, etc., recovering from this illness for only a few days, to take one last walk in the countryside. Touching. The *new* governess kept a diary, in which the most important of the records of this last month are to be found. (It's hardly the place, I suppose, for a little dictum on the reliability of diaries.) For example:

<u>26th May</u>: *The rector called... When leaving the rector remarked, in private, upon how inflamed the mistress' eyes showed themselves to be. It is true that she has great difficulty reading. It is left to my hands to write each and every letter for her.*

<u>30th May</u>: *The rector came to call. Dr Cross would not allow him into the house.*

<u>1st June</u>: *These last three days, the mistress is unable to eat...with no more than a cup of milk by her bed.*

On the night of the first of June the servants heard a series of screams,

---

7. It is of some small interest to note that 11 days after the execution, a niece of Dr Cross was charged with her own husband's death ("resulting from starvation from want of proper medical attendance and from neglect"). This husband's sister had, for some unknown reason, several years before bequeathed her entire property — inherited in place of her brother because of her father's disapproval with regard to his son's marriage (complicated, isn't it, when nothing follows its normal course) — to this same woman, her brother's wife, on the condition that he be supplied from it "...with farming stock, implements, et cetera, and provide him during her mortal life with house, room, support, sustenance and comfort, such as she herself had." The court heard one witness describe a visit to this house, in which the deceased's private chamber - husband and wife no longer sharing a bed — "...had the appearance of utter filth and neglect." Even before the trial ended the local paper chose to sum it all up with: DEATH OF SIMON COOKE — INQUEST AT DRIPSEY — SHOCKING DISCLOSURES — DECEASED'S WIFE INCRIMINATED. The Justice advised the 12 men of the Grand Jury that though this woman's conduct might be morally blameworthy, this was a different thing from being legally criminal. Nice to know he'd been reading Montaigne.

with Mrs Cross' chamber as their source, though the sounds died away again almost at once, returning the household to silence.[8] To all appearances the two young daughters did not understand what had come to pass. In a journal to which my father also submits, a local historian, Anthony Greene, describes the preparations that followed:

> Dr Cross then went upstairs and, with the assistance of one young maid, washed the body clean and laid it out. They dressed Mrs Cross in a white vest, a nightdress, blue stockings and a band around her head, to keep her mouth closed.[9]

After the exhumation the remains were brought to Cork, to the city courthouse, where they were to be stored until the trial, but were then transferred, with the rest of the proceedings, to the larger function rooms of Burke's Hotel, to facilitate the crowds. Greene insists on giving us the details:

> Meanwhile Dr Pearson [the coroner] removed parts of the body, which he took to Cork City for analysis. The body was then returned to the graveyard in a donkey cart and reinterred. On the following day Dr Pearson returned, re-exhumed the unfortunate body and removed further samples...using Marsh's test, then relatively new, [he] established the presence of arsenic in the body. These findings were conveyed to the police.[10]

Next day Philip Cross travelled the nine miles to Cork City to meet a train. Instead he was himself met on the platform, by three constables and an inspector. After a minor scuffle, he was taken into custody, where he was to be charged with the wilful murder of his first wife.[11]

Cross appeared in court wearing a green tweed suit with matching scarf. He was otherwise described by one reporter as:

> ...no ordinary man. With his upright, martial bearing and well-cut features, he has often, while following the hounds, evoked general admi-

---

8. Her husband had — no doubt on medical grounds — by that stage decided it best that he share the same room as his wife. Taking a separate bed, naturally.
9. Anthony Greene, "Reasonable Doubt: The Trial and Execution of Dr Philip Cross", *The Coachford Record*, Vol 1, p. 43.
10. Ibid., pp. 49-50.
11. Cross at once applied to the Queen's Bench (The High Court) to have his trial transferred to Dublin, on the grounds that it would be impossible to have a fair one in Cork, because of the various rumours then in circulation, his unpopularity, and the "heightened feelings caused by press reports." Pure Chomsky. The trial was indeed transferred, but then immediately moved back when the prosecutor *swore* that no such rumours were currently circulating in the city. (Greene describes this declaration as "incredible," but does not say why. He goes on to describe the trial as a "media sensation," and how "...applications for tickets were received from some 5,000 people, including *ladies of quality!*" I'd imagine that his quote is not reliable here, that the exclamation mark is his own.)

ration from his neighbours... It was remarked that the prisoner's beard was noticeably more grey than hitherto.[12]

The jury, at the request of the defence, were all members of the Church of England.

The prosecution's case goes over most of what I've related so far — the affair, etc., adding only several medical opinions about typhoid, toxins, Mrs Cross' health, and so on.[13]

The servants testified to having supplied their mistress with a diet of macaroni, cornflower, and sago[14] (declaring that she was "addicted" to this last substance). They also confessed to having seen Dr Cross give his wife chlorodyne[15] on many occasions, and to having seen "a bottle of white powder" amongst the possessions of her chamber. (Despite extensive questioning, they remained ignorant as to what this "white powder" might have consisted of.)

A hotel manager kindly made the journey from Dublin to give evidence. So did his receptionist. Yes, he did think it strange that a man whose bags were marked "*P.X.*" would sign himself "*Mr Osborne*".

One Denis Griffin, Sub-Postmaster at Dripsey gave evidence of the contents of various correspondences between Dr Cross and Miss Skinner.

On cross-examination — were I less of a writer, I'd follow my father's example and make something of the pun — the coroner admitted to:

1. Having placed more than one of the organs examined in the same dish.
2. Having never previously examined an alleged murder victim.
3. Having no previous — professional — experience of arsenic poisoning.
4. Having never previously performed Marsh's Test, nor — in the case at hand — having tested for two other substances [their names are not relevant] which also produce positive results to the said test.
5. Having carried out the necropsy without assistance.
6. Having neglected to retain the samples.

The witnesses seem bent on proving themselves — to borrow, for once, a phrase of my father's — "*of weak intellect*", and little else.[16] Maybe I should

---

12. *The Cork Evening Examiner,* 15-12-1898, p. 2. This same reporter, obviously oblivious to the prevailing conditions of the 19th century gaol, remarks upon the moral significance of this variation.

13. One such "expert" opinion came from a friend of the deceased who had discussed poisons with a brother-in-law several years previously, and once read a book on the subject. This witness also "...saw Dr Cross give his wife a bowl of chicken broth on one occasion."

14. A form of starch.

15. A mild form of analgesic.

16. One witness, for instance, could offer nothing new other than that she had offered champagne to the sick woman. I couldn't discover whether or not the offer was accepted.

give them the benefit of the doubt; maybe intermarriage was widespread in the general population also.[17]

The defence called only one witness — Henrietta Cross, the accused's sister. She told of having discussed, both with the deceased and with her own dentist(?), the use of arsenic for certain cosmetic purposes[18] and to having obtained — from a respectable chemist in the city — several prescriptions of it for the deceased *"on word of such express purpose"*. (The Justice, however, believing Miss Cross to be doing all in her power to protect her brother, rather than serve the interests of justice, invited her to leave the stand. Her evidence was struck from the books. And from the memories of the jurymen, no doubt.)

The assigned Justice[19] summed up the case before sending the jury out, as remains the practice to this day. His address repeatedly brings their attention to the fact that Philip Cross was charged with murder, not with having "illicit relations", as if there were another kind. Nevertheless he dwelled for over an hour on the "improper conduct" of the accused. His speech also includes amongst its suggestions:

Let them put arsenic for the complexion out of the question — the idea of a lady eighteen years married and her two daughters using arsenic!

The judge also ventures interpretations of a kinesic nature — remarking, in one instance, on the prisoner's announcement of his wife's death to the staff as having been *"...without any sign of natural feeling on his part, no wailing or expression of grief."*[20] Maybe I'm wrong, maybe it isn't life that's so melodramatic, only people's expectations of it.

Greene's own account of what happened next is better than any wording I could ever contrive:

It suddenly occurred to the learned Judge that the body had never been identified and a Dr Crowley was called for this purpose, which he did. The jury was then sent out. The jury reappeared twice, first to ask Dr Pearson [the coroner, if you remember] *if he would swear on the*

---

17. Nor does the tone of the prosecutor's speech add much to the proceedings. He describes, for instance, the "crime" as "...one of the most horrible that has ever disgraced our common humanity...in order that he might gratify his lust for the young woman he had seduced." (How is it men always get the blame for seducing then, but never the credit now?) This same prosecutor insists on referring throughout to the prisoner's wife as "the mother of his innocent children." What have they do do with it?
18. At that time, arsenic was commonly used to whiten the skin. (Perhaps it might also be noted now, seeing as how we're in our historical materialist phase, that up until the Criminal Evidence Act of 1900, "an accused person may not give evidence at his [sic] own trial.")
19. Possessing, for the time, the peculiarly Irish name of Murphy.
20. This man also seems to have been affected by the prosecutor's verbal dramatics, insofar as he repeatedly refers to Miss Skinner as "governess to his innocent children." I wonder does the same use of language indicate similarity of perspective.

> *Bible that Mrs Cross had died of arsenic poisoning, which he did at the judge's request, and the second time to ask for a photograph of Miss Skinner. This was provided. Several minutes later they returned and delivered a verdict of GUILTY.*[21]

Cross' *"have–you–anything–to–say–prior–to–the–sentence's–being–pronounced"* speech — he most certainly had, he spoke for over 40 minutes — protests his complete innocence,[22] refers innumerable times to injustice in general, the miscarriage of justice in particular, and so on, but asks as its last sentence if it were likely that a man of his age would commit murder for such a *"slip"* of a girl, answering that he'd have too much to lose. Being taken from the court, the prisoner was hissed, booed, and spat upon by his audience.

Philip Cross' appeal to the Queen, in the form of the Irish Lord Lieutenant, was denied.

A gentleman from Peterborough, one Mr Berry, was sent for, to perform his 114th execution.

The local newspapers advertised and published a series of articles and "letters to the editor", generally in support of the outcome of the case, and also printed accounts of:

1. Dr Philip Cross' defiant attitude.
2. Dr Philip Cross' *"sang froid"*. (?)
3. Dr Philip Cross' heartless rejection of his wife and family.
4. Dr Philip Cross' complaints about prison food.

They also insisted on repeating a rumour — which our Mr Greene reports as untrue, claiming that the prisoner maintained his innocence to the end — proclaiming that Cross confessed at the last minute.[23]

All applications of the press to be present at "the event" were denied, leading one editorial to complain of the authorities' having "...*acted very*

---

21. Greene, pp. 57-8. This same Dr C.Y. Pearson later wrote an article (entitled "The Medico-legal Aspects of the Case of Philip Cross" in the quarterly *Journal of the Medical Profession of Ireland*, Spring 1899, pp. 25-41) a draft of which had been sent to the press and from which extracts were printed — in an attempt to both vindicate himself and leave "a permanent record for future readers who can have no other means of becoming acquainted with the true facts and history of the case." Its essential point is that any member of Cross' profession could easily have obtained a poison not traceable in the body. (Yet he later undermines this insinuation with a remark which "praises" Cross' "choice" of poison - one described as "without odour, taste, or colour — therefore most easy of administration.") Elsewhere in this article, Pearson refers to the likening, by the defence attorney, of the liver to a sponge, in an attempt to prove that the organ could not possibly have "soaked up" as much arsenic as the corner testified it did. Dr Pearson denies the accuracy of the "metaphor" saying that this "goes to show the utter absurdity of anyone trying to deal with scientific matters on [sic] which they are wholly ignorant."
22. "...of his crime," writes Greene.
23. In the three weeks between sentence and execution, the chaplain continued to visit the prisoner regularly, despite always meeting with a "polite but firm" refusal of his ministrations.

improperly in thus declining to gratify the natural curiosity of the public."[24] Nevertheless, full accounts of "the event" appeared in this very same paper on the very same day, describing what the prisoner wore, how he walked, and — more expectations "gratified" — how

> *When the rope had been adjusted, he turned to the chaplain, as if desirous of uttering a few words to him. But, before he could frame a sentence, the trap on which he stood fell apart beneath his feet, and, the next moment, Philip Cross was launched into eternity.*[25]

In the next paragraph of this same article a portrait is given of the man from Peterborough:

> *In his private capacity, Mr Beery* [sic] *does a considerable business in selling bacon on commission. He is also an ardent pigeon-fancier. Another of his hobbies is fishing, and, in his leisure hours, he is a keen disciple of Izaac Walton.*

Another member of this same newspaper's staff is reported to have overheard this same Mr Berry tell of the prisoner's passing away "*...as peaceful as a summer eve.*"[26]

Yet another newspaper, *The Evening Echo*,[27] was alone in printing extracts from a statement submitted by the coroner[28] to all members of the press. From those extracts I include these:

> *No external marks of violence were discernible. A rigorous internal examination showed, after some difficulty, due to the firmness of the tissue resisting the various manipulations necessarily performed upon it, the absence of any evidence of violence to the larynx, trachea, vagina, anus or rectum, or inner surfaces or borders of the mouth*[29]*... The only evidences of putrefaction present in the abdomen were found in the liver; the gall-bladder contained a small amount of bile; the spleen and kidneys were healthy; the bladder was empty; the uterus and ovaries presented a healthy appearance. I shall now describe the appearance found on examining the interior of the alimentary canal...* [etc]

In this same release (in a section not selected for publication), Dr Pearson vari-

---

24. *The Cork Evening Examiner*, 12-1-1899, p. 2.
25. Ibid., p. 12.
26. The autopsy of the executed, which could not take place without the presence of this same executioner, is of interest only insofar as it mentions several "decorations" which were found on the remains, one of which is playfully described as consisting of "...a pack of hounds tattooed down the back with the fox going to earth in the appropriate place." Although there was still space available in the family plot, Cross had been condemned to be buried in prison grounds.
27. The interest in partiality, at least, is commendable.
28. Cf. fn. 20-21
29. A subsequent section of this same text — which failed to reach print — describes *rigor mortis* as "a state which is of transient duration [what other type of duration is there?] lasting no more than the several hours which follow after death."

ously refers to his own testimony in support of his various claims[30] concluding:
> ...*he* [Cross] *exhibited it* [the arsenic] *in repeated doses, so as to produce a prolonged illness, and gave chlorodyne to mask the painful symptoms; he prepared her* [Mrs Cross] *relatives and friends for her inevitable, approaching death.*

The conclusions Greene draws — though I'd always presumed historians not to have any — from these aspects of the case are probably worth noting here, in turn, if nowhere else:
> *Owing to the fact that repeated doses must have been administered in order to produce the symptoms present in this case, the possibility of accidental administration cannot be admitted, whereas if it was put forward that Laura, with the object of taking her own life, deliberately took the poisons herself on repeated occasions, I should be led to believe that she subjected herself to a slow and painful form of lingering torture* [not unlike this sentence] *such as is rarely to be found recorded in all of toxicological literature.*[31]

He goes on again, to conclude:
> *Despite the good judge's disbelief, arsenic was commonly used for the complexion, and we know that Mrs Cross did indeed discuss its use for that purpose. Despite the good judge's disbelief* [32] *arsenic was used for stomach upsets and 'feminine complaints'* [indicating the lack of its use on the part(s) of men?] — *Milner's Medical Dictionary, a common text-book at the time, makes several references to its use.*[33]

He offers us just three possibilities to choose from, best juxtaposed as:
1. Laura Cross was poisoned by her husband.
2. Laura Cross poisoned herself, accidentally.
3. Laura Cross poisoned herself, deliberately.

Greene himself prefers the last of these, as it allows him to use phrases such as "*...leave this world...*", "*...cruel wrongs suffered at the hands of her husband...*", "*...in order that he should be convicted...*", and even "*...courage and single mindedness* [sic] *to go ahead with such a plan.*" He knows why — he pro-

---

30. Where, for example, he stated that the administration of a narcotic would have the effect of diminishing or preventing the painful symptoms which arsenic might cause, and how one such narcotic - chlorodyne - was on record as having been frequently ingested by Mrs Cross.
31. Greene, pp. 60-1. He also makes a brief mention of the fable of the arsenic-eaters of Syria and of Mrs Cross' servants' conviction that her mistress shared in this practice, though adding nothing further on the subject. (He also offers alternative strategies that might have been used by the defence, supposedly to more success.)
32. Here even the quality of the writing can't be blamed on my father, who simply transcribed it.
33. Summing up the case Greene makes a first mention of what I, uneasy about any kind of "retrospective irony", would like to have known earlier - that Cross' is the signature which appears on his own wife's death certificate.

nounces simply, but solemnly: "*She was indeed, 'a woman scorned'.*"

At the bottom of the file was quite an amount of background material not really relevant to the case at all — court records, newspapers, family trees, etc. — so I sorted through the lot and picked out a few I thought I might incorporate into the story I was going to write. A newspaper article entitled "*A HANGMAN'S REMINISCENCES*" (but with the subtitle "*HOW BERRY DISGUISED HIMSELF IN CORK*") is the best:

> On Tuesday Berry, the executioner, after having carried out a double execution at Hereford, took the train for Birmingham and on the way confided his reminiscences to his fellow passengers in a most remarkable manner. He said — "Let me tell you about the time I went to Cork to hang Dr Cross; in order to elude the crowd waiting on the platform I made myself up in a pair of black eyes with charcoal. I bound my head as if my skull had been recently broken, and put some horse halters around my waist. Once outside I asked what was everyone looking after, and on hearing the name Berry, said I would not go two yards to see a creature of such a profession, and so I got quietly away to the goal [sic]. Next morning I left again disguised as an officer with complete uniform, except the sword, with this beneath my belt —" and here Berry pulled a revolver out of his pocket, frightening several of the female members of his audience. He informed us that he had taught his wife to use it as a precaution, against burglars or other attackers. Indeed he himself wore a scar received from one while serving in the police force. Replying to a fellow traveller Berry bid us take note that his was a scientific mode of hanging, and that he did not altogether approve of the old plan of letting them struggle for a quarter of an hour. He broke their neck, and they suffered no more pain than the prick of a pin — though he added that it must be a dreadful thing for them to feel themselves going off the trap, not knowing where to, an opinion concurred with by all present. He was, he added, very particular as to what company he kept, and believed himself to be the only executioner who ever mixed with magistrates, baronets, lords and dukes, and this on a regular and ongoing basis. When attending to carry out an execution he was obliged to sleep in the gaol. He had slept in 52 prisons. In his opinion it would be better to send all people condemned to death to London.[34] They might be hanged there in batches — he could hang a dozen as easily as two.[35]

The worst is an "epic" poem by a local woman who thinks she's a poet, a drinking friend of my father's, who therefore sings her praises, without the

---

34. Punishment enough in itself?
35. *The Evening Eagle*, 24-3-1899, pp.1, 12.

Cormac Mac Cárthaigh

slightest knowledge of whatever literary standards might temper the enthusiasm. I've yet to decide which of the two deserves my sympathy more.

Here's a typical extract:

> The local surgeon[36] had, going off far away
> For a full month's hard-earned holiday,
> Handed over his patient-list to the charge
> Of that so hated lunatic at large
> The more infamous than famous Dr. Cross, to be soon after hanged
> For poisoning his poor wife. The doctor was wronged
> In this I do believe, although he declared
> An hour before being hanged how little he cared
> For this stroke of mischance, being sure
> He'd done very many things certainly worth swinging for.

My father has Xeroxed rather than transcribed a lot of the newspaper accounts of the trials, etc., which means that parts of adjacent articles are there to be read also. I came across one about some dinner the Earl of Grey[37] attended at Edinburgh:

> *The Pavilion in which his lordship was entertained was most magnificent. It was supported by sixteen pillars with gilt capitals, the shafts being surrounded with wreaths of gilt laurel. The walls were ornamented with appropriate devices...The Lord Advocate briefly proposed the health of the Earl of Durham* (cheers) *and the reformers of England.* (immense cheering) *The Earl of Durham came forward to speak amidst the most rapturous cheering..."How often have we been told by our Tory opponents — for you must allow me to use an expression which they are ashamed of, and have therefore dropped — how often have we been told by our Tory opponents that the spirit of reform was dying away, that liberal feelings were no longer predominant, and that the day was fast approaching, when the people of England would return like repentant sinners to their Tory homes, to be received with forgiveness by their Tory master!* (cheers and great laughter) *Can any such absurd and wanton abandonment of your hardly won and inestimable privileges be read in these proceedings of to-day? No is the answer. No; the gathering of this day — to use a Scottish phrase* (cheers) *— at which are the wisest, the best, and the most influential persons in Scotland, proves, without a doubt, the contrary...I have now been some twenty years in public life, during which time I have felt it both duty*

---

36. Is it just me, or does the whole countryside seem to have been filled with doctors?
37. Not, unfortunately, a little research of my own has shown, the one who gave his name to the tea.

and pleasure to act with my noble relative, differing from him occasionally, as all men of independence must occasionally differ from one another, but following him steadily and firmly in all the great objects of his political life (cheers) *and I now tell you what I believe him to be — an unflinching but safe and practical reformer — a determined corrector of all abuses, upholding the legitimate influence of the crown and the due privileges of the nobility, but at the same time advocating the extension of the liberties of the people, and their adaptation to the increased and increasing intelligence of the age.* (loud cheers) *One word more and I have done.* (cries of no, no, go on) *My noble and learned relative and friend has been pleased to give me some advice, which I have no doubt he deems very sound, to some class of persons — I know nor mix with none such — who evince too strong a desire to get rid of ancient abuses. Now I frankly confess that I am one of those persons who see with regret every hour which passes over the existence of recognised and unreformed abuses.* (immense cheering) *I am, however, perfectly willing to accept the correction of them as deliberately as our good rulers, and my noble friend among them, can wish, but on one condition alone — that every measure should be proposed in conformity with those common principles for which we all contend.* (prolonged cheering)

 The report is not cut off here exactly, but rather a couple of lines further down. I've no idea of what's excluded, only that it probably runs to a few additional columns.

Claire Ingham

Her Song (a short screenplay)

Claire Ingham, 24, is a graduate of the universites of Stirling and California, where she started writing for film. Previous jobs have included writing and directing trailers for Granada and Central Television, reporting for radio stations in Scotland and Wales, throwing children around as a gymnastics teacher, and day-dreaming on the production line of a peanut butter factory...

FADE UP TO PATTERNS OF INTENSE WHITE LIGHT.

As the camera moves gently from side to side, we should gradually become aware that we are looking through several layers of curved glass — each layer bouncing light back to our eyes. Faintly we hear the sloweddown hum of running machines. A blurred white shape appears behind the glass, increasing in size. It is MARLENE.

MARLENE: (echoing off-camera) Ann. Ann!

Cut to the camera moving upwards unsteadily to look at the flushed, round, overall-filling supervisor Marlene, and we see that we are now

INTERIOR SHOT: YELLOW-TILED FACTORY ROOM. AFTERNOON. SUMMER.

The camera cuts to MARI-ANN as she finishes standing up from behind a tall pallet of glass jars, and we should realise that everything before has been from her point of view. She is a small woman, athletically built, darkeyed, and dressed in the factory uniform of white overall, cap, hairnet and gloves. With one hand she plucks a cracked glass jar from the centre of the pallet and with the other pulls off her ear defenders. The noise of the factory immediately snaps into a several decibel din. Without looking Mari-Ann throws the cracked jar over her shoulder into an industrial green bin. Her eyes are focused hard and unblinking on Marlene — challenging.

MARLENE: (clearly now, sharply) Well, glad you could join us — for the last few minutes at least...(She nods at the feeding-in table on the production line.) Work!

Mari-Ann watches her walk away, her face perfectly still. Suddenly she glances round at the table, replaces her ear defenders, and with mechanical actions begins to scoop jars from the top layer of the pallet onto the table — ten jars at a time, one for each finger. She hums as she works, although for us the humming and the noise of the factory fade into voiceover, the tone intimate, close, confessional.

MARI-ANN: (In voiceover, her voice has a Gaelic lilt.) Sometimes I think it would have been quite easy for us to go mad...Don't you think? To just stand lost in a strange wood, while my brain went soft-brown and sticky like the pickle when it oozes from the filler...

The camera revolves around Mari-Ann as we hear her words. In the background we see the whizzing of empty jars into the filler and full jars leaving it. A buzzer sounds and a stream of women enters the factory for the next shift.

CUT TO INTERIOR SHOT: CLOAKROOM. AFTERNOON.
Women are shedding their overalls, and there is a buzz of gossip and calling of goodbyes. The camera discovers MARI-ANN in a corner, unzipping her overall to reveal a pair of battered shorts.

MARI-ANN: (in V.O.) ...I used to watch the others, their eyes empty...Every night factory gossip and soap plots, and I'd force myself to think — to count the jars — to work out how much I was getting paid to the second...Anything...

CUT TO INTERIOR SHOT: LADIES TOILETS. CONTINUING
Mari-Ann is standing in front of a long mirror, staring at herself as she pulls her cap and hairnet away. Other women buzz constantly around her.

MARI ANN: (in V.O.) ...That's when I discovered talking to you. Well not talking really — Like this.

CUT TO EXTERIOR: A STATIC LONG SHOT OF A SOLITARY ROW OF TERRACED HOUSES.
Behind, the moors rise, golden in the late sun. Mari-Ann walks across frame, the only figure in the landscape.

MARI-ANN: (in V.O.) ...It was songs first. Songs I knew all the words to, and I'd sing them over and over until you'd tell me to change the record.

Her Song

CUT TO INTERIOR SHOT: A SITTING ROOM. EVENING.
The camera moves past a photograph of a younger Mari-Ann and a man, to discover her sitting on a window sill, watching children playing football on the sloping moorside pitch outside. She is rocking backwards and forwards, humming to herself.

MARI-ANN: (in V.O) I think I must have said something to Alan once too, because he bought me a poetry book — said poems'd be easy to remember too, because of the rhythm. I think it was to help with my English really — that he liked the Uist Gaelic lilt, but not the stumbling over simple English words.

CUT TO INTERIOR SHOT: A BEDROOM. NIGHT.
Although a bedside clock says 9 pm, light is still streaming in through the window onto the bed. Mari-Ann crawls on top of the covers and picks up a book. She finds her place in the well-thumbed pages, marked by a piece of dried white heather. As background sound we hear her trying to form words as her finger traces the first lines of a poem called *Her Song*. The sounds are barely recognisable, and her face twists with the effort.

MARI ANN: (in V.O.) ...I'm not used to the sound of my own voice any more. You say it's dry as bible-pressed flowers. I wish Alan was still here so I could read to him like before. Sometimes I just wish — Like you.

CUT TO HAND-HELD CAMERA
From Mari-Ann's point of view we enter the yellow-tiled room of the factory just as the buzzer sounds. A quick shot/glance at the clock tells us it's exactly 6am. A WOMAN's face looks up at Mari-Ann as she feeds jars onto the line. She has the purple shadows under her eyes of the night shift worker.

WOMAN: Thank God! Cop this.

Mari-Ann slips on her gloves and they change over in mid-feed, effortless with the benefit of long practise. As Mari-Ann glances around the rest of the line we see Marlene, a FOREWOMAN, and a young girl (MADDY) framed in the open loading doors at the far end of the room. The two older women are talking together, glancing occasionally at Mari-Ann. Marlene jerks her head at Maddy and the threesome walk towards the camera.

145

MARI-ANN: (in V.O.) You've told me before that they're watching me, and I know it's true. They think we're strange. Flies in the ointment.

As the three women approach we have a quick succession of shots of each of their faces. Marlene — red and pointed, the Forewoman dark and mannish. MADDY is wide-eyed, her overall too big, her cap and hairnet too perfect.

MARLENE: Ann....This is Maddy, she'll be in here on spare for the summer, stacking and glass. Alright Maddy? Ann'll show you what to do.

She begins to walk away with the Forewoman, and the two giggle together at something which Marlene cannot resist sharing.

MARLENE: Oh, and be careful what you say. She's the boss's daughter, aren't you Maddy?

Maddy squirms as the older women leave, then she turns to Mari-Ann embarrassed, yet expectant. Mari-Ann hold up her hands indicating the gloves and points.

MADDY: Oh, right.

She moves to the side of the feeding-in table and takes a pair of plastic gloves from a box perched on one of the table supports. The camera shows us the two women facing each other across the frame, the pallet of glass jars between them. Mari-Ann picks up ten jars as before and waggles them at Maddy to make sure she's watching. Then she begins her short, precise movements once more. Maddy awkwardly picks up four jars in each hand and tries to follow suit, nervously aware that she is only inches away from knocking over a tower of glass.

MADDY: (embarrassed by the silence) My dad didn't get me the job here you know. I didn't even tell him I applied — I'm not a spy or anything... I need the money for when I go back to college.

She looks up as MARI-ANN continues working, sees that her chat isn't going anywhere and concentrates once more on the job in hand, her tongue between her teeth in concentration.

Her Song

CUT TO INTERIOR SHOT: WENDY HOUSE (Cubicle in the corner of the factory room). LATE MORNING.

At one end of the Wendy House there is a Maxpax coffee machine. Along each side are benches, and in front of each bench, narrow white tables stand attached to the floor. The air is blue with cigarette smoke as the first coffee break of the morning gets under way. EILEEN, a woman of about fifty, muscular and small, passes Maddy a brown plastic cup and sits heavily next to her on one of the benches. Facing them are BET, LIZ and two other younger girls.

EILEEN: Gettin' on alright then? Maddy in't it? Ann showing you the ropes is she, chuck?

MADDY: She doesn't talk much, does she?

BET: Don't get chance to talk much in 'ere, love. Too noisy. Sign language, that's what we're good at! (She makes a crude gesture, and the others hoot with laughter.)

LIZ: Don't go teaching the girl that!

EILEEN: Aye, but you're right. Ann don't talk much. Never heard her for ages anyway. She's a bit, you know, weird in the head like.

BET: Like they say, you don't have to be out of your tree to work here, but it helps. You're not the only maddy round 'ere, that's for sure.

MADDY: Oh.

Maddy watches Mari-Ann through the glass window of the Wendy House as she uses a hand-operated truck to line up another pallet of glass with the table.

CUT TO Mari-Ann as she lowers the empty pallet to the ground and slides it out of the way. Rapidly she cuts away the plastic wrapping of the next pallet with her knife and quickly scoops a few jars onto the line to buy herself some time. The noise of the factory fades into voiceover once more.

MARI-ANN: Stop nagging me. Alright, so she's the boss' daughter. If she's good they'll get rid of you...me...They'll send us onto custard powder with the purple waves and the varicose veins.... I used to want out before I had you to listen to. They listen to Radio Two in custard.

Claire Ingham

One of the jars on the line falls on its side and gets caught in the machinery. Without a second thought Mari-Ann goes to the affected part of the machine, lifts the safety guard and frees the jar, her hand vulnerable in the interior space of the machine.

MADDY: Can I help?

Mari-Ann jumps, snatching her hand quickly away from the machine, and turns to Maddy shaking her head fiercely. She walks out of shot leaving Maddy staring after her.

MADDY: (To herself) No, thank you anyway. You're welcome.

From her desk in the centre of the room Marlene nods grudging approval at Mari-Ann.

CUT TO INTERIOR SHOT: CLOAKROOM CORNER. MIDDAY.
Mari-Ann is curled up between two sets of lockers, dog-eared poetry book in hand. her mouth is moving, but there is no sound. Maddy sees Mari-Ann sitting alone, hesitates for a moment, then goes over to join her.

MADDY: (tipping the book gently to see the title) The Liverpool Poets! My fifth form teacher went out with Brian Patten in the sixties. We did their stuff a lot. Not surprising really, I s'pose. Do you know this one? (Reciting softly):
> *For no other reason than I love him wholly I am here.*
> *For this one night at least, the world has shrunk to*
> *a boyish breast, on which my head...*

Faintly we hear Maddy continue, but prominence is given to Mari-Ann reciting the same words passionately in voiceover. She is watching Maddy's profile as she recites in complete wonder. There is a connection.

MARI-ANN: (in V.O.) ...Brilliant and exhausted rests, and can know of nothing more complete...

MIX TO EXTERIOR SHOT: TRIG POINT (The highest point of the moor). EVENING.
Mari-Ann is perched on top of the trig point swinging her legs beneath her as an aeroplane flies far overhead. She waves frantically at it, then shades her eyes watching it fly on.

Her Song

MARI-ANN: (in V.O.) I am as far beyond doubt as the sun...I am as far beyond doubt as is possible. (Whispering hoarsely) Are you still there?

MIX TO the camera looking into a machine, its housing framing the picture. Trays of six jars are coming through on the belt, and plastic sheeting is being heat-wrapped onto them, the warm air making the picture quiver. Suddenly Mari-Ann leans into frame, her back to the camera, scoops up the tray of jars and turns. We turn with her and watch her stacking the full trays onto a pallet. Ambient sound fades once again as we go into voiceover.

MARI-ANN: (In V.O.) You're sulking aren't you? Because I listened to someone else. Even at Alan's funeral you sulked...

Eileen walks over and waits for Mari-Ann to notice her. Then she taps on her watch and begins to take over stacking. Mari-Ann walks to the other end of the room, pulling on her gloves. At the feeding-in table Maddy is now coping well with the jars, her speed improved.

MARI-ANN: (in V.O.) ..She's only a kid. She'd never understand — would you Maddy. Would you?

MADDY: (Fading in) Break time? Brilliant. Back at ten to?

The camera follows Maddy as she walks towards the Wendy House, as if from Mari-Ann's point of view. Marlene walks across the shot, however, stops and stares at Mari-Ann, who bends to her work once more. Marlene's eyes then follow Maddy.

CUT TO INTERIOR SHOT: WENDY HOUSE. LATE MORNING.
Bet enters the room as Maddy sits looking out of the windows towards Mari-Ann. Her cup of coffee is nearly empty and she swirls what is left around absently. Bet presses her back against the door, struggles to fish her cigarettes out of her overall pocket, lights one, and then relaxes. She swings herself down into the seat next to Maddy.

BET: How's the maddy today, then?

MADDY: I'm fine

BET; Not you...Your baby sitter — Ann. Spoken to you yet has she?

MADDY: She's just quiet.

Maddy takes the last of her coffee and stands up, making for the door.

BET: Suit yourself...(Mouthing as Maddy exits) Boss' daughter.

She grins around the Wendy House at the other girls as Maddy shuts the door firmly behind her.

CUT TO INTERIOR SHOT: FACTORY ROOM. LATER THAT MORNING.
Mari-Ann is lifting a cardboard lid off a new pallet of jars, so that at first all we see is the brown card filling screen, and then her face. A jar wobbles on the corner of the pallet furthest from her, and she bites her lip in concentration as she takes the lid slowly away. Maddy steadies the precarious jar.

MADDY: Go on. Go for your break.

Mari-Ann looks surprised but pleased, and gives Maddy a striking smile as she pulls off her gloves. She begins to walk away, her back to the camera, the camera tight on her back.

MARI-ANN: (In V.O.) What do you think she thinks about? Maybe she's writing songs in her head...Weaving stories...lost in a strange wood where words are silent, where touch is dead, where the loudest thing is the blood singing in her ears...I wonder what it would be like...

Over the last of these words the camera catches Mari-Ann looking over her shoulder. All we can see are her eyes, large and luminous. It is a disconcerting look straight at us, and suddenly the expression in her eyes changes.

MARI-ANN: (shouting) NO!

The word echoes over the noise of the factory as Mari-Ann runs back towards the camera in slow motion. From her point of view we can see Maddy reaching into the machine to free a fallen glass, the moving parts of the machine frighteningly close. Mari-Ann whirls towards Maddy, plunging both hands into the machine and pulling Maddy's hand free with one of her own. An alarm sounds, the machinery grinds to a halt and the sound of

Her Song

Mari-Ann's cry echoes round the tiled room, blending with the endless grating of the machine brakes.

CUT TO INTERIOR OF A HOSPITAL WARD. EVENING.
　　Mari-Ann is lying in bed, her hand heavily bandaged. Maddy is sitting on the bed, her back to the camera. As the camera moves towards the bed we see Maddy rise. She turns towards the camera and walks out of shot. As Mari-Ann watches her walk down the corridor we hear her in voiceover for the last time.

MARI ANN: (in V.O.) Have you gone? (Whispering) You're not going to speak to me again, are you?

CUT TO EXTERIOR SHOT: TRIG POINT. LATE SUMMER. EVENING.
　　The green ferns of the moor have turned to rust-brown bracken. As the camera moves upwards we can see Mari-Ann and Maddy running up towards the trig point. As a plane flies over, Mari-Ann spins round. Maddy watches her smiling.

MARI-ANN: (shouting) Wave at me! Wave at me!

　　The camera stays close on Mari-Ann twirling and laughing.

MADDY: (in V.O.) How right...To shrug off real and invented grief..When being lost seems so much more like being found...And you find all that is lost is all that weighed you down.

　　Over Maddy's last words we cut back to a wide shot of Mari-Ann silhouetted against the evening sky. We see now that she is alone, spinning.

Martin Aaron

From *Reptiles*

Martin Aaron, born 1970, lives in South London.

"Rob! Rob!"

The voice dies slowly in my dream and is reborn screaming into my waking consciousness. "Yes" I shout back, a pained bellow that lasts until the shrieking stops. With half-closed eyes I spy the Mickey Mouse clock I've had since I was six. The American rodent cheerfully points his big stubby fingers between the nine and the ten. Bastard. Why does he look so cheerful every damn morning? Bastard. I can't move. I'm dead.

"Rob!"

No, I'm alive and I think I can just make it out of bed.

When I come downstairs I see my mother raising her shoulders over the ironing board. So tired, so tired, she presses down on the iron as she presses down on change, a crease is flattened, steam rises, the sweat of her soul. My mother turns from the ironing board as I enter the kitchen and, without looking at me, points at some thick black marks on the lino.

"Don't ever clean your bloody bike in here again."

"Morning."

"Don't ever ever again, the tea towels are ruined."

"Mmm sorry."

"You can get rid of that oil on the floor now."

The ironing board creaks as she slams a pair of pants into submission.

"I have to go to work, remember." I drop my baseball cap onto my head, shuffle quickly into the hall. I can still hear her shrieking at top volume as I close the front door behind me. That was my mother and that's all you need to know about her.

Down at the supermarket I chuck my cap into a locker, put on my lovely brown workcoat and clip the knotted tie onto my shirt. The beautiful brown tie is industrial safety issue; two plastic branches slide under my collar so that it pulls off with the slightest yank. Yeah, like I'm in real danger of grisly death from getting my tie caught in a shelf of cup-a-soup sachets. I am a 'shop floor assistant' — basically hard labour in unsuitable clothes. The supermarket is a fucking million aisles wide and I get to carry huge boxes of everything — baked beans, cat litter, probably anvils — from one side to the other.

Out on the shop floor Akeem, my manager, shows me which boxes he wants moving. I nod, Akeem shambles down some infinite isle, fuck, I'm still half-asleep. Whack. I'm hit by a fist in my spine. I turn around, head back, gasping.

"Orright."

It's Liam, a big boxer from Ireland with pig-pink skin and thin blond hair. He's over here to make it; he's already been on the telly once. He lives in Merton and works here when he's not skipping or spreading someone's face over canvas. I understand about four percent of the words he speaks. Most of the time I just nod or shake my head at the droning Belfast burr, desperately hoping I get the gist right. To smile or frown at the wrong part of his Hoover monologue has fearful consequences. He shimmies around me like a cyclone, throwing awesome punches that stop millimetres from my face. The only defence is to stand stock still and close my eyes until he softly slaps my face and walks away grinning. Stupid Irish bastard.

Still, he keeps me awake.

"All right mate," I wheeze, clutching my ruined back.

He chats away but I can't pick out any words. After a few minutes of really straining my ears I gather he's telling me about having sex with his landlady. This is his usual topic so I feel fairly safe, but I can never work out whether these lavish tales are reality, fantasy or a long joke with a punchline I never quite catch. Anyway, I've been pretending to understand perfectly for too long now so I just nod and laugh when he does.

"Shacunacooaglosin!"

"Ha, ha!"

I should get an Oscar for this. Fortunately Akeem appears and in his fake friendly, condescending, obviously-been-on-a-course-about-motivating-employees type way "suggests" we get on with our work and stop messing about. Liam shirks off, Akeem offers some Cheshire cat encouragement, thumbs aloft. Does the little turd really expect me to find job satisfaction in stacking baked beans in ordered lines?

"Well done Rob! Great job!"

Each time he talks to me like this I stare at him with an ever more disgusted expression of disbelief. But the little shit is too stupid to realise his own stupidity.

It's Friday and I'm looking forward to the evening. The hours hurt,

Reptiles

hanging on my nerves. I catch myself counting seconds. My mind slows down until I feel only half awake, carrying out my work like a robot. They're training me to stop thinking. One of my tasks is to make sure the shelves are full with all the proper produce. I've got, say, a twenty-four-inch gap to place the packets of beef flavour noodles, then I've got twenty-four inches either side for the prawn flavour and the chicken flavour, and the packets all have to be neatly stacked and the old packets have to be moved to the front before they go out of date and the front packets have to be in a straight line right along the lip of the shelf and the AAAARGGH! FOR FUCK'S SAKE! I used to think only idiots worked stacking shelves. Now I realise that's all upside down. Concentrating on the symmetry of duck liver dog food kills anyone's mind. Give me a genius — I will give him a brown uniform and a knotted tie that slots under his collar and I will give him seventy-eight Toblerones (which, in case you didn't know, are triangular and bastards to stack neatly) and after two hours of fretting over their arrangement I guarantee his mind will be empty, no thoughts at all, his skull a ghost town echoing with brand names. 'You don't have to be stupid to work here...' is a nauseous cliché that cons the stupid into thinking it somehow funny to be useless. Sometimes I read my sister's books, and one of these books — Saturday Night, Sunday Morning — has this northern bloke who works in a shit job like me and he goes on about how he likes doing his job because it gives him time to think, time to think about machine-gunning his fat bosses and rising up, taking on the world.

Well bollocks. My mind is being sucked like an egg. Every can of beans I lug is another straw on my back. And I'm one fucking tired camel.

I'm going to talk about me. I work at the supermarket during the week and at the pet shop on occasional Saturdays when I need the cash.

My mum does the laundry at the hospital, my dad drives a bus all day then sits in a chair and watches T.V. He doesn't talk to me, in fact he rarely even looks my way. The last time he spoke he said he didn't want me calling him dad anymore and I should call him by his name — Barry. I look at my parents and wish they were criminals or separated or one of them was missing — run off, dead — I don't care how, just so that I could have an excuse for any behaviour like almost every kid on the estate. It's no fun being "normal" (notice my socially aware inverted commas).

My sister I'll talk about another time.

We have a mongrel dog called Bonza.

I live in Roehampton Village. Ha! Village! Since when has a maze of concrete boxes piled on top of each other been a village? Oh yes, we're sandwiched between Wimbledon Common and Richmond Park, the two biggest daubs of green on the London map but all *we* get is concrete. Our delightful village residence is halfway up the estate's central tower block, the one hanging over the library, looking down over the shops like it could spit, gazing wistfully towards the City.

The main street is Danebury Avenue. The planners who fucked us all decided if you planted trees either side of a grotty little road it became an avenue. What a laugh. Recently, all along the rows of concrete boxes, satellite dishes have sprung up like fungi enabling the dead-eyed residents to watch even more T.V. Well, if you can't live in the real world. The concrete boxes are piled on top of each with a front door reached by a stairwell and balcony.

Some of these balconies are covered with a wire grill. I never know whether the wire is put up by the people who live there to stop stones getting lobbed through their windows or whether the wire's put there by the council to stop the people who live there chucking stuff down. It's a weird zoo with no one quite sure who the animals are.

But this is my home, lying like London's gutter on the outskirts of oh-so-pleasant affluence.

I go straight to Clem's house after work. Clem is my best mate. This particular Friday we're going out with the others uptown.

Clem doesn't live in a tower block like me, he has one of the matchboxes by the park. His mum opens the door. She's 35 years old, she's nearly six foot tall, she's got a plastic bag on her head covered in thick purple goo, strands of hair are pulled through tiny holes in the bag, there's purple goo splurging out the sides. She looks terrifying.

"Hello Rob love, he's upstairs."

The pulse of Aphex is shaking the stairs so I figure I can creep up on Clem and give him a scare. Gently opening the door the full force of the music pours out and I catch him kneeling on the floor by his bed. With popping eyes he whips around to face me and shoves a sparkling treasure trove under the mattress. Then he sees it's me and he closes his eyes and smiles. He reaches over to the stereo and turns down the sound.

"You cunt Rob I thought you was me mum."

From under the mattress he pulls out a handbag brimming with gold chains, pearl earrings and jewelled rings.

"I thought your mum knows about the nicking?"

"Yeah but I got these doing over an ol' dear's place."

"Yeah?"

"An' m'mum's funny about doin' old people."

"Who were you with?"

"Dog."

"What about the others?"

"They did a house in Putney, got wads of cash and a VCR for that guy down the pub."
"Why's your mum got a plastic bag on her head?"
"She's doin' her hair."
Sitting down on the bed we go through the stuff together. I'm a bit worried about getting my fingerprints on hot stuff so I pick up the sparkling pieces with my grubby fingernails. Clem takes the piss about this. I laugh with him but it brings back all the nightmares.

I dredge this memory reluctantly, a corpse exhumed only for essential post-mortem. I suppose like a rape victim, like an abused child, I've blocked out the whole episode, erasure being the only way to deal with horror. Like a forest fire which seems burnt out but then flickers up and consumes again with only the tiniest blow of encouragement, so this memory will have to be quashed again, a blanket of willed amnesia chucked over the facts that burn.
Play.
The flashbacks come worse than any acid. The chain of events play in my mind then rewind and repeat all over again. The jar of syrup into my pocket. In the open aisle instead of at the crowded till. Complacency, so foolish. If only I could rewind the events myself, splice them differently, rearrange things so I don't get caught. But no, the nightmare drama performs once again. Outside the shop, a little local shop, a hand slaps onto my sleeve. Burning white-hot manacle. Would you come inside the shop please. Absent question mark. My heart is set to explode but I try to sound calm. He's gesturing towards the shop. Yes of course. I pretend I'm a posh kid, pretend he must be absurdly mistaken. But he knows. He's a young kid, my age. Why? What's in it for him?
Rewind.
Would you come inside the shop please. Yes of course. Fear is weird. Shoals of people blur past, I'm floating, barely aware of anything. At that moment only I exist. Me and his hand on my forearm. My dry mouth and his shiny, excited eyes. His straight mouth quivering with adrenaline.
Rewind.
I place the syrup in my pocket. Why there? Why there in the open aisle where anyone could spot me? Idiot.
Fast Forward.
Waiting in a tiny storeroom for the police. Swaying, sweat pouring off me, feel I'm going to faint. The bastard stands, arms folded, watching me, making sure I don't make a run for it. Dumb staff peer in through the window of the storeroom: their glares are judging, fascinated, scared, amused. I'm going to faint. I could kill this bastard if only I could pull myself together. But my legs just aren't there. I am jelly. Mario wouldn't be like this. If the guy had snatched Mario's arm Mario would have broken his face and been laughing half-way home before the guy had hit the

159

ground. But not me. Coward.

Rewind.

"YES OF COURSE." Oh idiot honesty never pays. I tried to bluff but they knew with one glance. One glance at my white face — a waterfall of sweat rushing from my brow, I slapped a hand on the back of a chair to save myself from fainting. Not the behaviour of an innocent man, innocently carrying a jar of syrup, quite wrongly accused of shoplifting.

Fast Forward.

I can't bear it. Two pigs, one big and tough, the other ginger hair, quiet, calm. No handcuffs but they hold me by my sleeve. Down the precinct, through the crowd. Feel like Jesus. So many nosy scum, staring eyes, sneers, necks craning, whispers, a homeboy laughing and shouting but I don't hear the words. In the patrol car Big Bastard is nasty, Ginger is nice and sympathetic, like in films.

In a concrete windowless room, a desk in front of me, lots of talking. A transparent bag with a yellow zip eats my possessions — bus ticket, chewing gum, ten-pound note. Outside a cell they take my belt and trainers. I'm in the cell for ages. Nothing to scratch my name on the walls with. Later paperwork. I stick to my story. I'd already bought the syrup when I went into the damned shop. Ginger pig lets me read back what he's written. He's changed sentences around, altered how I said things so I sound even more guilty. Reluctantly he makes corrections, I initial them.

Five hours later I step outside, there's a group of crusty travellers hanging about outside on the steps. They see me threading my belt back on and give me a big cheer. I suppose I feel quite cool — fuck the police and all that. Mind you, Lyons syrup, hardly the Krays is it.

Fast Forward.

A brown envelope arrives. Court summons. Have to bunk off the afternoon at work. Change into jacket and tie in the toilets at lunch time. Borrowed from Dad's wardrobe without him knowing. The collar's too tight, sweating again. Catch a bus to court. Past the cemetery. Wish the ground would take me. Quick chat with a guy from legal aid. Little guy with thick moustache.

"Plead guilty."

"Okay."

In the court an old man in uniform is nice to me. Winks. Don't worry he says. Say nothing says the moustache. Three old cunts come out and listen to the story. The moustache says that I'm very sorry and I plead guilty. Man in uniform pats my arm. The three cunts disappear through a panelled door then reappear. Fined seventy-five pounds with twenty-five-pound costs. I'm free to go.

It's in the paper. A tiny column about a youth fined ninety-five pounds for a jar of syrup costing ninety-five pence. The youth is named. There's my name in fucking black and white. How the folks never hear about it I don't know. Maybe none of the gossips dare mention it. The youth is referred to as smartly dressed, didn't they see *that top button choking me? Clem, Dog and the others find it all hilarious. Clem sticks the clipping on his wall.*

After a while of just chilling out to Kiss and nattering we go downstairs to score off Clem's mum. She's in the kitchen with some scales and some red seal. We get an eighth off her and laugh at her purple head. Then we go back upstairs and skin up, both of us rolling. Clem turns his spliff round, bites on the roach, leans his full lips towards me and blows into my open mouth. I must look like a baby bird.

Judith Rawnsley

Into the Light

Judith Rawnsley was born in Rugby in 1964. After Cambridge, she worked as London correspondent for a Japanese newspaper. From 1988 to 1993 she worked in Tokyo, first as a stockbroker, then as a correspondent for London-based publications. She has written a collection of short stories, *Turning Bamboo*. *Into the Light* is her first novel.

I found my father much as I had left him four months before — alone, surrounded only by his books and his flowers. He collected me from the station in the Morris Minor he still drives even though he is 75. He calls her Viva, meaning she is his lifeline. He has had her almost as long as I can remember, but she is still in immaculate condition and with so few miles on the clock that she could have been driven out of the showroom last year. He took the plastic covers off the seats only three summers ago.

As we drove, it took him some time to find his voice again — he rarely ventures into the outside world anymore and he'd not had time to get used to the idea that I was coming. I imagined that my voice must have seemed to him like a distant crackle on the World Service and that it was taking him time to tune in. But in the half-hour drive he warmed to my presence again, and I began to feel nervous about how I was going to tell him about Michael.

The pebble-dash of the house glinted in the sunshine like a wet beach as we drove up. I am still surprised by how much smaller the house is in reality than the childhood image I carry in my head, reduced to the size and compactness of a doll's house as the world around me has grown steadily larger.

My father stood on the doorstep nervously twisting the keys round and round in his hand, trying to find the right one. He has experienced much in his long life, including a war and the loss of my mother, and this must have alerted him to my mood, made him wary of my visit. As he fumbled with the lock I could tell he sensed the presence of impending doom. His face reflected what he must have seen in mine.

Instead of going straight into the kitchen and sitting down with him as I normally would have done, I went upstairs to my old room and began to unpack my bag, throwing my clothes on hangers, arranging and rearranging my toiletries on the dressing table.

I did not know how to phrase what I had to tell him. My father had taken immediately to Michael, assimilating him into his life from the day they met. Perhaps he trusted my judgement, or, more likely, he felt immediately drawn by Michael's ease with people and his interest in my father's life and Yorkshire background. The first time I took Michael to Scarborough, he sat in front of the fire with my father and listened patiently to the tales of his days in the military and how he had been forced to leave after National Service because his Yorkshire accent had determined that he would never be promoted above the rank of lieutenant.

My father followed me upstairs and stood watching me in the doorway for a while as I clattered about trying to stave off the moment, then he reached out and grabbed my wrist, drawing me to him, holding me still. "What is it love? What's happened? Were the results of the test bad?" I nodded. He fell silent and looked at his toes for a moment, then put his arms around me and rocked me back and forth as he used to do when I was small. Then he left me alone, knowing that what I needed before I could tell him was a little time on my own.

When I went downstairs Dad was making a pot of tea. I held out to him a copy of my latest museum paper on Celtic burial rituals, which I knew would interest him, as if the extension of a present would somehow act as a buffer against the harshness of what I was really about to give him. He accepted it silently, acknowledging with a quick glance and a nod of the head what it was, then put it down on the kitchen top and looked at me directly, drawing himself up a little straighter in preparation for the news he was about to receive.

"Michael's blood markers have gone up again. It's spread to his lungs. They say he has an excellent prognosis, but I don't know...I couldn't, didn't know how to tell you on the phone."

My father has never been one to attempt to bridge the gap between what he wants to say and what it is possible to verbalise and he simply put down the pot of tea he was holding and placed his hands on the tops of my arms with a slight pressure, steadying. His eyes were brimming with tears which seemed to leak from the corners of his eyes and bathe me in sympathy. I choked back tears myself and reached up for his hands and squeezed the fingers tightly. "I'm not sure how I'm going to cope with it this time. He seems to be turning in on himself, away from me."

My father swallowed. "It may be the only way for him to cope with it himself; sometimes, with the big things, it's only possible to face up to them alone. I know that's hard for you. You'll have to be brave."

Into the Light

There was no need for further words. Beyond the physical expressions, my father did not want to communicate his sorrow, knowing that it would only add to my burden. He released one of my hands, laced his fingers into the other in a gentle clasp and led me out of the back door and into the sunshine. In silence we walked around the garden arm in arm, the garden he has been creating since his retirement 15 years ago. When I was a child, it was no different from the gardens of our neighbours behind the drystone walls which lay on either side. There was a small lawn with a flower bed in the middle, where roses blossomed in the salt air, and one of those whirligig washing lines which I bent by swinging round on it the day my mother brought it back from the shop. At the end of the garden was a rough area of land we called the Patch, where briars and broom covered the sandy soil like tangles of green wire and rose bay willow herb rose up, careering on the sea breeze like the purple horses' manes in fairy tales. I used to tunnel through the Patch with my friends who lived in the street, and to us the tunnels and dens we created were a fantasy land better than anything we could read in *Swallows and Amazons* or the Famous Five books. But it was the bane of my father's life — this unruly, undisciplined piece of land which had grown out of his control. He longed to have time to tame it, to create something beautiful from its natural chaos.

Now the garden has been transformed. Gone is the rough lawn with its buttercups and springy pads of moss, with the cement path which shot down the middle like a small airport runway and stopped abruptly where the washing line stood. Gone too are the woody roses and the flower-bed and gone is the Patch and my childhood fantasies. The small lawn has been clipped into a green circle as finely manicured as snooker cloth, neatly bordered by a riot of flowers. Beyond this lies a herb garden with thyme and lemon verbena and mature bushes of rosemary, all bordered by a thick haze of lavender upon which the cabbage whites dance. Along the small paths which weave in between the beds are terracotta pots of sweet basil like those I grow at home.

Where the Patch used to be there is now a wonderful vegetable garden set among apple and pear trees where, my father tells me, he potters about on summer evenings as the gnats begin to cloud beneath the trees, and talks to his onions and his tomato plants, or sits in his greenhouse listening to the radio and watching his strawberries grow.

We came to a stop at the end of the garden and stood for a few moments in the doorway of the greenhouse. The interior reflected the same orderly concern as the inside of the house and the garden: cleaned and sharpened hand-tools in their proper places in a rack, a garden hose neatly coiled on its drum, rows of seedlings sprouting under cloches, each tray with its own white plastic tag neatly labelled in black felt-tip. But in one corner a butter-

Judith Rawnsley

fly was trapped: it battered itself repeatedly against the pane in an attempt to break through to the world outside, the powder from its wings leaving smudges of purple on the glass. In the harmony of the setting even the soft sound of its struggle seemed a gross disturbance. I leaned forward and gently scooped it out into the open in the palm of my hand. And as I looked back at the garden, a wave of something akin to nostalgia washed over me. I thought of how it used to be when I was small, and part of me suddenly mourned the annihilation of its wildness. It was as if the discipline of everything I saw around me suggested the loss of everything which had been natural, fertile and creative.

"Remember the nettles, Dad? The permanent raspberry-coloured rashes I had on my arms and legs in the summer?"

"Bandaged you up in dock leaves and you were right as rain. You could hardly bear to stop for treatment." He turned his gaze away from the garden as he said this and back into the greenhouse, his eyes resting on a group of single flowers, each solitary in its own pot, each protected by its own polythene bag. He gently lifted the covering from one of them. "Now look at this will you? I've been trying to get these to grow for years. Never could understand it..." I bent closer to look at the orchid, at the delicate pink tracery of its petals, the proud rigidity of its stem, and took a deep draught of its sweet musky fragrance. It was too beautiful to be kept hidden in a plastic bag.

"Taken me years to realise how to grow them. Like anything, I suppose, just takes a bit of nurturing."

"Perhaps the hot weather has helped them."

We wandered back towards the lawn, Dad leaning heavily on my arm, a slight wheezing sound coming from his chest as if something was trapped inside him. I fetched the tea from the kitchen, and we sat down in the deck-chairs faded to a salty aquamarine by the breeze which blows sand and salt across the garden, listening to the waves pounding against the cliffs below. And I suddenly realised that my father has grown old without my noticing it. The backs of his hands are stained with the coins of old age and his thumbs twitch of their own accord. The hair on the top of his head has become the soft, fine down of a baby's. As we sat there, I saw his eyes reach to the skies as the gulls wheeled overhead and knew that he was thinking of his air rifle still kept in a cupboard somewhere. I was expecting him to start telling me the tale of how he and his father used to shoot the gulls when he was a boy and force my grandmother to bake them in a pie. But instead he broke off a piece of the scone he was balancing on a plate on his knee and threw it a little way in front of him, smiling as he watched the gulls loop and circle down, their orange feet dangling like ribbons below their ungainly bodies, listening to their harsh cries, which even in Scarborough evoke images of sea mariners and distant shores. The gulls seemed to know him as a provider as they circled in, and I understood that this was a regular thing, this breaking of bread for the seagulls that he had always hated. And I thought, something in my father has changed; it was as if he was no longer trying to hold on, as if the anger which had always threatened my youth, appearing like a sea squall which passed as quickly as it had come, had been replaced by permanent summer weather. I would have called it happiness but for what he said later and for the shock I was to feel when I finally understood that he meant it.

Dusk settled slowly across the garden as we sat there so that shadows crept like fingers across the lawn and bats began to draw hoops in the dusk around our heads. Eventually we moved indoors and sat by the hearth, sipping the gin and tonics my father has grown so fond of. I made a light supper of scrambled eggs on toast which we ate from trays on our laps.

For a long time we didn't speak, and then, in the quiet intimacy which grew between us, I found space to mull over what had been bothering me, the questions I wanted to ask. But it was difficult to think of a subtle way to bring up the subject and the precise importance of my enquiries began to elude me as I realised that the subject might be painful for my father. A good 15 minutes must have passed before I finally came out with it: "What happened between you and Mum?"

He has rarely spoken of her, and throughout the years I was growing up, perhaps because of the joint force of my father and grandmother, I never noticed that one dimension of parenthood was missing from my life. And I know next to nothing about how she and my father met, why they married or why and how she had left. I wanted to know how he had coped with the loss of her and whether he had considered it a loss. Why I hadn't asked this before, I don't know. Only it had never seemed important, nor had it ever seemed as if there might come a time when I wouldn't be able to ask about it. It is difficult at any time to accept that your mother and father are anything other than parents, are people in their own right who have made decisions and choices in their lives quite independently of you, that they are often strangers to their own children.

My father looked up. His eyes, blue as the afternoon sky, were clouded with bewilderment, but he must have seen the earnest expression on my face. He phrased a careful reply behind the defenses of the biography of Churchill he had begun reading.

"Your mother was a good woman. Too good for me." He was being cryptic, did not want to have to pursue this line of discussion, but I couldn't let it go.

"In what way too good?"

"She was somehow more committed to life, to people, than I am, if you can say such a thing, whereas I, well, I have always been able to find my peace in the world within." The book rested in his lap now and his insect-legs were crossed, a triangle of white skin showing between his sock and trouser leg like a flag of kid leather. "You see Samuel," — the spaniel was sitting on my father's slippers like a muffler — "he's like me, content to remain on his own patch — never so much as sniffs at the neighbour's fence. But there are other dogs I've known that would run and run given the chance, need to go off and explore as far as they can." He paused for a moment. "I couldn't stop her from going, wouldn't have stopped her for the world. It was her life. Not my place to impose limitations."

His face was flushed as he thought about her, and I thought I detected something akin to irritation in his eyes.

"Do you think about her?"

"Not much. It was a long time ago and now she's dead, well, what does it matter?" He looked up at me and I saw his eyes trace the contours of my face, coming to rest on my hair-line. "When I see you I do. You remind me of her, the way you look sometimes. There's a look of enquiry in you too, questioning, confronting the world. That's what irritated me about your mother after a while: the constant need to delve beneath the surface of people, things. It's not right."

I asked him if he felt bitter about the fact that she had run off with another man, but he replied that there was no room for bitterness, that he had ultimately been better off on his own. "People hurt, complicate one another. I've learned that people are better off alone."

"What's the point of being alive if you don't communicate with the world?"

"You don't need to talk to other people to understand what it's all about."

"But if people aren't important to you, what is?"

"God is important. I don't suppose you believe in Him. Gone out of fashion these days, but it would help, you know, at times like these." He paused for a while and I saw his gaze reach into the distance; when he began to speak again it was as if I was no longer in the room. "Used to see Him sometimes, quite vividly, in the war. Yes, it was then. When you step outside yourself for a moment and realise that you are just an ordinary man holding a gun and firing at another ordinary man, no better or worse than yourself, for the sake of what we call civilisation. That's evil for you. And when you've seen evil in the making, it's not hard to see God right behind. Saw my whole life flashing before me — my hopes, my dreams — being shot down, falling on the mud like spent bullets. It's at those moments you realise what's important. You know you need something else to hold on to. No good holding on to your friend who lies dead at your feet, his own dreams shattered around him."

Into the Light

I couldn't pin-point exactly what it was he was trying to say or why it disturbed me so much. I thought that perhaps in talking about having some*thing* rather than some*one* else to hold on to, he was referring to Michael and I, to Michael's illness, to how he thought I might be feeling; yet there was something missing. There was no easy connection between my father's eremitical way of thinking and the sense I had of my own childhood; the sense that there definitely had been, still were, bonds between my father, my grandmother, my mother and I. It was as if he was now trying to deny something which to me is an integral part of my past and, by virtue of that, of the person I am now.

"If people don't matter to you, why did you get married?"

"I was young then and it was the age for marriage. It was what we all did then. D'you know, your mother hadn't seen my feet before the night of our wedding? She had sent off for a mixed bag of contraceptives, hilarious assortment of things we had no clue what to do with, including a bag with a draw-string top and a small sponge at the bottom. That was how you arrived. You do things differently now. Young people take each other for granted. I'm not saying that's the way with you and Michael. You always seemed to make each other happy enough. But that's exactly what it boils down to: happiness. Young people always expect to be happy now. Happiness. What is it anyway?"

I felt frustrated by his passive cynicism and my mind moved back to Michael. I pictured him lying in the hospital with the thin plastic tubes conveying yellow fluids into his system, nurturing him, helping to keep him alive. I reflected on how the last year has found us striving again and again to adapt to changed circumstances, struggling to maintain our happiness, still trying to seek out and relish the good moments while they last. In his phrasing, my father seemed to be negating all this, to be saying it was worthless to try to pursue it at all.

"Why shouldn't we be happy? What's so wrong with trying to be happy?"

"It's not a question of should or shouldn't. It's the expectation, as if it's some kind of right you have. You lot expect it to be given to you on a plate. Don't expect to have to strive for anything anymore, not for contentment anyway. There's no questioning, no self-doubt, no taking the wrong path and in doing so finding the right one, or just accepting that you made a wrong choice and living with it. It's when people stop asking questions about themselves, stop being interested in the how and why of things that society breaks down. You lot think you can change the world just by voicing an opinion and look what's happened. When things go wrong there's no mechanism for coping."

"But we *can* change things. People *can* change, *do* change."

171

Judith Rawnsley

"No. A man is just a man, no more or less than he is."

"No, Dad. We're free to choose what we become. No one's anything but what he makes of himself. And if individuals can change, so can society. All things are possible..."

My father put down his empty gin glass on the side table and, placing a palm on each arm of the chair, raised himself slowly, taking the weight on his hands. He shuffled over to me and leaned over to kiss me on the forehead. "Time I turned in. Goodnight. Sleep tight." Our conversation had been closed.

I sat for a while in the armchair and tried to drink another gin and tonic, but I no longer had the heart for it. The room seemed as empty as my father's glass without his presence, suddenly drained, except for our words which lingered in the air, heavy as the damask curtains blocking out the night sky. I felt our discussion had in many ways opened up a gap, rather than forged a connection. I felt dissatisfied, as though there was something more I had to uncover.

In response to this feeling I went upstairs to my old room and began to root around in the bottom of my wardrobe as if in search of some object, long forgotten, or as yet unknown. It is strange, the ease with which a whole past can be captured in the contents of one cupboard, which random fate has destined to be rediscovered at a date when the items themselves are no longer bound by their specific time and context. I found the collection of polished stones I had assembled when I was 11 and going through a phase when I thought I might become a geologist. I held up a piece of amber and twisted it round in the pool of light from the bedside lamp, saw the tiny remnants of insects suspended in the fossilised sap. I remembered the unpleasant texture of the polishing powder, like the harshest toothpaste, caught the smell of the chamois leather I used to polish it off. There was a pile of shells I had collected from the beach over the course of several years, tied up in one of Dad's handkerchiefs, in the bottom of which grains of sand had gathered like dust. That loose, dry sand seemed somehow out of place. I wanted then and there to go down to the shore and toss the shells back to the sea, to watch the water sparkle across them, revive their colour, bring them back to life. And I found other things as well: an old biscuit tin stuffed with childhood nicknacks like a set of jacks, and a pair of fluorescent green Clackers I never mastered, plastic toys from Christmas crackers.

It was hot in my room and too much was revolving in my mind for me to sleep. I threw open the windows and stared down into the darkness of the street and memories floated up of torchlight flashing on the window pane from Janet's house opposite, of slipping on a swimsuit and stealing downstairs for biscuits, then out into the garden to meet her on hot summer nights. Behind me the house resounded with a silence underscored by the notes of my father's deep rhythmical snores.

I went into the spare room which my father uses as a study and began to open the drawers of the desk. I suppose I was prying, transgressing my father's private space, but I still felt somehow indignant about our conversation, as if there was a piece of mosaic which he had denied me and to which I felt I had a right. In the second drawer down I found a leather-bound book filled with neat lines of poetry. It was military mostly, some about loss and isolation. The poems were good, some a little bitter, some too pared, too brutally lonely to be readable, but it was full of genuine emotion. I knew the handwriting.

In the heavy quietude of the house the effect of the poetry was suddenly overwhelming. I felt drained by the despair it suggested, the finality of its loneliness, and was left with a sense of nothingness, as if I had been digging through layer upon layer of earth towards a burial tomb only to find that the body had been snatched. It was as if I was being given a glimpse of something which I was about to experience myself and my heart felt as if it had been scooped out with a sharp knife, a pain so acute that it threatened to engulf me if I did not resist. I snapped the book shut and went straight to bed.

"The poetry, why haven't you ever sent it to a publisher?" I asked as I stuck my knife into the jar of Chivers Thick Cut.

My father froze with a napkin to his mouth, his eyes suddenly darkened above the gingham barricade which protected his expression. Then he drew it in one deft movement across his face and emerged with his lips pressed into a line of virulent composure. "It's not for public consumption."

"But it's good. Some of it's very good. People would enjoy reading it."

"That's not the point. I write for myself."

I looked at him for the first time with clear eyes and saw not my father but an old burned-leather man who had put up defenses against the world and found contentment within his own being. It is not a form of contentment, an isolation I want for myself, but it suited him, fitting around his shoulders as neatly as an old corduroy jacket which had worn to his shape. For the first time in his life he looked comfortable. And for the first time in my life I began really to question my own values, to think about what I have been doing with my life, which now seems as fragile as an ancient piece of pottery about to collapse in my palm.

I watched from the train window as he stood on the platform waving, diminishing by the second as the train pulled away, until we swung round a bend and I could no longer see him. I settled back in my seat and closed my eyes and it was Michael's face which appeared against the dewy membrane of my eyelids.

Judith Rawnsley

The thought that Michael might die illuminates for me how little we have done with our love. I don't mean there's been a lack of it. We love each other very much, have never stopped loving each other. And yet we have failed to do anything with that love. We have never stopped to question the basis for our love or looked to see in what direction we might take it, how we might more usefully employ it. Instead of letting it flow between us, beyond us, we have kept it locked in a neat little box labelled marriage which we bring out on birthdays and anniversaries — as if to remind ourselves that we possess it — and congratulate each other on having found it. There are no words to describe what we have not done with our love. We have little to show of our seven years together other than a house full of furniture, a mortgage and some holiday snaps.

We have not had sex for weeks now. For months the zest and tenderness of this side of our marriage has been slipping away so that now it is virtually nonexistent. This withdrawal from physical love is possibly worse for me than anything else; for without that special bond between us we are little to each other but good friends, and even our friendship has been eroded of late. Although I can rationalise Michael's lassitude, understand it in the context of his illness, it does not lessen my need for this expression of our love, and this worry and confusion about my emotional needs is making me feel guilty and frightened. I wonder how other women of my age have coped?

We have argued again. Michael is masking all his feelings of fear and sadness with anger. He has been constantly impatient with me, irritated by the smallest things, like the way I take so long in the bathroom in the mornings, the food I prepare for him. I know this is not a personal attack but he won't even talk to me about it. When he's not shouting at me, he's withdrawn and quiet. I want to share this time with him but he won't let me in.

It was Sunday yesterday. Nick and Julie came over with their toddler Harry and we enjoyed a relaxed lunch together and sat around afterwards, chatting and drinking red wine, the usual mouth-scouring muck the French palm off on the British. Michael was in good spirits and he and Nick talked for ages about Michael's book which Nick is helping to edit, while Julie and I played with Harry and his Duplex on the rug. But as soon as they had left, Michael retreated back into himself.

Instead of helping me to clear up and chatting to me about how the lunch had gone, as he would have done in the past, Michael sat down at the table and buried himself in the newspapers while I washed up. As I stood at the sink, I caught my reflection in the glass. My rubber-gloved arms were plunged into the soapsuds, my hair had flopped across my face. Me, Helen, 33 years old, with shadows under my eyes and coarse white hairs stealthily sprouting among the dark roots of my scalp. I could see Michael hunched over the newspaper behind me and I realised just how far apart we had become. I thought of how we were allowing this thing to stop our lives, that we didn't know what might happen and that we couldn't let life keep flowing around us, carrying us downstream without fighting against the current, trying to cling to a shore somewhere. And in my mind I could picture that shore quite clearly, a life force that we had the power to create.

I stopped scrubbing the dishes and stood with the brush poised in the air in front of me, dripping soapsuds.

"I want to have a baby."

There was silence from the table behind me and I wondered for a moment whether I had actually said it, then I heard Michael folding up the newspaper and putting it on the chair.

"Give me a break."

"No. I think we should talk about it."

"We've been through all this before. I don't want to talk about it again."

I turned round to face him, with my gloved hands crossed in the air to stop them dripping. "Michael, I know it's hardly the best time to ask, but I'm 33. You know how much I want this. I'm just really worried. We might not get another chance."

"Don't use my chemotherapy as an excuse. You've been on at me about this for years. You know I'm not ready to have kids."

"You might not always feel like that. It's not as if we have a choice is it? Please try and think about it."

"Of course we have a choice."

"But we don't." There was a long silence and Michael got up as if he was going to leave. "You're so damned *selfish*. You think this illness is yours alone. Well, it isn't. You're not thinking of me at all. You don't even talk to me anymore. You're scared, I understand that, but you could at least let me in. You're frightened that you might not be around to see a baby if we have one. But think about me for once. Think about what I'll be left with..."

"If you're that bloody frustrated, why don't you just go out and get laid? Don't give me this baby crap."

"For Christ's sake. You could be sterile in two months' time..."

"Well, fuck you." He didn't wait to hear anymore. He stormed out of the room and went upstairs to his study, where I heard him banging around in the filing cabinets for a while, and then there was silence. He stayed up there for the next couple of hours and I presumed he had gone to bed.

I finished washing up and thought about going to him, apologising for what I had said, but I was frightened to — he seemed to be angry rather than hurt. And besides, I thought I had a point and that he should think about what I had said.

I went out into the garden for a few hours and raked up the leaves which had formed a carpet of spun gold across the lawn. All around us nature is despairing, and yet I like this time of year, when there is a mellowness, as if in every ending there is the suggestion of a new beginning.

It began to get cold around four-thirty so I went indoors and sat at my desk in the living room overlooking the graveyard of St. Mark's. I watched as the colours slowly drained from the landscape and the sky draped itself in indigo, pleated with subtle shading. The evening deepened and deepened and the trees outside faded to smudges. Eventually the street lamps came on in distant streets like frozen stars and one by one the lights were switched on in the houses on the opposite side of the graveyard, blushing oblongs which sent out a glow to me. Below me, the graveyard became an inky pool, but through the open window I could smell the heady perfume of the cedars, imagine the gravestones nestling like weathered teeth among their roots.

Friends have often commented that this must be a depressing view, have voiced fears of ghosts and uncanny happenings round here, but I find a strange comfort in being surrounded by the spirits of the dead, enfolding us like luminous envelopes. I feel it in our home too, which is so old that the oak beams have scars in them, where, over the years, people have felt the need to inscribe their names and the dates when they lived here, as if to leave some mark of themselves behind, to make themselves more substantial.

Michael had obviously been asleep. I heard him coughing and then the shuffle of his bare feet across the boards and the click of the bathroom light. I held my breath waiting to see whether he would call out to me or whether he would go back to bed, and in those minutes time was suspended, stretched out like a taut wire which might snap.

Then I heard the floorboards creaking on the stairs as he came down. For a moment I sat staring straight ahead, rigid as a block of wood. I wasn't going to turn round and be drawn into a continuation of the argument. Having said my piece I wanted to leave it at that. But I could feel his eyes burning on my back. We were at stalemate.

Then he did something that surprised me. Michael is never the first to make up after an argument, but last night he came up behind me and put his arms around my neck, kneading my shoulders with his fingers. He has good hands, as fine as the earth, with deep grooves on the palms like maps. I clasped his fingers in my own and squeezed them slightly, then turned round to face him. He smiled a thin smile like the first crack of light round a blind drawn down.

"Sorry. You're right. I haven't been thinking about you at all."

"No, it's my fault. I shouldn't have said what I did. It was stupid, cruel."

"It's just that it's all gone wrong somehow..."

"Don't. We have to share this. If it's happening to you, it's happening to me. We're a team, aren't we?"

"Of course we are. It's just that there's been a change in the team rules... I love you, Helen. Whatever happens, don't forget that."

We held each other for a moment and stood revolving round and round in a tight little circle on the spot. "Why don't you come back to bed with me for a cuddle?"

We lay on the bed in the darkness for a while, forming a double O with our arms, sharing our skin as if like that we could somehow draw the essence from each other. A souvenir to bottle up and keep.

Let me love you, he seemed to say silently. Let me trace your shadows with my fingers and inhale your skin's perfume of fresh rain. He drew me gently into him and I felt the warmth radiating from him like the lost rays of the sun. The middle of my body buckled softly.

We fell apart to rest, our heads still together, the sides of our faces touching. His skin felt rough and warm like golden sand; mine like the coating of a pearl. Then suddenly he said into the darkness: "Don't you think there's something like death in making love?"

And I thought perhaps he meant that to divide, to give oneself, is to die in part, the spilling of one's own vital essence.

I was suddenly aware of existing in my own body in our shared space.— the quickened drumming of my heart, the gentle roar of a shell in my ears — and yet of standing alone on a distant shore. A tear ran down my cheek.

He gently ran his forefinger across my face, tracing the dips of my eyes, the straightness of my nose, coming to rest on my full lips where it pressed on them as if to read my thoughts, my hopes, by Braille, and in doing so, silence them.

We lay on the bed side by side for a while, not touching, creating a small force-field between us in the darkness until suddenly we could no longer bear even this hair's breadth of distance between us and were drawn to one another again, like magnets.

Stephanie Newell

Circles and Stops

Stephanie Newell was born in Kent in 1968. She started to write short stories while at Anglia Polytechnic-University, and is currently working on a novel.

Kate rolled up her sleeve and stretched her arm to the back of the 'Home Baking' shelf. She experienced a shudder of nervous excitement at the thought of disturbing a snake or scorpion or black widow spider that was waking and crouching, sliding, crawling, poised to sting her scrabbling fingers. It was in the morning paper: Sunny Weather Keeps Scorpions Alive in Kent. A woman had picked a bunch of bananas from its box, and a black scorpion had scuttled onto the back of her hand.

Kate quickly pulled out a bag of Be-Ro flour from the back row, shook it to make sure it did not trickle a trail of white powder across the floor from any loose seams or torn corners, placed it in the trolley, wrote its price on her pad, and calculated the sub-total so far.

"Flour. Milk, eggs, bread, oil," she muttered, gazing over at the stacked tins of fruit.

Her son skidded around the corner, past the blur of reds, yellows, oranges and whites in the Co-Op's cheese counter, past queuing people's legs, their fidgeting children and their tapping feet, down the aisle towards Kate. He clutched a packet of chocolate biscuits to his chest and made a staccato rat tat machine gun noise from the back of his throat, although it might have been the noise of a baa-ing sheep or goat. A Horrible Hobgoblin with a sharp knife, a long red nose and a green suede jerkin leapt out of the previous night's storybook pages. It hobbled towards him, through the fire from the Frightened Dragon's nostrils, preparing to attack Jack Tucker, who fled towards the pizza bases for refuge.

Just before reaching his mother Jack halted, silenced. An angular, white-faced, white-haired woman with brown, horn-rimmed glasses was jumping from one foot to the other in front of him, elbowing the air, quietly articulating no-things at no one in the aisle. Loose tomatoes and apples rolled around in her basket, and brightly coloured sweets dropped through its mesh to the floor.

"Please go away, nasty little man. Shoo!" She launched her body away from the Pick'n'Mix sweets shelf, flapping her hands and swaying in a half-dance. Each part of her body seemed autonomous from the whole; each part signed the air in a constant movement of its own.

Jack looked around for an explanation: the other shoppers smirked secretly at their toes or studied the shelves or their trolleys. Transfixed, he clasped his hands together around the packet of biscuits and, blinking heavily, focused a long, curious stare upon the woman.

(Cain was creeping up on her, now leering from the crevice under the grocery shelves where He could leap up her skirt and tear down her tights; now hurtling His jaws at her neck from the unseen behind, from where He would squeeze His hairy hand around her mouth and force-pump His Thing in her. Now scuttling along the shelf tops above her, poised to leap gnawing and scratching into her cranium like a rodent with sharp yellow teeth.)

She gave a brief shriek, cranking her head round so that muscles and veins stuck out in her neck. Her eyes strained to capture the malign figure, which slipped away wriggling its fingers towards her petticoat from the shadows behind. Her green tweed skirt swayed with her body's syncopated circles, and a grey handkerchief fell to the floor from her pocket.

(Because Cain — and this occurred increasingly in shops, supermarkets and public places since Mother passed away — because Cain — and this was the reason she so rarely felt sufficiently free to shop for herself — Cain was still refusing to accept, after ten years of struggle, that she was not going to let Him, Not Now Nor Ever, have His evil-minded way. In revenge, He was attempting to publicly humiliate her by tracking her, sniffing at her scent as if she were a wild beast on heat.)

Jack moved towards the handkerchief. He felt possessed by the need to pick it and the sweets up for her. He was fascinated by the unique patterns that the strange woman's limbs carved into the Co-Op's space. Her hips gyrated slightly and her toes shuffled, chasing her head's spinning movements. Her mouth mumbled strange words. She suddenly flew round on him, glaring.

"Get away from There this instant," she hissed, covering her groin with the basket.

(Last night Cain leapt out at There from beneath the bed. She shrieked, and tried to lock herself in the bathroom. Then He started rushing with a Whoosh! up and out of the lavatory bowl just as she was lowering There into position on the seat. She fainted when He tried to cram His head

Circles and Stops

inside, but when she came to, she quickly leapt from the lavatory seat and pulled the flush. Tonight and for always, she would use only her mother's commode, then empty it down the drain in the back garden. Another of His recent tricks, now the house was empty, was to hurtle out from behind open doors, screaming silent "Boo!" noises which shattered her fragile nervous system.)

"I'll call the Police," she warned.

(Over time, Cain had grown grotesque. He never came when Father was alive. Each of her bereavements and her spiralling sense of loss seemed to have fed His virility and strength of purpose. Now He was shouting sexually explicit insults that everybody in the Co-Op would be able to hear if she did not attempt to halt Him, swiftly.)

"Now, you'll leave me this instant, or I shall be perfectly within my rights to call the Police, and you heard what they threatened to do the last time. 'Careful, or we'll lock you up,' they shouted. 'You are a persistent trespasser.'" She rubbed a hand between her legs as she spoke.

"Now, be gone with you! If my father had found out..." She made a revolted, shuddering noise and wagged a finger in Jack's direction, tut-tutting through the air. Jack snapped out of his reverie and ran to Kate for security.

In embarrassment, the Co-Op staff carved wide arcs through the space around the woman. Round and round she turned in tight circles, her eyes rolling to capture what she thought was behind her.

(Each night when she put her hair into curlers, spray-fixing the loose strands, His lecherous red eye would gleam through the keyhole, and He would draw a hiss of breath in through teeth wet with spittle for her. Since Mother's passing, Cain had even run rampant through Tend-Pa's oak wardrobe. Perhaps Cain had killed Tend-Pa? This would explain a lot of things. It was certain that Tend-Pa was dead. When she gently called his name, the amber stone dangled limply from its raffia thread on the clothes rail. A medium for nothing, swaying gently in the breeze of the opening door. Not like before, when her dead father's spirit was summoned into Tend-Pa by Mother's incantations.)

Jack clasped Kate's hand and stared past her wrist-watch.

(Together, she and her mother called up Father's authority: "Portend, Father," they would command, and off the amber stone tick-tocked, side to side signifying Yes! and forwards and backwards from the rail for No! They consulted him about every household matter. Father's spirit communicated, dictated and responded through Tend-Pa, endowing order and sanity upon their daily routines: assenting, refusing, he sustained their lives. With Mother's death, however, she had become preoccupied with grief and with Cain's increased assaults. She was also trying to cope with the Fifth Years at school. She neglected the routines, the order, the household, the paternal authority, and Tend-Pa, the amber spirit, had vanished. Now Father refused to respond. She would drop to her knees before the amber, pleading that it tell her what to do about Cain. But her father's spirit had gone with Mother, and left her alone to run or be ravaged.)

"MummyMummyMummy! What's wrong with that funny lady?" Jack screeched, tugging Kate's handbag.

"Shut up," she told him.

"Why's that funny lady dancing like that?" Jack was loud and insistent. Other shoppers sent awkward looks over, and seemed to drift into earshot for Kate's response.

"Shut up and don't stare: it's rude," she snapped.

Made curious by her child's curiosity, Kate looked up, saw the woman and dizzied. A large fist clenched inside her stomach. Bang, bang. Bang, bang, bang. The tightening fist pounded on the years and the doors that had sealed off her personal history. The hand formed into a single finger, pointing at the memory door which had closed on that woman five years before. Miss Stone. Stepping back into view.

Kate's experience with the music teacher had refused to be neutralised over time: it had lodged inside her, clasped with anger, resisting transformation into a comic narrative where the characters and events occupied a safe, sealed-off time-world with a beginning, a middle and an end. While she relived the consequences almost daily in her mind, Kate had never succeeded in erecting an explanatory frame around Miss Stone's garbled story. Yet somehow the teacher's secret male tormentors had caused Kate's expulsion from school, just four months before her 'O' level exams. And Kate, standing over her supermarket trolley, looking with hindsight upon the young Self of Then, seated at the organ in Forestham Church, still did not understand the tale or the events as they occurred. She felt the old anger and sense of injustice surging through her stomach, though, and wanted to pelt the music teacher with the can of baked beans her fingers had wound around, white-knuckled.

Perhaps, she thought, the story was becoming clearer today in the Co-Op, now that it had run out of control. For Miss Stone performed openly to the shoppers, miming her life-text up and down the aisles, living her punishment. And it looked as if Cain had come into the open.

(And with Mother gone, Tend-Pa had vanished and everything was falling apart. The quiet wisdom of Father's spirit, manifested through the amber sphere, all this had gone. Tend-Pa dangled limply in the wardrobe's dullness.)

They had been sitting side-by-side on the great organ stool in Forestham

Circles and Stops

Church when Miss Stone started speaking in a high-pitched, warbling voice. She explained that Cain dripped and grasped at her from Forestham's alleyways, from in front, from all-ways and shadow-ways, forcing His intolerable desires on her.

"He's lurking outside the church itself!" she had half-shrieked at Kate's face, wiping a tear-streaked cheek with her handkerchief.

"At this very moment Cain is plotting to drive me insane. He is lurking out there, amongst the nettles in the graveyard, dancing and yelping with big-eyed glee, jubilant at my mother's illness. If she passes away, He will be free to tease, poke and petrify me. He is rubbing His fantasies up against the headstones, staring at me, staring from everywhere. He was never able to torment me like this when Father was fully alive. In those days, He had to content Himself with being a mere peeper. He stayed outside the room to I-Spy my body through keyholes and to push Himself over the door handles."

But Kate had heard only strange combinations of words, strung together at random and expressed by a voice that was straining and cracking from years filled with fear. Running from a man who was constantly before her, within her, His sweaty hands reaching out inside of her. Kate sat still at the organ, her hands and feet poised to pump "Once in Royal David's City" through the vast pipes which stretched to the roof. Miss Stone lifted her bluish-veined hands to wipe more wet drops from her fearful eyes. Then she rested her head on Kate's shoulder to whimper for her dying mother, her dead father, for Tend-Pa and Cain.

"He wouldn't dare come in, not here, you see," Miss Stone had continued, "but He's out there, now. You'll see the tip of His black nose and one of His bulging red eyes peeping around the edge of a gravestone when you leave."

All the girl could think to say, having looked at Miss Stone's greyish flesh, worn-out tweed skirt and thick grey tights, was, "But, Miss, your mother must be very, very old."

"She's only 75!" the teacher whined, staring at the organ keys and lifting the grey handkerchief to her nose.

Then Miss Stone seemed to recover herself. "Oh goodness me, 'Once in Royal David's City.' Play! Play the organ! You shan't tell a soul about this. Of course not, particularly your mother and those girls at school?"

And Kate had shivered, staring at the stops, the pedals, the pipes and the sheets of handwritten music clipped into place in front of her.

Miss Stone's indiscretion in Forestham Church had caused her to fear the young Kate with almost the same intensity that she felt towards Cain. Her passion initiated a new pattern whereby the hunted one turned briefly, in the early spring term of Kate's final year, into the hunter.

185

She walked to the front school gate. She stood, a stern white sentry, and waited there until the girl chattered up the path with her friends. She said, "Your music, Kate. Open it at home." A deadly tone. A brown package thrust from flaking blue-veined hands into nail-bitten young hands. Eyes beading out behind horn-rims, lids snapping up and down. A worried stare.

"Whooo-eee! A gift from your girlfriend!" The chorus went up as they passed through the gate. And Kate, penetrated, blushed a deep, deep red and started to feel the first surges of hate and dread. Underneath the paper, two boxes of chocolate Matchmakers and a short note etched on a small card: Please try to forget what I told you, Kate. Silence is Golden. My mother died shortly after we spoke. Yours, Mabel Stone.

After that, Miss Stone lingered, during playground duty, within sight and earshot of Kate's group, watching and tracking the girl. She stared obsessively, trying to overhear everything they said, straining for the mention of her own name. She exposed herself to their titters, their gossip, giggles and stares.

"She fancies you, Kate."

"Why's she always eyeing you up, eh?"

"Coo-ee! Mabel Dyke! Katie's over here."

Kate nervously watched back. In Miss Stone's music class Kate's classroom reaction was an instinctive response to the taunts of her friends.

"Lyn, 'ere, I'm a Gonnor!" Kate shouted.

"You're a Wott-Or?"

"Look 'ere, I'm a Gonorr-hoea!"

"Hey, Miss Stone, there's a Gonnor over 'ere!"

"Oh Yeah, Cain and Mabel, I'm a real Gonnor 'ere!" sang Kate, pummelling the desk.

"Ain't that King Lear's daughter, then, Gonorrhoea?" Lyn asked, waving her 'O' level text in the air.

Miss Stone stood rigid and pale-faced, her eyes flashing fury behind their horn-rimmed frames.

"Kate Tucker, yer old Fucker!" Lyn shouted.

Miss Stone stood so still, white and tight-lipped, that her skin had become almost translucent. "Out," she said.

"Oops! I'm a Gonnor!" As she said it, Kate's heart pounded so hard that her hands shook.

The taut line of tolerance had snapped. Kate scraped her chair along the floor, stamped her feet, dropped a pile of music books on the floor, and stalked towards the door. Miss Stone cried as she handed over the letter for Kate to carry to the Head. Kate vaguely heard her panted words, "I heard you telling them. You promised. That's it."

Kate flicked fingers through her fringe, frowned and rushed off, blowing clouds of hot anger into the icy February air. Again and again, she had trudged up this gravel path, past the graveyard with its flint boundary walls, its Headless Man and its five-foot stinging nettles, past the art block, the science block, the cookery rooms, away from Miss Stone's mobile music room. Miss Richardson sometimes waved a hand in support, lifting her paint-loaded brush at the window. This afternoon, she stared at the Fifth Year for a long time after she had disappeared through the door to the main school.

The school building was cold, wrapped in silence. The only noises were teachers' muffled voices, droning lessons through the numbered doors, and the creak of Mr Whitehead's chair when he turned to see Kate. He let her stand for 15 minutes, biting her nails with worry outside his office door, before he hissed "Come in!"

This was it. Her mother would be telephoned to collect her from school.

Mr Whitehead had tried to intercede in January, taking pains to explain to the student a number of confidential details concerning Miss Stone. He had extended a bony finger with a manicured nail in her direction, and adopted the tone of the lay preacher he was to become: "It is imperative that what I shall impart remains within these four walls."

Like an air hostess indicating escape routes, the bony forefingers from his left and right hands had formed parallel lines pointing forwards, the fingers then parting to point sideways at the walls before swooping in a loop to indicate the window behind his ears, from which, when he swivelled his seat, he could gaze at the sports on the playing field behind the school.

"Let it not pass beyond these walls, that Miss Stone's dear mother, whom she cared for single-handedly for many years, sadly passed away during the Christmas holidays."

Kate had been agitated. She knew this already.

"Now, Miss Stone has also been suffering from Some Other Problems."

He had been speaking so softly by the end of this sentence that Kate could scarcely hear him, despite leaning forwards into the stream of his breath, craning over from her high-backed, hard-seated chair. Mr Whitehead's verbiage and his emphasis on 'Other Problems' had left a void in Kate's stomach. Spoken as if sufficient, when everything still had to be explained. But he had allowed no openings for questions. Kate urgently needed to ask him if he knew about Cain—or was she the only one?—and she had needed Mr Whitehead to convey to Miss Stone the message that not a single person knew about Tend-Pa, or Cain. Mr Whitehead, however, had only nodded at Kate, flicked his strands of hair back into place, and warned her that her next transgression would result in her expulsion from school. He had swivelled his spindly legs and chair back towards the playing fields. And, by the end of February, she was gone.

Stephanie Newell

Pinned down by confusion and anger, Kate placed the tin of baked beans in her trolley. Jack tugged at her sleeve, chanting, "Why's she dancing?"

She tried to force the images back behind their memory door, but they thrust their limbs in the gaps.

Miss Stone spun around in circles in the aisle ahead: hectic, tired and panting beside the tinned fruit. Her curly hair, blanched white, stuck out in wiry tufts. Its colour matched the pale of her skin, which drooped from her face in the shape of her miseries and fears.

The Co-Op manageress was approaching with two men. They were asking that the aisle be cleared of all customers.

"Now you're for it," Miss Stone told Cain.

A smile spread across Kate's face and she started to laugh as her son tugged at her hand, pulling her back to the present.

"Please tell me," Jack whimpered, hanging his full weight off his mother's arm, so that when Kate pulled herself away from Miss Stone, her son's shoes scraped a shrill noise along the tiled floor.

"If I'm good, can we have these biscuits, then? And can I ride in the trolley?" He started a throaty wailing noise as they moved away.

Jeremy Page

Mise-En-Abyme

Jeremy Page was born in Cambridge in 1969. His writing has received awards from the BBC, *The Guardian*, and the London Short Story Competition.

You alone?
 "What?"
 "Is someone there?"
 "No."
 "In the background."
 "...no. Maybe down in the street. Yeah — the street."
 "What's going on?"
 "Don't know. Hang on."
 She would hear the distance ricochet. The sound of the phone being put down at the other end. Then silence. She would hear the latch being released, and then the vibration as the tightly sealed window swung away from the frame. Long high windows she remembered. Curtains like mist, blowing in waves. He would probably open the curved window at the side of the bay. The one he always opens. He always sits there looking down upon the street. She would imagine him returning to the phone, having to squeeze past the table.
 She has a flash of the two of them sitting there, having breakfast together. With the morning sunlight flooding into the room. Tall glasses filled with grapefruit juice, beads of water clinging down the outside of the jug, threads of the fruit's flesh spiralling through the drink. And he, preferring not to speak, casually tracing the pattern of the tablecloth with his finger, looking sad because he believes in drama and he believes in making moments special, being silent because that's how he thinks breakfast should be.
 "Iona?"
 And maybe the sun didn't reach the window till noon.
 "Still here."

"That better?"
"Not sure."
"Wait — I'll pull the phone to the window."
Again, she would listen to the distance. Clunking, banging. His voice would become briefly strained, and louder, as the mouth-piece hooked under his chin:
"Oops — you still there..? It's the tail end of an argument. She's in trouble; I think he might hit her. He's waving a chain about."
"A chain?"
"Yes. Some sort of a...it's a bike chain I think. Or a very big necklace."
"Doing what with it?"
"It's a necklace, definitely. Just waving it about. Phew — made it, I'm at the window now. Can you hear?"
"...no...I...Is it all over?"
"There's no one there."
"What?"
"I was joking."
"Joking?"
"Yeah."
"But I heard something. Thought I heard a voice. A woman's voice."
"Really."
"In the street."
"The street."
"Calling up at you."
"Well there's no one there."
"Who is it?"
"Iona! There's no one there. The street's empty. It's very early. Listen."
He would go silent. She would listen to the gentle fuzz, the dust of static along the line. And there was a lot of distance which stretched between them now. She would vaguely think about rows of telegraph poles. In the twilight. Cables strung over field after field. Wind whistling through the wires. But her lasting impressions would be of staring into a cave. Staring into its darkness. Staring. Until she feels that there is something — maybe just the dark — but something there, in front of her. And it is staring back at her. She would feel her fear rising, would let it rise, would continue to stare, watching the darkness, wanting to know what lay beyond. Then, a voice would creep faintly onto the wire, lifting itself through the waves of interference, like a coarse grained photograph — the figure of a woman looming out of the shadows.
She would listen, pressing the cold plastic of the receiver firmly against her ear. She would listen to the voice...
"Iona? ...What's the matter?"

Mise-en-Abyme

"Nothing Jack. Your voice shocked me that's all."
"Sorry. Still think you can hear someone?"
"Yes."
"You're not making much sense."
"No."
"It's probably only...Hey I know — got it! It's a cat. Kitten. Next door found it last week. It was — they found it on the river bank — all wet and muddy. They think it was probably part of a — a litter — you know — they bag them up and throw them in the river."
"That's horrible."
"Yeah. Weighted down. They think it got out. Got out in time. Called it Lucky. Crap name isn't it? Oh...Iona — I'm sorry...I wasn't thinking..."
"What?"
"...you know...about the..."
"...the river?"
"Yes."
"It's OK. It's OK Jack. Happened a long time ago. It's alright...now."
"Right."
"You haven't said."
"Said what?"
"The noise. What is it."
"Oh...Oh yes. Well it's odd. I was watching it yesterday. Here in the window. I can see — you know I can see into their bedroom..."
"Their what?"
"...bedroom. Next door. Just the corner of it. Well there's a mirror there, in the corner. Dress mirror. And that cat — *Lucky* — it was, you know, arching its back — making that awful noise — like cats do. All day."
"At its reflection."
"Yeah. And pouncing as well — at the mirror. Jumping up and — with its claws out. Irritating really...Iona?"
"Yeah — sorry...I was just trying to listen. Has it gone?"
"No. It's just shut up."
"Given up?"
"Doubt it."
"You should say something to them."
"Funny thing was — I was watching — when it pounced and hit the glass it would sort of — bounce off, slide off. And it would just — immediately — just forget everything. Lie on the carpet and lick its paws. Walk off all indifferent."
"...I hate cats..."
"...ten minutes later it was back there. Screaming. Hackles up."
"And it hasn't learnt yet."

193

"Unfortunately."
"Maybe it won't."
"Pathetic thing. Pathetic."
"It's a nice view there isn't it."
"Yeah. See a lot of life going by."
"You once said it was more like a river than a street."
"Did I? Suppose it is. No ducks though. Oh — that's a shame — there was someone here yesterday doing pavement art with some chalks. Took them ages. Underneath here. Everybody's walked over it, and rain last night. It's all smudged."
"Some things aren't made to last."
"...no..."
"Is it sunny there? In the flat?"
"Sunny...? Bit overcast really. Bit grey."
"It's still dark here."
"Really? So you're in bed?"
"Yeah. It's snowing outside."
"Are you alone?"
"I'm isolated."
"There's no one there?"
"You know how it is. That's the last thing I'd want. Is that the cat again?"
"Yeah. And you're not lonely?"
"I've never been so busy."
"It's crawling at the mirror — no — it's stopped. Looks terrified. Can you hear?"
"Think so. The line's not too good."
"This phone's bad."
"And the distance."
"What was that?"
"Um — don't know — probably just snow sliding off the roof. You'd think it would be silent here. I thought it would be. Everything white, covered up. It's minus twelve you know, the air — think even the trees are frozen. But the sound — and all this silence — sometimes I think it's the loudest noise I've ever heard."
"When are you coming back?"
"Please don't ask. I don't want you to ask."
"But you're happy?"
"I'm happy."
"...though God knows what you do all day."
"Well...I walk."
"In the forest?"
"Or on the lake."

Mise-en-Abyme

"What?"
"It's frozen. The ice is about a metre thick. Sometimes I drive on it."
"You drive!"
"Short cut to town."
"Wow."
"Short cut to town but I never go. It's easier looking across the lake at the lights in the evening. It's prettier that way. You can believe anything you want about that place when you look at the lights. But not when you're there. Suppose some of them might even look at my light."
"Can I have your number? ...Iona?"
"Jack. It's better this way."
"OK. Sorry. You need space."
"Lots of it."
"You will call?"
"I'll call."
"Hello — there it goes..."
"...what?"
"Pounced at the mirror."
"So now it licks its paws and forgets the whole thing."
"By the way...about the letter..."
"...we'll talk about it another time. I'd better go."
"Right."
"Jack? Please don't. Now's not the time. I'm still recovering."
"Sorry. I...it's just we never seem to talk. That's all."
"We talk."
"Do we? Sometimes I forget — so much — forget the sound of your voice. And it's only — your voice — it's the only thing I seem to have of you, now. When we speak you — youre voice seems so distant. I want it to be special but, then we talk and it's just ordinary. Oh forget it! I've never made a good speech."
"I have to go."
"Yes. Sorry. It's difficult that's all."
"I know."
"Ring me soon."
"I will. Look remember...when we talk — it's not just words. There's always more. Always."
"Yeah. Yeah you're right."
"I'll speak to you soon."
"OK."
"...and Jack — wait. Just a minute — I have to know — what were you looking at?"
"What?"

"The chalk drawing in the street. What's it of?"
"Funny question. It's a — it's a fish. It's a snake."
"Oh."
"I think."
"Yeah. Oh well — speak to you soon."
"OK. Bye."
"Bye."

She would wait until she heard the click of his phone being put down. Because when she heard that click she would see his action, not just a voice, or words, but a hand placing a receiver on to a phone, a man in a flat, a man she had once known very well, getting up and pulling the phone back to where it always was. The phone was pulled all round that flat but it would never be left where the call was made. Order restored.

Only by listening to the dead tone could she feel his touch. Feel that she was still connected to that other place, that flat so far away. But a connection which was gentle, not fully formed, like a whisper. As long as she held the phone against her ear, she would remain, in contact, there in his flat; silent, and able to watch him move about the room, perhaps taking a drink, perhaps going once more to the window to glance down the street. Movements a man makes when he is readjusting back to his life, his own situation, his own set of rules, readjusting, returning, but still in his mind connected to a conversation which he has just had. A conversation he didn't really want to leave. She would feel close to him, intimate, while she listened to the dead tone. With him, but on her own terms; to watch him, not to touch him, not to be seen by him. Her presence in his flat was nothing but vapourous — the space where her body should be, if anything, it was just a shape of hollow air, of air without substance. She imagined it to be silent and breathless. And from within this space she can slowly turn, watching him as he moves about the room. His face, the furniture and the shapes of the room, flickering like pale reflections on the periphery of her world. Her silent, empty world.

A world of ice. Where ice cracks. The lake bleeds through, already congealing. And the water is black. Sluggish. Beyond the pale there is just a greater darkness. A further deception.

She watches as he begins to fade from her mind, resolutely, both of their lives pulling apart, stretching, regaining the stability which would have been there before she called.

The disintegration becomes cloudy. Different objects begin to assemble around her, and as she watches the interior of Jack's flat becoming overgrown with the shapes and angles of her own room, like crystals growing out from the walls and floor, furniture, where Jack has spaces, darkness, where Jack has light, colours spreading like ink-blots, she suddenly hears a

Mise-en Abyme

voice. That voice, far away, shards of ice, rising up from a far off street — fleeing the confines of the street in the echo of a phone line. A voice which she knows, a voice she recognises. The voice has sought her out, it has penetrated her, there in the dark. And the voice abruptly halts the growth of her room around her. Half in the life and shapes of Jack's flat, half in her own. And all of it seems alien.

The dead tone in the ear-piece would come to a brusque end. Replaced by a nothingness, just a fuzz, a sound with no shape or dimension to it. Somewhere, an exchange would have had enough, a switch would click, a connection would be severed. And it would give her an impetus, a chance for her to feel that she must do something to govern her thoughts, to divide her worlds. She would put the receiver down.

In the bathroom next door, he had finished his shower. She heard the indeterminate sound of a towel rack, taps being turned, the brief burst of a hair dryer. And silences. Gazing into mirror silences. Then there were other sounds; sounds coming into the room from outside. An electric tram, slowing down to go over the junction where the old paving began. A barge laboriously churning up the river. Ice cracking under an iron bow. She suspected that he wouldn't come back into the room. He was the kind of man that once he's left the bed doesn't want to see it again, and particularly not the woman still in it. He would go downstairs and have some salami on rye bread, and coffee. And he would phone her up from work later on. He would come back in the evening with a bunch of flowers — and if she had taken her case and left, then the flowers would go into a vase on the table.

She turned on to her side, away from the emptiness of the mattress next to her. She looked at the smooth glow falling from the bedside light. A pool of warmth amongst ice and shadows. And the glow poured down the edges of a simple silver frame. She had seen the photograph the night before but deliberately ignored it. A young man and a woman on the Richelieu Steps at Odessa. The man's arms were reaching round the woman's waist, and he was pulling her off balance as the picture was taken. The girl's hair was quite long and was swinging slightly away from her head as she fell towards him. She looked very young, the surprise on her face opening her eyes wide. And he was smiling too, grinning full of teeth with one large hand splayed across the flat of her belly, grinning because he knew that after the picture had been taken she would turn to him and pretend to be angry. But she wouldn't really be angry; she would be happy. She would say his name and tell him that he was a child. And that was why he was smiling. But he hadn't smiled like that last night.

Again, the shadowy angles of the room seemed imperfect to her. She was unsettled, there was a disruption, somewhere, without form, near her — and it was affecting her. But it wasn't the photograph of the girl being pulled off balance by the young man in military uniform. It wasn't the sight of her suitcase, way across the room in the corner with its lid open, the dress she had bought in Hamburg, the one she had worn yesterday, the dress she had thrown towards the suitcase in the middle of the night. An empty dress. She had no particular feelings for these things. But none the less she felt cautious, as if any minute she would begin to feel sadness, regret, pity. Things she couldn't afford to carry around.

Through the walls she listened to the iron grille of the elevator rattling shut. A distant bell, then a faint whirr beginning to sink through the storeys of the building. The sound pulled away from her into a darkness she could not see. Sounds of taut cables, the slow turn of cog-wheels smeared with thick grease, a counterweight rising, swiftly, through the depths of the shaft. And the sounds fell away from her, becoming more distant, until she was sure that it had, at last, become silent. Not noticing the point when the noise had ended, in her mind she was still listening, making up the sounds, listening to the elevators which leave us behind, which thread away from us into the dark to scenes we cannot hear. Scenes which we imagine and watch, and listen to over and over. Over again.

The long empty corridor. So many doors on to so many worlds, all closed, all being listened to, all returning to a single, darkened passageway. Once more the faint bell of the elevator rings. Now quick footsteps on the polished tiles. A key jangling into lock turning. Metal bolts springing back a door swinging open so close so close. Slams. And the door seems to slam again, repeatedly, fading each time, throughout the building. Then the electric hum of the light in the corridor, joining the pitch of another light, fainter, and another, further away, further away.

She knows she will probably turn and reach across the cold mattress, she will pick up the phone and dial, thinking of the alleyway stretching down from Jack's flat, the long curving slope towards the old stone bridge, the river, the meadows.

"Hi."

"Sadie."

"Of all the people! Thought perhaps you might've slipped away for good."

"You're out of breath."

"Yeah! I was out. Had to dash in when I heard the phone. You back?"

"No."

"No? So...wow! All this time; what have you been up to? My God — she's met a man!"

"Is that what it means?"

"Probably. Knowing you."

"...maybe you don't."

"So I'm wrong? Huh?"

"I've left Finland."
"Really?"
"Week or two ago."
"Now?"
"Now? I'm still moving. How are things with you?"
"Fine. Saw Jack the other day."
"I've just been talking to him."
"Free phone?"
"You could say..."
"...how is he?"
"Jack? OK. A bit odd. Bit strained, you know."
"I bet! I saw him — didn't talk to him. At the station. Mind — I always found him a bit hard to get on with. After that business. Did you know he's grown his hair long?"
"Hair? No. I...I didn't know."
"Looks good. Had mine cut. It's awful."
"Do you see him often?"
"Nah."
"Oh. Look...if you do...he — he doesn't know..."
"...what?"
"...I've moved..."
"...don't be silly. Won't say a thing darling! We've always had our little secrets haven't we. Best that way."
"Thanks."
"You be mysterious, be mysterious — what's it to me? I never see him anyway. So — you haven't said — how are you? You drab wench. How are things?"
"Am I being cryptic?"
"A bit. Yeah you bitch — quite a lot!"
"Sorry!"
"No need to laugh about it!"
"...you *make* me laugh Sadie! You've always made me laugh. That's why we're friends isn't it? Why I've called. That's — actually that's not why I called. Look, it may seem a strange thing to ask but can you see out of the window?"
"Window?"
"Sound so worried! Yeah the window."
"Oh I get it! You're the psycho in the phone box by the bridge. Is that it?"
"Maybe."
"...*watch me change every night*...Yeah. Why?"
"Nothing really. I was...it's just, on the phone, with Jack, there was a — there was this woman walking by — you know — under his window

in the street..."

"Feeling a bit weird are we?"

"...can you see her?"

"What'd I look for?"

"Her voice. It sounds like a cat. Screaming."

"Cat?"

"See her?"

"Er...don't...what d'you mean sounds like a cat?"

"I don't know. Jack said."

"There's no one there."

"Oh. Oh well — it was just a guess. You can see all way up the hill?"

"Scale Street. So Jack took a fancy to this woman or what?"

"No! No. She was — I could hear over the phone — she was shouting."

"...this is a very strange call Iona."

"I'm sorry."

"Should think so. Christ it's early! I mean, where are you going next? Or don't you...I hear from you for the first time in months and we're...I don't know; what's got into you?"

"You angry?"

"God no! Just care that's all. Worried. Don't even know why you left really. Bad memories? Is that it? Bad memories?"

"It was all too much."

"But...maybe I don't know — is it going to...where are you going to find any answers? You should come back. It's here you know, you might not even realise it. Tell me to shut up...or...Iona?..."

"I'm in St. Petersburg."

"Oh."

"Sorry. I...I just wanted to tell you where I am. I think I feel a little better now."

"St. Petersburg?"

"...yeah. It...but it means nothing. It means nothing to me."

"With a man?"

"No."

"Not that I'm prying."

"That's OK. I'm not doing anything. Looking at train timetables I suppose. Yeah — that's what you could say I'm doing."

"...and you've no idea when..."

"...that's her! I can hear her!"

"What?"

"Outside. You can see her. You must see her. The woman."

"...no — I don't think..."

"What's she doing? Sadie? *Sadie?*"

"...I — there's no-one outside. There's no-one there."
"Can you hear her? I can't quite make out the words."
"What *on Earth* are you talking about? I don't understand. You making all this up?"
"...look on the bridge."
"It's empty."
"You can't hear her?"
"No!"
"So that means I'm making it all up. That I'm lying..."
"I didn't say that."
"Yes you did."
"I meant — well you're mistaken aren't you. That's all. Mistaken. There's no one out there. I'd tell you if — why the hell would I lie anyway?"
"...but I'm sure..."
"For God's sake! ...Iona?"
"I suppose you're right. Sorry."
"Forget it. Let's forget it all."
"OK...Maybe a crossed line or..."
"Probably."
"I'm being stupid. Oh I'm sorry. It's funny, I can hear the church bell. That's something I *can* hear."
"Can you? Yeah. I think there's a...is that a bell I can hear there — with you, in the background?"
"Yes. Yes I think so. There are lots of bells here."
"That's odd isn't it? Isn't that odd?"
"It only means there's a new hour."
"Eight."
"Six."
"Six! God can't you sleep. Not sleeping Iona? Can't remember the last time I got up so early. Probably when the..."
"No!"
"...Iona..."
"It's me! My name. The woman's shouting my name — over and over. It all makes sense. You've been lying. Lying all along haven't you."
"...no...no Iona. Stop. You must stop this..."
"Tell me. Tell me now."
"Don't do this. Don't do this to yourself. Oh — God not again. I thought...no...What's happening to you? You mustn't!...*Not again!*...What's going on!"
"You're seeing Jack aren't you."
"No! No."
"Tell me. Now."

"No! Oh no Iona."
"He told me."
"Jack."
"Jack told me."
"No! He's lying. Lying! Oh Iona no. You mustn't start. Please! Not now. He could never say that."
"He didn't have to."
"...oh please — you must control yourself. Do it now! Do it for me — it's so important. So important. Lies! Not again Iona. Has nothing changed? Please oh God what can I say..."
"Lies."
"...yes! Lies. It's all lies. It's all...it's only ever been lies. All of it. You can see that? You can see that now can't you. Tell me you can see that..."
"I can see. I can see."

She would place her hand over the cradle of the phone. She would press down. Hear the ricochet split through the receiver. Axe. The crack of ice. And then as she places the receiver down, gently, delicately, she would see a woman on the parapet of the stone bridge, so far away, frozen, staring, pointing a finger with venom at a nearby window, at a woman in a window, gripped by horror, a phone still held in her hand, a woman listening to the dead tone.

And as the church bells stop ringing across Europe, she sees the woman leap from the old stone bridge. Her name gasping into the air, sweeping down the river and echoing back from its banks, abruptly ceasing, becoming a gargled cry. A body spearing through murky water, a crowd of bubbles spinning and wobbling up to the surface. And in the wobble of each bubble, rising, is the last of her name, held captive, seeking the air.

...she lay back onto the bed. She felt for the warmth that her body had made in the mattress. She lay on top of it...

The body torpedoes into the soft mud, right up to the knees. All action ceases. Swaying arms of river weed. The splash marks float down the river, through the town, through the estuary, through the sea.

She pretends to pick up the packet of Russian cigarettes he had been smoking the night before. She pretends to hold one in her hand, to put it between her lips, to light it. She breathes in deeply and holds the air. Then she exhales and watches smoke blowing into a cloud above the bed. She sees the smoke billow and twist. And she follows the path of each individual ribbon and swirl, each descending layer of smoke, thinking of lies and truths in sinuous tangles, intricately diverting, over writing, crossing and re-crossing, pulling in her memory, her life, her movements, her self. Forming networks seeking victims and hiding, running, never stopping from ever

Mise-en-Abyme

complicating, ever expanding. Layer upon layer. Layers of suspicion. And the cloud drifts away from her, fading into the shadows of the room. Drifting away — unable to be held, or contained; refusing to be mapped. It has all been delusion. Everything, perhaps even for years of her life. And nothing has importance for her now. She is free. Alone and free. Always moving, always searching. But never escaping the maelstrom. And still she searches for truth in the clouds she sees.

Under every rock there lies a toad. But sometimes, bending down to pick up the toad it is found to be just another rock. And under that, again, the mistake that now a toad has been found. But it is never found. Never. And yet, it is true, under every rock there lies a toad.

She knew that her life was in turmoil, that it twisted in her grasp. That it urged her forward, propelled her further from the sources of her trauma — but that each step she took was only taking her further into her memories. Deeper, always deeper, out-manoeuvring herself constantly, at every junction, every decision. She knew all this. She was accelerating, hurtling towards a destination, any destination. But always approaching the mirror. Each step she took enclosing the space between world and reflection. Her hands outstretched to touch hands that approach. Her face growing toward face. Eyes converging on eyes. Face to face, hand to hand. Closer, closer, pushing into the crystal perfection of glass. And there she would find the seconds compressing, piling up, falling about her in disarray...

...then streaming back behind her, time would elongate, reassemble, fasten itself through the points of her life, of her memory. And she would be pulled, detached from the reflection, forced to return, forced to return.

If only she could hold on to — grasp some splinter of her life. Hold on to the jagged shape, contain it, press it into the softness of her palm. That pure, searing pain — knowing that she could catch, possess a few passing seconds. Is it too much to ask? A splinter. That's all.

It was silent outside. There had been noise, such noise, of cities, of travel, of voices. Voices which span and coiled, writhing in the room. They had all drained away. Now she didn't really know where she was. She was in a room; it was foreign. Bed, open suitcase, dress, photograph, phone, lamp, window. Silence. The man has left.

She looks at the bedside photograph again. She has to return to it. She has no choice. Choices are not her own. Something in that photograph has made a connection with her. It has addressed her. And the photograph will not let her be. She looks closer, closer to that sunny day in Odessa.

That split second of time, that capture of a love, that unbearable happiness. The tumbling girl had fallen into his arms and vanished within a year.

Jeremy Page

Passed through his life with a momentum which could not be stopped. As if she were smoke, a vision, she could not be grasped. Only the clutch of the photograph had managed to give the girl any kind of permanence, her form any kind of substance.

She thinks the girl from Odessa is dead. She thinks of the silence of the night before. Two shadows pulling each other into the dark room. He had seen her eyes turn to the photograph. He had not tried to make her jealous. He had not made reference to a girl so obviously missing from his life. When the sheets had flown from the bed, she had thought of swans from the lake rising like vapour through the dark. The picture had not been turned to the wall. In the morning he had been quiet. Sitting on the edge of the bed pulling a gown across his shoulders he had glanced at her open suitcase. For all these reasons she knew the girl had died. Despite youth, despite happiness, despite love — in the girl's eyes, now she sees death.

Had the young couple climbed up the steps or gone down? Somehow, that is the only thing which remains of any importance. Up the steps, down the steps. But sometimes answers aren't even important. Maybe they don't exist. It seemed appropriate that they were going in no particular direction. They were there — in the middle — for all time — and nowhere else. Love had permanence, a stability, unafraid to run, to hide. Love had a home. She felt the eternity, vanishing briefly.

The pendulum stops mid swing. The depths of her eyes grow sour. She feels suddenly so tired, so weary. And as she moves back away from the photograph she sees her own reflection in the ornately-carved brass lampstand. In coils and spheres of polished metal she sees her face at least a dozen times. A shattered reflection, fractured, dislocated. A twisted reflection.

She looks at what she has become, at what will become of her, she counts ten, twenty, twenty-five times until the phone by the bed stops ringing.

Nicky Röhl

Celebration

Nicky Röhl, son of a German mother and an English father, was born in Brighton in 1967. He went to Cambridge where he received a degree in Social and Political Sciences. For three years he lived in Japan, where he worked and went to film school. His short films have been shown at Brighton and Edinbugh film festivals.

I have heard the key
Turn in the door once and turn once only
We think of the key, each in his prison
Thinking of the key, each confirms a prison
Only at nightfall, aethereal rumours
Revive for a moment a broken Coriolanus
                    T. S. *Eliot,* The Waste Land

INTERIOR: DETACHED ESTATE HOUSE — EARLY EVENING THROUGH TO NIGHT
EDWARD walks in through the front door of a detached estate house. He is middle-aged and looks preoccupied. He moves, tired, across the entrance hall. The sound of voices as from a dinner or cocktail party emanate from the living room just off the hall.

He takes off his scarf and then his overcoat, hanging each on the coat stand in turn. A GIRL, maybe in her early twenties, emerges from the living room and leans against the door frame. She has a glass of wine in her hand, which she holds up to her mouth, biting the rim of the glass as she looks, unblinking, at the man. Edward stays where he is for much longer than he should, facing the coat stand with one hand resting gently on his coat.

A clap of laughter forces itself into the hall. Edward hesitatingly turns his head and sees the girl looking at him from across the rim of the glass. No words are spoken. He then turns with his whole body to face her.

He takes a step towards her, all the time holding her gaze. At the door he looks up from her face and turns to the room. The camera tracks behind him and we see from over his shoulder that a cocktail party is in progress. Edward stands next to the girl in the doorway for a suspended moment without being noticed. Then a voice is heard shouting above the din:

MAN A: (Out of shot) Ah! Here he is at last!

The camera picks up a number of faces turning in Edward's direction, and there is a general crescendo of oohs and ahs.

Nicky Röhl

MAN A: (Out of shot) Make way for the consultant!

As Edward enters the room to the sound of clapping, the camera rests on the face of the girl, who watches the proceedings from the sidelines. She nonchalantly pushes herself away from the door frame and steps across the entrance hall to the coat stand. She checks the pockets of the overcoat Edward has just hung up. From the inside pocket she pulls out a wallet and opens it. Inside are photographs, which she looks at one after the other. She lingers on one depicting a younger Edward with two of his children. She continues flicking through the photographs, then puts them back. She opens another section of the wallet. This time she finds a small passport photograph of herself. She looks up towards the doorway, and then replaces the wallet in the coat pocket.

She places her glass of wine down on an empty chair standing to the side of the living room door, then goes to the toilet opposite and closes the door behind her.

The camera roams slowly back to the open door of the living room. Inside, we are just able to see Edward talking to a number of people. He looks in the direction of the camera, puts down his glass, excuses himself, and makes his way towards the camera. He passes the camera and attempts to open the toilet door, which is of course locked. He looks around him quickly and sees the wine glass sitting on the empty chair. He hesitates, and then goes up the stairs.

At the top of the stairs is a small rectangular landing from which lead three doors. Two of the doors are at the far end of the landing, the third immediately to Edward's right as he stands at the top of the stairs. Edward crosses over to this closed door to his right. He puts his ear against it. He hears nothing except for the reverberations of the party continuing downstairs. Always the reverberations of the party continuing downstairs.

He walks, floorboards creaking, to a second closed door at the far end of the landing and quietly opens it. It is the bathroom. A white shower curtain hangs over the bath, which is located opposite the sink and to the right of Edward as he enters. Beyond the bath and totally obscured by the curtain is a toilet, which only comes into view as he heads for a mirror cabinet hanging above the sink. Edward looks at himself in the mirror and suddenly notices a pair of legs protruding from behind the shower curtain. A pair of tights lies in a ragged pool around the ankles.

Edward stares for a stunned moment and then walks quickly out, closing the door quietly behind him. He disappears into the master bedroom, which is just to the left of the bathroom.

The toilet flushes.

An elderly woman, MOTHER, comes out of the bathroom, looking

Celebration

about her, obviously worried. She closes the bathroom door and moves to the far end of the landing, over to the closed door to which Edward had put his ear minutes before.

Just as the woman is opening this door, Edward comes out of the bedroom and calls out. When Edward speaks it is haltingly, and he often forgets to finish his sentences, his voice trailing off into difficult silence.

EDWARD: Hello Mother.

MOTHER: Oh! It's you Edward...I thought someone from the party...

EDWARD: (Glancing over to the bathroom door) I ...er...

Mother is playing with a simple gold wedding ring. She slides the ring up and down on her finger. Up and down, up down. She is clearly upset. She says nothing. Suddenly the ring drops to the carpeted floor and rolls away towards Edward. He hesitates and then stoops and picks it up.

MOTHER: You don't need to worry about me. Really you don't.

EDWARD: No. I...I just needed to use the bathroom...I didn't realise...

MOTHER: Oh! Well...

Edward steps forward and hands Mother her ring. She takes it, although she looks as if she hardly knows what she is doing. She smiles absently and then turns, opens the door, and goes into the room.

Edward stands a while alone on the landing and then he too turns and goes into the bathroom, closing the door softly behind him. He goes to the mirror cabinet above the sink and opens it. From inside he takes out a key and locks the bathroom door. He sits on the side of the bath with his head in his hands, swaying slightly. He rubs his temples with his fingers, then gets up and disappears behind the shower curtain. The sound of the lid of the toilet touching china is heard.

The camera tracks slowly around from the white of the shower curtain to the mirror cabinet on the wall. Edward's back is seen in the mirror as he pisses.

He unlocks the door quietly, and comes out of the bathroom, clutching the key in his fist, and then putting it in his pocket as he begins walking down the stairs. Suddenly he hears a thud against glass from Mother's room, followed by a quiet cry of surprise. Edward stops in his tracks and listens. He hears the window being opened. He turns and hurriedly retraces his steps to the landing, opens the door to the room without knocking and steps halfway into a very small room. It is almost wholly taken up by a chest of drawers and a bed. Mother is standing with her back to him, the window wide open. There is a slight breeze, and strands of his mother's hair shift slightly. The breeze is eerily silent. She belatedly turns to face Edward.

MOTHER: It must have been a bird. Did you hear it?

Without answering Edward closes the window. A number of small grey feathers are stuck to the glass where the bird hit.

MOTHER: Why is it only humans that commit suicide, Edward. Do you know?

EDWARD: Mother...please don't start now.

MOTHER: We have too much. (Pauses) We can't cope, can we, Edward?

Everything is still in the room except for the low hum of the party downstairs. Edward's mother moves away from the window and opens a cupboard drawer. She takes out a small wrapped box.

MOTHER: You thought I had forgotten, didn't you?

EDWARD: It's not important.

MOTHER: Your father would have been so proud...(Pauses) I hope you like it.

She hands him the box.

MOTHER: Aren't you going to open it?

EDWARD: I already know what it is.

MOTHER: (Slightly angry) Don't be silly, it's wrapped.

Edward is silent. A woman's voice breaks in from the hallway.

ELIZABETH: (Out of shot) Edward? Edward? What are you doing up here? They're all asking for you...

ELIZABETH, also middle-aged (around 45), enters the room and shoots a

Celebration

cold glance at Mother. She takes Edward by the arm and pulls him out of the room. Edward lets himself be pulled. They stop together on the landing.

ELIZABETH: (Annoyed and in a whisper) What *are* you doing?

EDWARD: (Haltingly) Elizabeth, I can manage...

Elizabeth glances again at the doorway leading to Mother's room. Mother is not visible, but her reflection in the glossy white door is. She is standing by the doorway listening.

ELIZABETH: (Interrupting) Have you given her her pills? She'll be all worked up about the party downstairs.

We follow Elizabeth to the previous bedroom with the double bed. She goes to the far corner and opens the drawer of a bedside table. She takes out a key and then stretches up and opens a cupboard above her. There are a number of identical after-shave bottles, unopened and unused, stacked on one shelf. Some are even still in their wrapping paper — the same wrapping paper Mother has used to wrap her present to Edward. From the top shelf above her Elizabeth takes down a large metal box and unlocks it. Inside are numerous bottles of medicine and pills.

As Elizabeth takes out a bottle of Mogadon and shakes two pills onto the palm of her hand, she looks through the opening of the door and sees Edward standing on the landing with his mother holding his hands. For a split second Mother looks at Elizabeth, but Elizabeth has already turned her back again to close the metal box and put it away.

EDWARD: Why don't you come down for a while, Mother?

Elizabeth goes into the bathroom and fills a glass of water, then comes out and hands it to Mother.

ELIZABETH: (Coming from the bathroom) You should be in bed. Is the noise disturbing you?

MOTHER: (Smiling artificially) Oh no, Elizabeth. I quite like listening to all those voices. It keeps me company.

EDWARD: Why don't you...

ELIZABETH (Interrupting.): Will you please take these pills. It'll calm you down.

Edward glances at his wife and then back at his mother.

MOTHER: Alright, Elizabeth.

Mother turns and her face drops, the artificial smile vanishing.

ELIZABETH: I want to see you take them. I won't be able to relax until you do.

Mother turns round and looks Elizabeth steadily in the face.

MOTHER: (Calmly) Alright, Elizabeth.

EDWARD: (Overlapping and almost in the background) Elizabeth, is this really necessary...

While still looking at Elizabeth, Mother puts the two pills in her mouth and takes a drink from the glass of water. She hands the glass back to Elizabeth.

ELIZABETH: (Fading into the background) Edward, sometimes I fail to understand you, you know...

While Elizabeth is speaking, we follow Mother back into her bedroom. Her face is screwed up. She goes over to a mirror hanging on the wall and looks at herself. Suddenly she opens her mouth and spits out the two white pills. She begins to cry in sobs.

★★★

It is some time later, and down in the entrance hall, the girl we saw earlier is standing very close to Edward, who is leaning with his back against the wall. The girl is still holding her glass of white wine.

GIRL: (Coquettishly) Tell me how the consultant feels.

As she begins talking she places her free hand in between the lower buttons of his light blue shirt, so that she touches the naked skin of his stomach. He grabs her wrist and holds it. The girl smiles.

GIRL: You should let yourself go. Let go.

His hand relaxes and she places her hand back on his stomach.

GIRL: (Taking a sip from her glass of wine) Talk to me. (Pauses) Tell me something.

She presses herself lightly against him and feels the key in his pocket pressing into her.

GIRL: What's that?

EDWARD: (Feeling his pocket) Oh, a key.

Edward leans his head against the wall behind him. JOHN, a young man about the same age as the girl, comes out of the living room. Edward panics momentarily, again grabbing her wrist. The girl spills a little wine on her lip and wipes it off with the hand holding the glass. John grins at them and then heads drunkenly for the toilet. The loud noise of him pissing is heard for some time through the scene.

GIRL: You're hurting me. It hurts.

There is a rustle on the stairs and Edward looks up. His mother is standing on the stairs. She smiles. Edward releases his grip on the girl's wrist and her hand drops by her side. She turns and puts the glass on the empty chair again, and then faces Edward's mother.
At this moment, John comes out of the toilet. He hesitates in front of the scene in the entrance hall. He looks up at Edward's mother.
She walks some way down the stairs, carefully taking one step at a time. She smiles self-deprecatingly.

MOTHER: I thought I'd come and...

JOHN: (Posh voice, slightly drunk) You must be Edward's...(Looks at Edward)...uh!...It's just I thought that...well...Elizabeth told us that you were...

MOTHER: (Distressed and nervous, and again playing with her wedding ring) Well, I suppose I am in a manner of speaking. You see, my husband...you might have heard of him, he was very well known, you know, in...

213

EDWARD: (Interrupting) Mother, why don't you come down and join the party?

MOTHER: (Continuing) Circles...

JOHN: (Overlapping) Yes...I was very sorry to hear...(Looking at Edward) I don't know what to say really...er...

MOTHER: (Overlapping) I miss him terribly, you understand...(voice pitching higher) As a matter of fact, I...

EDWARD: (Interrupting) Mother, come down here and we'll say hello. John, please...Go inside, will you?

MOTHER: (Overlapping) What? Oh! Well...Hang on, I'll just get something to put on, then.

Edward leaves his position near the girl and mounts the stairs to where his mother is turning to go back up the stairs. John vanishes into the living room.

EDWARD: You're fine like that, Mother.

He takes her by the arm and leads her down the stairs. As they pass the girl, Mother stops and puts her palm on the girl's cheek.

MOTHER: (Turning to Edward) She is much more beautiful than Elizabeth was at that age, Edward...

The girl blushes and steals a glance at Edward. Mother's hand drops and takes the girl's hand as Edward again steers her to the open doorway of the living room.

MOTHER: (To the girl) Wish me good luck!

As Edward and his mother are about to enter the living room, Elizabeth comes out. She has a silver tray of cheese and pineapple bits shafted with toothpicks, which she wants to put on the chair, but cannot because of the girl's glass of wine. She places the tray on the edge of the chair and takes the glass, looking around her for a place to put it. She is about to put it on the floor, when the girl comes up to her and takes the glass. They look at each

Celebration

other for a moment. The camera again tracks around them so that the party going on behind them can be seen in snippets.

ELIZABETH: Edward, you're insane!

(Pause.)

EDWARD: Elizabeth, I think...

ELIZABETH: They're all terribly drunk. Edward, listen to reason, for Christ's sake!

At this point two people come through the door of the living room. They push into Elizabeth so as to get through.

MAN B: (Shouting manically) Oah! Oh oh oh! Woa! Won't believe this!

WOMAN (Overlapping, posh.): Elizabeth and Edward, you must come and see this...It's fucking hilarious!

The man heads for the front door.

MAN B: (Continuing) Pissed as farts, Jesus to God! Hah! Woa! (Etc. etc.)

He opens the front door. A number of other guests are emerging from the party, all drunk, when the burglar alarm goes off, sending a shrill shock through the house. Outside on the lawn and in the pool of light shed by the spotlight of the burglar alarm, two naked men have appeared, both of them running with their legs close together. They have their penises tucked behind them so that they look as if they have no genitalia. One is older than the other and has a large beer belly. Elizabeth turns in panic and begins to scrabble behind the coats and scarves in an attempt to switch the alarm off, shouting all the while at Edward.

ELIZABETH: Where's the bloody key, Edward? Don't just stand there, for crying out loud! Where have you put the key?

The guests are still streaming from the living room into the garden, all of them impervious to the unbearable noise of the alarm. Many of them are laughing and shouting hysterically. Edward, his mother and the girl stay where they are, motionless. Edward's mother turns to him and shouts in his ear.

215

Nicky Röhl

MOTHER: Never mind, Edward. It'll still be all right, you know.

As she finishes the sentence the alarm is turned off and her voice rings out in the relative silence. She turns and goes back up the stairs. Dishevelled and breathless, Elizabeth frees herself from the coats, looks around her and sees Mother disappearing upstairs. A man appears from outside and grabs Edward's arm.

MAN A: Edward, come and have a look at this. It's madness, it really is! You've never seen anything like it. Come on, man; you're meant to be celebrating!

The man vanishes into the garden again. Edward hardly reacts to what the man has said; he looks as if he has understood nothing. He stands facing his wife and the girl, the three of them making a ragged triangle in the hall. The girl moves first, backing away into the living room.

ELIZABETH: I think we should see what's going on, don't you?

She stumbles past Edward into the garden, leaving him on his own. After a moment, he slowly closes the front door and moves into the living room.
The patio doors are open and most of the people are outside, laughing and screaming at the spectacle. Someone is lying sprawled out on the sofa, dead drunk. Otherwise Edward is alone with the girl.

GIRL: Do you want another drink?

EDWARD: No. No thank you.

The girl starts humming. She picks up some food and starts eating. Edward stands in the middle of the room. A silent, favonian breeze comes in from the open window and he repositions his lank, ruffled hair. The girl looks at him and chews. Edward doesn't move. She laughs through her nose. She goes on eating. The atmosphere is sordid.

She lights up a cigarette and walks up to Edward, who is still standing in the middle of the room. She puts it between his lips. Edward doesn't move. He squints from the smoke. She moves away from him. He takes the cigarette from his mouth and stubs it out.

EDWARD: Why did you do that?

GIRL: Doctors shouldn't smoke, that's all.

Celebration

A bout of laughter comes through the patio doors. Edward looks behind him. No one is to be seen.

GIRL: (Derisively) Look at you!

The girl gets up and leaves the room, leaving Edward to stand there stupidly on his own.

The girl climbs the stairs. She begins opening doors, starting with the one to her right. It is Edward's mother's door. She is sitting on her bed with a metal box open beside her. It is the same one from which Elizabeth took the sleeping pills. Mother looks up, surprised. She has a glass of water in her hand. She doesn't try to hide the box. Neither woman says anything; they just stare at each other. Edward appears from behind the girl, and gently closes the door without bothering to look inside. He then walks across the landing to the master bedroom. She hesitates and then follows.

Edward enters the bedroom while the girl stands outside the door and feels the lock for a key. There is none. Through the window of the bedroom behind them the two naked men are seen running through the street. More men are now trying to take their trousers off.

GIRL: There's no key.

Edward does not answer; nor does he move in the semi-darkness of the room. The girl goes to him and pulls the key from his pocket. She tries to lock the door with it; it doesn't fit. She leaves it hanging in the lock and takes slow steps towards him.

They lie down together on the bed. His face is covered with a thin film of sweat like cellophane, which gleams in the light coming from outside. He swallows hard but is otherwise impassive, staring up at the ceiling. Lying to the side of him, the girl begins to stroke his large head.

The key drops from the lock of door. Edward jumps. He switches on the reading lamp by the bed. The room is illuminated for the first time. The girl is stunned and stops, looking at him. She then looks at the door. No one is there. Edward doesn't even look towards the door. He lies on his back staring up at the ceiling.

Cut to open drawer from which the metal box was taken.

Cut to the closed door of Mother's bedroom. Under the door is a strip of light. There is a click and the light goes out. A quiet crying can be heard.

Cut back to the bedroom. The girl reaches over and turns the lamp off. As the bedroom becomes dark again, a flashing blue light from outside becomes noticeable. She whispers into his ear.

217

GIRL: It'll be all right, Edward.

Cut to scene outside. A police car has arrived, and two policeman are talking to Elizabeth. The naked men have stopped fooling around now, and are meekly allowing themselves to be led back into the house. The house is momentarily calm.

The burglar alarm goes off again.

Ralph Goldswain

From *Natural Curriculum*

Ralph Goldswain has many interests and has tried more than one career but unfortunately for him he is fatally attracted to the most difficult: writing. *Natural Curriculum* is told by five narrators. This is a sample of one, pulled from the text like a thread from a length of fabric.

The family non-human animal companion's barking wakes me. He is responding to the delivery by an enslaved child of the reconstituted biomaterial containing the morning propaganda.

I am a method writer and my current project is a satirical novel. My protagonist is a sixth form student in a North London comprehensive school: although he himself is a white male he is a champion of the oppressed and insists on using the language of political correctness at all times, whatever subject he is talking about. Although I am not him I take the opportunity of my *mise-en-scene* to live his life during the school day and for my pains I am variously regarded as an idiot, buffoon, clown, comedian, jester, cuckoo and stooge as I move about my fictional world. I don't mind, however, as it's all in the interests of emerging as the major writer of the decade, and cutting a somewhat ludicrous figure I am in good company at Brunswick Comprehensive School.

The idea came in an English lesson while I was listening to Ms Duvall who is a charm-free, bovine-American possessing an alternative body image. I subsequently made a point of engaging her in conversation whenever possible to capture the flavour of the language. (I must include a footnote here to the effect that the term 'political correctness' is itself no longer 'politically correct': it is a hegemonic term co-opted by the white power elite as a weapon to attack culturally sensitive people. The acceptable term is 'appropriately inclusive'.) Ms Duvall uses elements of the appropriately inclusive discourse in her everyday language and I have learnt a great deal from that but also done my own research and taken the language into areas beyond her reach. All that, combined with my keen eye for observation and my opportunistic and manipulative talents, qualifies me for the task I have undertaken.

"Nigel!" my female parent calls. "Your breakfast's ready!" As method writing involves total immersion in the source world of the fiction, I enter that world every morning while dressing. I warm up on my mother then move on to school, documenting the day mentally as I journey through it, resuming my own persona in the evening to type up the day's events.

"Nigelll!"

"Alright, Parent," I call. "Coming."

During my consultations with Ms Duvall I have been taught that the head of the English department is a differently logical male who is frequently sobriety-deprived and interested only in DWEMs. He taught me last year and I have some reservations about that last point, having enjoyed Fay Weldon's she-devil under his auspices and frolicked in the linguistic sea of Stevie Smith's poetry. I have been rocked by the horror of Sylvia Plath, not to mention gobsmacked by *The Colour Purple* which I read on his recommendation. But yes, he is guilty of overemphasis on the literary canon. He led me to the wonders of Hemingway but I am forced to remain in the closet because the name is one of Ms Duvall's triggers. I have the recurring dream that Ms Duvall has outlived her usefulness and I terminate her existence with a metabolically different non-human being mutilator's knife then shout Hemingway's name at her permanently inconvenienced body until I am hoarse. In the meantime, I have to accept that he's a rapist, wife-beater and bigot and read his texts under my duvet by torchlight. I've been taught that his cultural and social vandalism renders his fiction worthless and that all copies of his processed tree carcasses should be burnt. Even though such action would be environmentally unfriendly.

"Nigel! It's not funny!"

I grin at myself in the mirror. Gemma White calls me a Cheshire cat — she doesn't know what to make of me — but I have difficulty keeping a straight face at school.

I yearn to be puritanically non-lookist but that ambition is frustrated by Gemma White. If I had been more mature in Year ten when she showed an interest ...

"Breakfast going in the bin!" I hear. "One ... Two ..."

"Alright then, Forebear," I call. A delicious smell of frying eggs and bacon assails my nostrils.

"I wish you'd stop this nonsense," she says as I descend.

"Oh no," I say. "How can you serve up fried stolen non-human animal products and ribbons of flesh carved from the slaughtered carcasses of cruelly exploited non-human animals of the pig family?" I rub my hands and climb in.

"Oh Nigel." She's laughing. "You're a complete idiot."

"Parent," I say, my mouth stuffed with redundant non-human animal, "are you suggesting that I'm mentally disadvantaged? That I'm in need of additional preparation?"

"Yes!" she says, dumping a mug of coffee on the table.

I am a few minutes late to school and there are two police cars and an ambulance near the gates, beside the ditch. The Head is there too, talking to the police, so I quicken my step and overtake a group of Year tens who are talking about a nonviable adult male in the ditch. I hurry to my form room.

My tutor is a mathematics teacher who is differently appealing. I would not for the world be sizest and, indeed, Mr Warren is only selectively horizontally challenged, to wit, round his middle, but this combined with his refusal to wear size-friendly clothes exaggerates the condition. He is severely cosmetically different and apparently non-accepting of his follicular challenge, growing his hair very long on the one side and sweeping it over the top of his head, thus drawing attention to it and ensuring that all the world but himself sees at a glance that he is in a desperately different hirsute state

He is already there, as are Kenny, Hannah, Virginia, Sundi and Azeem and some others. They groan as I enter. They are watching Mr Warren trying to swat a fly with a copy of The Times and soon after I arrive he succeeds. He sweeps it into the wastepaper basket then smiles his satisfaction and lowers himself into his chair.

"Do you realise, Sir, that you have violated a dozen laws of nature?" I say, "and shown yourself to be culturally insensitive."

The others groan, louder this time.

"Oh sit down, Nigel," says Mr Warren.

"Blatant phylumism, not to mention non-humanslaughter," I mutter and sit down, knowing that, in spite of bitter experience, he will not be able to resist.

"What was that?" he says.

"What?" I say.

"Oh please don't get him started, Sir," says Sundi. "Give us a break, Nigel!"

"No, wait," says Mr Warren, gesturing to Sundi to be quiet. "What did you say, Nigel?"

"I said you've committed non-humanslaughter. "

"No, not that ," he says. "Before that. What did you say before that?"

"That you were phylumistic," I say.

"What's that?" he says.

More groans but I forgive them for they know not how well I'm going to entertain them.

"Phylumism?" I say.

He nods.

"It's a form of discriminatory thinking," I tell him. "Similar to sexism

Ralph Goldswain

and racism but extended to include such things as insectism." My classmates are beginning to show an interest. "Which is sorely frowned upon in this institution, due to its enlightened policies," I continue, watching Mr Warren's face. "It's the conviction that one's own biotype is intrinsically superior to another because of a perceived greater sophistication of its body structure."

Mr Warren looks at me, orally-challenged-founded. His two lower shirt buttons are missing and his melanin-impoverished belly heaves with each breath. The others laugh. No one could deny that Mr Warren has distinctly and clearly requested that.

The siren blasts. I go out with the mental image of him sitting there like that, it merges with the thought of the permanently inconvenienced individual in the ditch and it gives me an idea for a short story which I already know will not leave me in peace until I have written it.

History with Miss Stickert is profoundly differently interesting to most students but not to me. We all have our own agenda when we go to lessons, of course, and mine is not the acquisition of an A Level because, although I will achieve one, if I were dependent on Miss Stickert's pedagogical skills then I would be doomed to an eternal alternative schooled condition.

As usual she ignores us as we slink past her into the classroom. She is in the corridor, standing to attention, her back rigid, looking straight up into the face of a very vertically different Year ten boy. Miss Stickert is by contrast vertically constrained and as usual her voice rings clearly along the corridor.

"And how many times have I warned you about running?"
Mumble.
"What? Speak up, Shane."
"A couple."
"A couple, Shane?"
Mumble
"So how do you think you can make amends to me, Shane?"
Mumble.
"Do you think I enjoy standing out here all day trying to reason with you, Shane?"

Yes, I think, you do. It affords the greatest pleasure known to a person of your kind — perhaps the only pleasure. I know that's unkind, or would be if it were more than an idle thought. I would not, for all my reflections on her condition, actually be impolite to her in spite of her being a natural target, particularly as a Bible oriented individual. But as I listen to the capitalisticpatriarchalhegemonicdiscourse coming relentlessly from the corridor I begin to feel my tolerance slipping and that means a red warning light is flashing.

"Do you, Shane?"

"What, Miss?"

"Think I enjoy standing out here all day trying to turn you into a civilised human being when I have a class waiting for me?"

"No, Miss," says the economically marginalised individual.

"Well then. Shall it be litter patrol?" Even though I can't see them I know that her slight body is like a ramrod and that Shane's is drooping.

Silence.

"Alright then, Shane. Half past three. Don't be late." And then the clicking of her heels and she's in the classroom. "Come on, come on, books open," she says.

My goal for today is to draw her into a discussion of the nature of history but her goal is the usual — that the students read from the textbook in silence while she writes memos. She is a very senior individual in the school and it is common knowledge that the power structure is balanced in her favour. Younger staff live in fear of the appearance of the familiar handwriting in their pigeonholes — their name on a yellow sheet, folded over and stapled shut. It is during her A Level history lessons that she conducts her campaign of terror, writing the memos, the sight of which can turn glossy brown hair white. I open the processed tree carcass whose title I have artfully changed to read '*Hystery* of Eighteenth Century Europe' to the page whose number she has inscribed on the strongly pigmentedboard. It is the chapter dealing with the foreign policy of Frederick the Second. I read through it and note the falseconscious assumptions and blatant indoctrination techniques. Then I raise my hand.

"Yes, Nigel?" she says impatiently.

"Ms Stickert," I say with careful annunciation and there's no need to pause for effect. She is on her feet in an instant and bearing down on me.

"I am no feminist!" she booms. "I expect you to address me courteously!"

"I apologise," I say with the rapidity of a machine gun.

"I don't know what's got into you, Nigel," she says. "When you were in Year seven one could not have found a more hardworking, polite pupil."

"That was almost five years ago," I say. "I'm an adult now."

"I've had complaints about you from everyone," she says.

"Complaints, Miss Stickert?" I say. I am beginning to feel heavily oppressed. "I make a point of being courteous to staff," I tell her. "And I never neglect my work."

"What about your discourtesy to me?" She is still standing over me.

"I merely addressed you by the conventional appellation 'Ms', a mode of address which is correct and appropriate, the widely recognised modern feminine equivalent of 'Mr' and which appears in the Oxford English Dictionary." She is staring malevolently at me and I succumb to the temptation to shock her and to test the power relationship that exists between us. I consider this and I feel irresistibly that it is what I really want to do today. The urge to change my agenda is overpowering. The historiographical discussion can wait.

"Not that I'm so keen on the OED," I say. "An enormously influential book written in a style of language imposed on our culture by patriarchal caucasian lexicographers. As a result of that it is deeply phallocentric and should be called a dick-tionary, spelt d-i-c-k. Perhaps in the future, when the balance has been redressed, we may have a new form of lexicon which we will call a cuntionary, spelt c-u-n-t!"

I will draw a veil over the next scene, dear reader. Suffice it to say that it was worth it. I have been given the rest of the week off. I plan to use the time to follow up my idea for the short story.

THE TEACHER
A short story by Nigel Sterne

It took us a long time — a good ten minutes — to discover that our teacher was dead. Looking back on it we should have realised immediately, even though we hardly knew him, because when you think about it our behaviour — talking, shouting to each other, even overturning chairs, that kind of thing — shouldn't have been on while he was in the room, large as life, right in front of us, behind the teacher's table, sitting on the teacher's chair, his authority in open display.

Then one of us said that the teacher was behaving oddly. That made us take notice of him, and it was then that we realised the truth. We stopped what we were doing. An awed hush replaced the companionable turmoil. We went up to his table and gathered around in respectful silence. Of course it wasn't very serious because he was only a supply teacher: he hadn't taken us more than three times before. As we looked at him now, though, he was a whole new person, reborn as a splendidly interesting teacher.

He was about 40 with a grey-streaked beard. His eyes were closed and his mouth was slightly open: it was an expression that suggested that he had suddenly been struck by an interesting thought or a clever idea. One of us said that it was an expression of pain, but that's the same thing anyway. We went round in that unproductive circle for a while but then we got onto the more interesting ground of speculation about the manner of his death.

One of us, perhaps more romantic than the others, said that he

Natural Curriculum

had been murdered, but after considering that we rejected it because we couldn't see any signs of violence. She persisted, though, saying that he could have been poisoned. We conceded that it was a possibility and that opened the way for an exploration of motive.

Who would poison him? He hadn't offended anyone — quite the contrary, in fact, having been invisible during his lifetime — so why should anyone have bothered to murder him? If he had taken one of us to the Head for disrupting a lesson or not doing homework and therefore created the risk of a letter home then murder would have been entirely understandable, or if he had tried to make anyone do something they didn't want to and forced it to a showdown, then one could see that it might be a motive, but a man who had not made any impression and whom we hadn't even noticed when we'd first come in was not likely to attract an assassin.

Suicide, then. Now that seemed less unlikely so we examined him for signs of that. Perhaps the poison theory was right, but self-administered. It would have to be poison because there were still no signs of violence — no stab wounds, no severing of arteries, no bullet holes or anything like that. No weapon either.

But why would he want to kill himself? After all, he had a good job and it couldn't have been anything we had done. His professional life was a very attractive one as far as we could see. All he had to do was come in at about nine, get through the day the same as everyone else, and go home at half past three. Being a supply teacher he had no responsibilities either. So if it was suicide it must have been something to do with his home life. That led us to take a closer look at him.

One of us more observant than the others drew our attention to the fact that he always wore the same clothes: whenever she had seen him it had always been in the same clothes. So do all teachers, we argued, but she pointed to his tie. They don't always wear the same tie, she said. We went up close and saw that the knot was very tight and greasy and smooth, obviously because of constant rubbing against his beard. It was clear that he never undid the knot but slid it down the tie to make a noose which he then lifted over his head when he got undressed, doing the reverse when he got dressed. It was a dark grey tie with maroon stripes which did not go with his check shirt. The shirt was wrinkled and the bottom button was undone, parting the shirt, stretching it tight against a paunch of which two inches of white skin with wiry black hairs could be seen. Perhaps he had committed suicide because he had no wife to love him.

We were somewhat baffled. He was well-fed — there was no evidence to suggest that he had died of starvation — and while he was a little pale he looked healthy enough. That he had died at this age, apparently in the pink, everything to live for, was inexplicable and we gave up trying to explain it. However, we couldn't just leave him sitting there for eternity so we took him out on to the football pitch and buried him. It was quite difficult because we were left with a mound of earth and we were certain to get into trouble for digging up the turf. The only thing we could do was spread the soil out over a large area and rub it into the grass. After we had done that all that was left of the teacher was a pale brown patch on the field.

When we got back to the classroom the lesson was coming to an end and we went off to our next class. We didn't worry about the experience too much: we knew that there would be another teacher waiting for us when we turned up for maths the next day.

The School's brochure states that any pupil in breach of reasonable conduct may be suspended and re-instated only after guarantees of acceptable behaviour have been given by the pupil and his/her parents.

I am charged with having engaged in negative attention getting and am therefore required to deliver the necessary guarantees.

I am male parent-deprived and so I set out with my female parent who has had to fawn to her worker exploiter in order to find the time to be interviewed by the illustrious Roy Gearing, headteacher of Brunswick Comprehensive School. She is driving and I am listening.

"I'll do the talking, Nigel. I don't want you to say anything unless you're asked." I don't reply as I'm thinking of the opportunities which an interview with the *Duce* — whom I have seen very little of and never spoken to personally — will offer. I look out the window at the golf course. "Is that understood?" she says sharply. I nod but my fingers are crossed.

"Right," she says. "If you keep your mouth shut you'll be back in school before break."

She says it as though that's an advantage but I'm thinking of English with Mr Nicholson, my other English 'instructor'. I have him three and four. I'm wondering what the matter with me is today because I've always regarded every differently interesting situation as an opportunity. Moreover, Mr Nicholson is a caucasian male and I am therefore not obliged to mince words when applying my mind to him: it is even within the rules of a nonphallocentric philosophy to refer to him as a wanker. If I wanted to learn all there is to know about cliches, euphemisms and idioms I could do no better than pay attention to Mr Nicholson. From that point of view being in his group has its advantages. 'It's an ill wind that blows nobody any good!' I must not fall into the trap of myself being differently interested. That would be the death blow to my writing career.

"Alright Nigel?" my parent says. "I know you. I want you to promise."

"Yes, beloved Female Parent," I say. My fingers are still crossed.

"Cut it out now, Nigel. None of your political whatsit in Mr Gearing's office. You understand?"

"Yes Mum," I say and she turns her head and smiles.

"That's better, Nigel." My fingers are still crossed. I'm wondering whether I'll be able to maintain my principles in the face of *il Duce* — whether, if he addresses me directly, I'll be able to subordinate my personality to the purpose of this gathering, which is to secure my reinstatement.

Mr Gearing welcomes us, smiling hotly at my female parent.

I must pause here, to place my ancestor in perspective. She has long black hair and a face which has sent many a better man than Mr Gearing into a terminal spiral. It doesn't behove me to dwell on her figure but if forced to regard it as though she were not my parent I would say that it is particularly striking. In short, she is a magnet to the male eye (although I am no student of Freud I suspect that he would have had something to say about the relevancy of my parent's looks to the fact of my particular attraction to Gemma White). When my parent tells me to leave the talking to her I know that she's displaying her confidence in her ability to manipulate the weaker sex.

It looks as though Mr Gearing's smile has been painted onto his face like a ventriloquist's doll.

"Ah, Mrs. Sterne," he says. "Nigel." He looks at me, still smiling. I am wondering what the best approach would be. Would my inclusively sensitive persona be appropriate? If I were prepared to risk it it could be a valuable learning experience. I grin while this complex decision foments.

He invites us to sit in the low armchairs while he sits behind his desk, just in case we are confused as to who is oppressing who.

"Coffee?" he says and I say, "Yes, please," before my parent has a chance to respond. She gives me a look which says 'If you do that again...' Mr Gearing's look says 'I'll get you later.' Then he smiles and says, "Of course, Nigel: you're a sixth former now. Mrs Sterne?" "Thank you," my female parent says. "No sugar," and he pushes a button on his desk.

As he admires my begetter I assess him. I must admit he's not the grotesque that most of his staff are. He's well thought of and the younger children aren't afraid of him, which is something in his favour: as a younger person I enjoyed his assemblies — they were always careful sidesteppings of the Biblephile antics which some members of his staff adopt, and they were always thought-provoking, showing him to be in a different league from most of his colleagues, who arouse everything in me except my intellect. He doesn't have the downtrodden, shabby look of the other male teachers: on the contrary, he wears an expensive suit. There is almost nothing about him worthy of comment apart from some hair deprivation and the silly smile which my parent has evoked. It is hard to tell his age — he seems to have been the same age forever and I have never thought about it. If forced in the face of some lethal weapon to do so I would pinpoint him at fifty.

"Did you find your way here alright?" he says and my respect for him wavers. I have been coming here every day for five years.

The school secretary comes in and Mr Gearing says, "Ah, three coffees please, Jill." Jill — Mrs Armitage to me — glares at me as she goes out, no doubt vividly recalling one or two previous encounters, and I have a moment of panic, convinced that my cup will contain a substantial dose of arsenic. I recover rapidly, however. "No milk for me thank you," I call after her and grin as she pauses and glares at me again, even harder this time. My mother's eyes scream at me.

"Well, Mrs Sterne," says Mr Gearing.

My ancestor straightens up. I observe Mr Gearing's eye movements as she adjusts her skirt. "Well, Mr Gearing?" She says, echoing him and smiling. She is attempting to be relaxed but I know she's thinking 'What's Nigel going to do?' I grin at her.

Mr Gearing turns to me. "Nigel," he says. He places the tips of his fingers together and leans forward on to his elbows. His reflection shines on the surface of his desk. "It's unusual to suspend a sixth former, you know."

I nod. Mrs Armitage comes in and places a tray on his desk. Mr Gearing gets up and gives us each a cup.

He starts again. "It's unusual to suspend a sixth former, you know."

I nod again.

"Ah...as you know that was done by Miss Stickert," he says. "And I assure you," he continues, "that from what she told me the suspension was er...it was..." He looks at my antecedent. "....A quite supportable...." He clears his throat. "In short I supported her action."

"Yes, Mr Gearing," I say and, ignoring the pleading on my antecedent's face, I continue. "Ms Stickert raised an interesting question of semantics to which I responded and before we -"

"What Nigel is trying to say," my female parent says, "is that he has the highest regard for Miss Stickert's intellect and the greatest respect for her position" — fixing me with a controlling glare — "as his history teacher. He is very sorry -"

"About the misunderstanding -" I begin.

"About his behaviour towards Miss Stickert," my mother corrects me, using

Natural Curriculum

the steely voice which my experience tells me means business. "He values –"

"Her input to my understanding of our culture," I say, and grin.

They both give me a look of what I can only describe as hatred and I concede. "I believe that Ms Stickert was absolutely right."

"But that doesn't excuse the language you used in your ...ah ... exchange with her," says Mr Gearing. "She maintains that you used language that –"

"If we are talking semantics –" I begin and my female parent loses all patience.

"Nigel," she says. "Tell Mr Gearing that you're sorry."

"Nigel," says Mr Gearing. "We both know the score." His eyes dart towards my female parent. I don't like to be drawn into a consensual situation with him — a shared perception scenario — and my instinct is to take issue with that but my female parent is looking at her watch and I know that her worker exploiter will be looking at his watch too, so I nod. "We won't go into your daily confrontations with Mr Warren and your...ah...playful banter with other members of staff, which it would be far too time consuming to...ah...pursue, but we both know that Miss Stickert has the right to expect an ... ah ... absence of profane language, particularly given her...ah...religious convictions. Don't you agree, Nigel?"

"Well," I begin, but catching a glimpse of my female parent's eyes, I smile. "I couldn't agree with you more, Sir," I say. I feel that I have betrayed my principles and doffed my persona to make my beloved ancestor happy but her smile of relief and the affection in her eyes compensates for my humiliation and the feeling of being the oppressed-within-the-oppressed.

"Well then," says Mr Gearing. "We are in agreement. There's no need to waste any more time." He shakes hands with my mother and keeps her hand in his for longer than I think is necessary.

"Well done, Progenatrix," I say as I walk her to the car, hoping that my gender-ender has run her through to the heart, but she does not react to it. "You are a mistress of obfuscation."

"I have no idea what you're talking about," she says.

"Well, Mother," I say. "You have non-communicated extremely well today. Each time Mr Gearing and I were on the threshold of an exploration of some interesting aspect of the case you manipulated the narrative."

She examines the ground as she walks then stops beside her car. She puts her hand on my arm. "Listen, Nigel," she says. "From now on I live in dread that you and Mr Gearing are going to fall out and that you will find yourself face to face with him, alone in his office. It is something that's going to give me sleepless nights. I know that the time will come. I know it will happen and I know that when it does I won't be able to bail you out. That, dear descendent," she says, "is not something over which I have control. It is, as you would say, merely an idle observation."

She gets in the car.

My parent counsels me over the breakfast table. Instead of assuming her usual role of dining room attendant she joins me, bearing her cereal bowl. She has been performing this ritual since my suspension — a traumatic experience for her and something which appears to necessitate constant revisiting.

"There must be no more incidents," she informs me.

"My behaviour since my return has been indefectible," I assert. "As you well know. Apart from one small incident involving a particular favourite of mine — one Mr Nicholson — I have retained my unravished status."

"Stop it, Nigel," she complains. "Please, please, speak proper English. What happened with Mr Nicholson?"

"An inconsequential event," I tell her, "considering that he remained oblivious throughout the infliction of the wound, like an anaesthetically inconvenienced hospital guest enfolding a scalpel."

"But what happened?" she begs.

"You would not want to hear about it," I tell her. "I made available to him the most sumptuous of African-American invective, albeit linguistically disguised."

"Oh Nigel," she says. "What's the point of talking to you? It's as though you can't hear me."

"I hear you plainly," I tell her. "I am exceedingly aurally convenienced."

"Well promise me that if you are tempted by any teachers you will operate discretion and say nothing instead."

The thought of interpreting that literally interests me so I promise.

"Why are you wearing a bow tie?" she says. "It looks silly."

"The bow tie is a piece of ideology," I tell her. "As I am to survive in silence at school I am indicating visually that although I have been linguistically restrained I am nevertheless present and highly visible."

"Oh go to school," she says. "But please be careful: one more incident and they'll suspend you indefinitely."

As I walk out the door I have visions of myself hanging from a tree, remaining in that state for eternity. And as I perambulate I consider my position as a writer. Determined as I am to produce the great satirical novel of the decade, like all writers I am intermittently wracked with self-doubt. My dissatisfaction with my short story disturbs me and I wonder whether prose writing is my forte after all. This causes a deeper level of doubt and I begin to reflect generally upon the capitalistic nature of the practice.

Prose is a form of human expression and is therefore subject to political analysis in the same way as any other human endeavour is. I have begun to suspect that prose writing is inherently oppressive. In the first place it is time consuming and therefore requires its practitioners to be individuals of leisure. Furthermore, unless the amount of time required is multiplied, writers require such tools as typewriters and word processors, those items thus becoming weapons in the class war. Moreover, space, such as one's own writing environment — a house, a flat, or at the minimum, a room of one's own, is a requirement for such an activity. Finally one should not forget the amount of paper consumed (rendering the activity environmentally unfriendly in addition). Prose writing is therefore beyond the reach of the economically maginalised and is consequently an oppressive activity. This must give appropriately inclusive-minded writers pause.

I am approaching the school gates now and a solution is at hand (albeit academic as I shall no doubt overcome my reservations in the interests of my novel). Using the same technique I now look at poetry writing. It tends to be a secret activity, performed in corners, in military trenches, in the back row of classrooms. It can be conducted in short bursts and executed on waste paper, in textbooks and on desks and walls. It requires nothing more than a pencil by way of hardware. Poetry is thus the literary medium of choice. It will be the footsoldier in the war to reclaim literature.

I decide that, leaving decisions about the novel aside for the moment, I will try my hand at poetry, beginning with culturally sensitive translations of works in the canon. I want to make them accessible to those unable to read them for fear of being offended by their cultural insensitivity.

I speak no words to Mr Warren although he attempts to provoke me into breaking my vow of silence by asking after my health. That fails and he attacks again, saying: "Nice tie, Nigel." I grin.

I am free during the first two periods and after pulling the cord of the common room hi-fi set until it comes loose I settle down to read *Beloved*, the current subject of study with Ms Duvall, who is like the famed monkeys: if the names of a thousand tree carcasses pass her lips she will be bound to name some worthwhile novels. Someone comes in and tries to switch on the hi-fi. "What's the matter with this fucking thing?" she says, looking at me as though she knows something. I grin. "Arsehole," she says and walks out again.

Miss Stickert for hystery three and four. This is not the time to provoke an incident by raising the historiographical point I wish to pursue. A promise to one's parent is a promise. I feel deprived, however, for if a serious student wishes to raise an academic matter of great import who can he raise it with if not his history teacher? I console myself with the thought that I shall do it at some future date.

We are 'doing' the French Revolution now, all reading in silence while Miss Stickert makes short work of her mail tray. I am excruciatingly differently interested and I get up and approach Miss Stickert, first satisfying myself that I cannot be tempted — thereby retaining my parental, promise. "Yes, Nigel?" she says, looking up. "May I please leave the room Miss

Ralph Goldswain

Stickert?" I say. "Don't be long, Nigel, there's a good boy, " she says, choosing the terminology deliberately, I am convinced, because she knows that I am temporarily differently abled. What she cannot know is the extent to which she is fuelling the engine of my revenge. "Thank you, Miss," I say. I try not to grin as I anticipate some future debates with her.

Tracy Chevalier

You, She and Me

Tracy Chevalier was born in 1962 and grew up in Washington, D.C. She has lived in London since 1984 and worked for several years as an editor of literary reference books. She has had stories published in *Fiction* and *Acumen* magazines and is currently writing a novel about French Huguenots.

These days, almost all of your time is spent in your bedroom.
Your room is not big, but your bed is king-sized, much longer and wider than you. You lie on the left-hand side, wearing a white knee-length nightgown and a cotton housecoat with yellow flowers and green leaves on it. Your hair is blond and cut short, to just below your ears. You are covered with a white sheet and a light blue blanket. When it is warm the blanket is folded down so that it is still covering your legs and feet.
Sometimes when you are lying so still in bed, you look like a plow that has been left in a field.
On a square table next to your bed are a box of Kleenex, a glass of water, orange-flavored potassium tablets, a small lamp with a 40-watt bulb, and a book, *Our Hearts Were Young and Gay*, lying face down, open at pages 46 and 47. You have not turned a page in several weeks.
To the left of your bed, in front of the door, is a small rectangular rug with a blue and white woven pattern. The floor is made up of polished pine floorboards, scratched in places. When walked on, it creaks.
Against the wall to the left of the bed is a large bureau with five drawers that slide noiselessly along waxed grooves. On top of the bureau are scattered some coins, mascara and several lipsticks, a few pieces of jewelry in a dish, two bottles of perfume, and, near the wall, a white porcelain bowl covered with a silver lid. There is a straight-backed chair next to the bureau with your white terry-cloth bathrobe draped over its back.
There is a walk-in closet in the corner diagonally opposite the door. Inside, the shoulders of a rack full of dresses, blouses and jackets are gathering dust. On the closet door hangs a full-length mirror. You have not looked at yourself for a long time.

The last corner, away from the door, the bureau and the closet, is my corner.

These days you move slowly, and less often. You are tired every moment now. The back of your head pulls down so that if a pillow were not supporting it your head would be tilted all the way back with your chin pointed towards the ceiling. These days you are grateful for the pillows behind your head.

You have to steel yourself for the long walk to the bathroom twice a day, once in the morning and once at night. When you sit up and swing your legs off the side of the bed, your bare feet touch the rug. You place your hands on the bed on either side of your body, pause, and then in slow motion push yourself into a standing position. Your left hand goes out and grasps the back of the chair, and you straighten your knees and steady yourself. Then you pull at the bathrobe until it is free from the chair. You hold it up, and pull on first the left arm, then the right arm, stretching both arms wide until the bathrobe settles onto your shoulders. The stretching movement tires you, and you stand still for some time, holding on to the back of the chair. Then you wrap the robe around you, gather up the ends of the belt, and tie them in half a knot. You take small, slow steps towards the door; you breathe deeply. You reach for the door knob with your right hand, turn it, pause, and then open the door. You stand in the blast of light and air from the hall, blinking. Then you take two steps and disappear.

You look pleased when the door is shut and you are back in bed. You are exhausted.

The windows stay closed, though if it is very hot and still, you sometimes open slightly the window that does not face the street. It takes a great deal of your strength to open the window, but you do not ask someone else to do it. You also insist on changing your own sheets, once a week. On that day you hardly move in order to be ready with the extra bit of energy that will allow you to stretch over the vast bed and smooth the sheet down, to walk from one side to the other, pulling and tucking.

The curtains in your room are made of a blue and green plaid material. They are always drawn. During the day the sun pushes at them, succeeding only in outlining the windows so that they are pale smudges hovering on the walls. Sometimes you turn on the bedside lamp, but most of the time you are enfolded in an opaque darkness touched by fluttering hints of a different light. The atmosphere in the room is muffled and close, as if invaded by fog.

I do not think you are aware that I am here.

Above your head is mounted an intercom. You can push a button, speak into the microphone, and downstairs in the kitchen your family will hear you. You used to go to the top of the stairs and call down, but that required

You, She and Me

so much energy that the intercom was installed. But these days it is getting harder to hoist yourself upright, prop your back against the wall, and turn your head to the left to speak into the microphone, while also reaching up and pressing the button. These days you do not speak much into the intercom; sometimes you push the button that makes the intercom downstairs beep so that someone will come to you.

When pressed, another button on the intercom brings the sounds from the kitchen to you. You can hear your children setting the table, playing, laughing. Sometimes when they fight downstairs you can hear them without the help of the intercom.

She has begun coming to your room more often. At meal times, different members of the family used to bring you a tray, but for the last two weeks she has entered your room three times a day, bearing your tray with a place setting that she has put there herself. She has folded the paper napkin in half on the diagonal, as you taught her. The fork sits on it to the left of the plate, the knife to the right. Occasionally, if there is a dessert, she will have placed a spoon to the right of the knife.

At first you ate what you had cooked for years: meat, a starch, a green vegetable, and dessert. But these days meat exhausts you and tastes of nothing; you prefer a small slice of cheese, a piece of bread with no crusts, a spoonful of spinach. There is no salt in any of the food. There are not many desserts these days: you cannot eat sugar, and you are not very hungry. Occasionally you manage a sliver of pale orange cantaloupe, or sliced banana in milk.

You drink water and sometimes unsweetened orange juice.

Your meals are diminishing in size as your appetite dwindles. When you begin leaving things on your plate, the portions are adjusted at the next meal so that there is a little less for you to try to finish. You do not like leaving food on your plate. You were taught to clean your plate, a lesson you passed on to your children. It embarrasses you now that they see your food unfinished.

Whenever she enters with the tray there is a brief phrase of light from the hall, cut off abruptly when she nudges the door shut with her foot. She always says "Mommy?" when she comes in, her small voice always rising at the end although she knows that you will be there. She sets the tray down on the edge of the bed next to your left thigh, and switches on the lamp, if you have not done so yourself. Usually you have not.

After she has set the tray down she stays for a while. She sits on the chair next to the bureau and watches you eat, playing with the belt from your bathrobe. Or she walks over to the window facing the street, pulls the curtain open an inch, and looks out. Or she fiddles with the things on the bureau, which comes up to her chin. She is tall for her age. She picks up one of the perfume bottles, sprays the air, sniffs. She lines the stray coins up in the dust. She rolls a lipstick across the bureau top until the jewelry dish stops it, then uncaps it, twists the bottom, and squints at the rust color she cannot see well in this light. She draws her finger slowly around the curve of the porcelain bowl, pings the silver lid. At the noise you say, "Don't touch it, honey."

She draws her finger back. "When can I?"

"Not yet."

She has blond hair like yours but longer. She wears matching cotton shirt-and-shorts sets in red and blue, ordered from a catalogue. She has thin brown legs and is barefoot. Her eyes are pale blue, like your eyes, like the blanket on the bed. For a child she looks at things for a long time. These days her attention span is longer than yours.

Sometimes she waits for you to finish eating then takes the tray with her. Other times she gets impatient or embarrassed or angry, and goes away abruptly while you are still picking at your food.

The tray she leaves behind is metal. You decorated it once with little bits of colored tissue paper glued down into a collage. You arrange the cutlery carefully on the plate, and if the glass is empty you tip it onto its side. Then you slowly lift the tray up and over your body and set it down on the vast plain of the rest of the bed.

You do not sleep much during the day. Most of the time you lie with your eyes closed, but your face twitches and your limbs shift slightly and it is clear that you are not asleep.

At night you sleep more.

Occasionally at night I reach over and pinch your arm. Then your eyes snap wide open and you stare up at the ceiling. After a while you turn on the light, pick up the book and glance at pages 46 and 47, take a sip of water. You do not sleep for the rest of the night.

I was introduced to you some time ago. You were preoccupied with a virus. I saw my chance and slipped in.

She knows your room well. She has opened all five drawers of your bureau and rifled through the clothes inside. Her favorite drawer is the scarf drawer. The silk scarves smell faintly of the perfume you had on the last time you wore them. From the closet she has dug out old pairs of high heels you had forgotten you owned. She has crawled under your bed and found pennies and marbles among the dust mice.

She gazes at herself in the full-length mirror, an outline filled in with one dark shade, until she pulls open a curtain a few inches and colors splash all over her body.

"I have scabs on *both* knees," she announces.

"Close the curtain, honey."

With a flick of her wrist she jerks the curtain closed and stands for a moment holding the cloth in a tight fist.

She never comes into this corner.

Once she opens your door when it is not meal time.

"Mommy?"

"Yes, honey."

"Are you awake?"

You do not answer until I reach over and tug a corner of the sheet.

"I think so."

She steps inside, closes the door, and sits on the edge of the bed where she usually puts the tray.

There is a pause.

"Are you mad at me?"

"No."

She looks down at her toes, rubs one foot against the other. She glances quickly at you and then looks down again.

"When are you coming downstairs?"

"I don't know, honey. Maybe in a few days."

You close your eyes. She looks at your face and her jaw tightens, as if she is clenching her teeth hard. She slaps the bed with the palms of her hands and jumps to her feet. She swings open the door quickly, slips through, and pulls it hard behind her, only to stop it suddenly before it slams, and to click it softly closed.

Another time she comes in with a bunch of red geraniums you planted in the back yard the year before. She has not used gardening clippers or a knife to cut them; she has pulled or broken them off with her hands, and the roots still dangle from some of the stalks. She stands looking at you and shakes the flowers so that a few petals float to the floor.

"Look, Mommy."

You look.

I look.

The last time I visited your heart, it had grown larger. The muscular walls of the atrium and the ventricle had stretched three millimeters. It was becoming increasingly difficult for the muscles to contract, and the pumping action was weakening. Your blood was passing more slowly through your heart.

But your atrioventricular and aortic valves were still strong. They still sealed off the blood so that it did not surge with a murmur back into the chamber it had just left.

I am working on them.

She has begun to ask you about the bowl on the bureau at every meal. She wants to open it, but you always say no, it is not ready yet. It is tiring for you to say this, for she wants to argue with you, and these days you no longer have the capacity to combat a six-year-old's logic.

But today you say, "Bring it over to me."

She hops to the bureau, and you add, "Carefully." She lifts the bowl slowly down from the bureau and holds it to her chest, her arm curved around it. She places her small hand flat over the silver lid and brings the bowl to you. She sets it down on the bed next to the tray and grasps the knob in the center of the lid. She looks at you. You count "One, two, three" and she whisks the cover off. She gasps, and begins to laugh. "Bean sprouts! Bean sprouts!" she cries, waving the lid in one hand and dipping her other hand into the bowl, which seems to overflow with moist white shoots of life. You watch her laughing, stirring the bean sprouts, and you begin to smile. Finally you laugh too. This is a sound she has not heard for some time, and she laughs harder and harder with you until with a burst she throws the silver lid up into the air.

I watch it. It reaches the peak of its ascent and hovers for a second. As it turns slowly to begin its fall, it catches the one ray of light in the room and flashes it at me. I am, momentarily, blinded.

Mark Radcliffe

Giving Head

Mark Radcliffe was born in 1960 and lives in North London. He is perhaps the best footballer ever to do the MA course. *Giving Head* is an extract from his first novel.

A small room with old chairs and Dennis, and I am trying not to look at the clock. There are still some things I will not do in a session and looking at the clock is one of them. Yawning is another. This is an uninspiring place where people come and wait to leave. Almost full, with two well-worn red-cushioned chairs. They face each other like tired soldiers in a sterile war.

Dennis is a thin man. Wide-eyed and sexless, which is perhaps one of the things that drew me to him. A thick black untidy beard dominates his face and a thick relentless nihilism shades his words, his world. He speaks with a soft austerity. I can see no tension in his body but he is probably infested with it. I can see no violence, although he has a faded, half-hearted reputation. He is sheltered but not stupid. Aware of me as a woman but uninterested in my sex. If it affects him at all it is as an issue of stilted manners, nothing else. His voice is low and humming, monotonous and disinterested. He has the eyes of a man who, despite himself, knows his project. On the crudest of levels it may be the case that he understands also the projects of those around him.

"Do you see your symptoms in me?"

Rhetorical. Strategic. He emphasises the 'your' as though it is I who invented the language of his alleged disease. He pretends to seek out disdain. To expect me to despair of him. Yet it is me he talks to, in this small room, twice a week. Sometimes briefly, sometimes deeply, he talks. Dennis has not shared himself for a very long time. By his nature he spurns attention, yet there can be no doubt that attention is the drug of his choice. He honours me with his hopelessness. In return I jump through some hoops. That is our unspoken contract.

I have been on this ward for five months and have four weeks left. It is an orange-walled grey place. A place designed, seemingly, to ignore all natural light. It hides inside a large Victorian hospital that once housed 3,000 patients. There are 67 left. Only two wards remain open, both rehabilitation facilities — this one and the one next door. Together they form the annex. The rest of the hospital silently screams its decay. Sometimes, particularly in the evenings, you can hear rats upstairs. They are dancing in what used to be the acute wards. I don't know why. There is no music upstairs.

Dennis knows me. When I first came here he had not spoken to anyone — voluntarily — for a very long time. He went largely unnoticed despite the depletion in the ranks around him, unseen apart from the occasional badly-staged drama. As much to keep his bed secure as anything else, I suspect. I noticed him because I had to notice somebody. My overwhelming concern when I arrived was "how the hell am I going to get through this time?" As far as I could see there was nothing to be done short of razing the place to the ground. Worse still, there was clearly nothing to pretend to do. By the fourth day, I was desperate for a Dennis, a project.

At first I would just say hello. Later I started adding some conversation, some 'off the record' observation about my day: the illusion of equality is a powerful one here. He ignored me, of course. Once he screamed at me to fuck off. I carried on in the same vein, the same way, each day. Eventually he had to start talking back. When he did I kept it short, informal. He was checking me out. It was him who raised his 'problems', his depressions, his habits, his self-abuse. I listened and nodded.

"Maybe" I said sweetly, "It would be useful to talk about them."

I eased him in with milk and honey.

"What did you use to do that?"

He is showing me his arm. A grid of stale red lines pattern the skin between his shoulder and elbow. Dried blood. Perfectly ordered trails announcing his special needs and I think "not many veins there". In thinking it I realise how I feel today. I will have to be careful. Keep my disdain to myself or take it where it belongs.

"The blade from a pencil sharpener."

"Do you still have it?" Thinking, "Spare me this ritual." A silence means yes and is an invitation to coax the blade from him. A hoop. He gets to see me care right there in front of him, and if he enjoys it he can recreate the same theatre tomorrow, or the next day, or any day. I resent that. Perhaps I am a little tired of having to stroke men at the moment.

I need to dress up my disinterest. Lend it the language of concern (for that is the word given to my actions). My mind is elsewhere. He gives me the blade, he is clearly not set for that game today and I am relieved. It is tiny and blunt. He must have run out of paper clips. There is an embarrassed silence. It lasts maybe twenty seconds and I could have used a

longer one. Dennis speaks.
"Sorry."
"It's not my arm Dennis."
I hate it when they do that.

I have a lover and I love him. However, ours is a relationship that plays in the face of such things as love and so I keep it to myself and wait. He has beautiful hands and kind eyes which — quite irrationally — make me sometimes believe he can do me no harm. Still more beautiful is the point where his shoulder meets his chest. The place where I would rest my head and sleep, if I could, for a hundred years. I tell him this and he smiles. Men seem to perceive such things merely as aesthetics or semi-sexual flattery. Or worse, as something said when there is nothing else to say. I tell him because it is the difference between loving and fucking. It is the point I gather myself around. If I am to wait, I will wait there.

We will make love and his kind eyes become fixed. Travelling elsewhere, beyond me and now to him, just him, and wherever it is that I cannot go. When he is inside me I kiss his beautiful hands. I suck each of his fingers one by one. Concerned that they could be damaged on the journey. Sometimes I imagine them bruised and I lick them better like a cat licks her kittens. And then afterwards, I rest my head on his shoulder and I can smell us. I breathe in time with him, feel the echo of his pulse. I let him stroke my hair.

He is a gentle man. An honest and troubled man. So often the way these days, or so it seems. When he comes to me he wears his uncertainty with a shy and modern pride. Recently his life has changed but his fear and confusion have little to do with the reasons he describes. I can tell. I stroke him, one way or another, and he cries. And when he cries I don't quite believe him.

"Are you cross with me?"
"No Dennis. I am interested in the way it makes you feel. What do you feel when you look at the cuts?"

He shrugs. Dennis will never accede regret. Regret is a long and difficult path leading to the possibility of past volition. A responsibility for self that does not suit Dennis. His life is a series of events that occur on him. Collide like vindictive meteors. It is his special burden to withstand their random spite. Today Dennis as victim does not convince me. That may be my problem. Another short silence and then he speaks again.

"You seem distant today."

Unlike Dennis. Others might say such things. Invent an intimacy, a mutuality. It is something some people do in the face of their patientness. But it is out of character for Dennis and I am momentarily confused.

"Do I?"

He says nothing but glances up at me. For a moment his black eyes and broken shoulders appear to borrow some life, in passing, and then it is gone.

When I started working with people like Dennis I tried to imagine the terror of symptoms. Unattached voices that only they can hear, telling them how useless they are, how dirty, how they would be better off dead. If it wasn't voices it would be an unspoken communion with the television or the radio. Or feeling that their veins are full of insects. They try to scratch them out. If not a psychosis then a thick black depression. Treacle on the soul. I saw them every day. It was only a couple of months until watching people living these things became normal. I felt no terror, no sadness. Now, if anything makes me shudder it is looking into the eyes of those blinded by madness and seeing a flashing light of sanity. Like a drowning woman coming up for air. There is a woman on this ward about the same age as my mother. I have seen her exchange sex with dirty old men for biscuits. I did not like seeing that. It kept me awake at night. But I would rather that than the thought she might ever glimpse herself with the eyes she had before.

"Why did you cut yourself?"

"It makes me feel better."

"Is there no other way?"

"I don't need another way."

"Did you mean to harm yourself?"

"You mean kill myself."

"If you like."

"With the blade of a pencil sharpener?"

He is almost mocking. I am not at my best.

"How would you do it, Dennis?"

My eyes fix on him. For a moment I lend him the disdain he pretends to crave. Just long enough for him to know. He looks away. I expect him to cry or sulk or spit. Or maybe leave. I can see the muscles around his jaw tense. He is kneading his tongue with his teeth.

I met by chance a man who is becoming of increasing concern to me and I resent that. His name is Finn. I met him in a bar one night: he is a friend of a friend of my brother. He spent all evening talking earnestly at me. Telling me what he believed and who he was. Imagining that I was interested. Telling me who he had loved and who he had hated. The people he hated seemed far more significant to him. He told me about bad poetry and his favourite books, and invited me to read them. I did not like him but I was polite. I did not trust his eyes. Strobed in blue and burning. At first I thought he was trying to be friendly, then I thought he wanted to fuck me.

Giving Head

By the end of the evening I think he wanted to put me in his pocket, take me home and keep me in a box beside his bed. He asked me for my phone number, and I explained gently I had a boyfriend. I would not normally do that but he was unnerving. I wanted to make the message clear and simple. He started acting strangely and of course I wondered, albeit briefly, if I had done something wrong. Led him on. Then I thought "Sod him."

Two days later, when I got to work, there was a package for me. It contained a pair of gold earrings and a card saying simply "Love, Finn." That evening he phoned me. I have no idea how he got my number. He spoke with a familiarity that was neither earned or desired. I told him not to phone me again. I told him I would return the earrings. He was piggish and indignant. He hung up. The following day, however, he was outside the hospital when I left work.

"I know the date of my death. I have planned it. It will happen after you have left the ward." Dennis is speaking calmly. Challenging.

"Go on."

"I will go to the station on June the thirtieth. I will wait for the Intercity express. I can see it from the bridge. By 6:35 there are no staff left there. I will go under that train. Quick and painless."

And unequivocal.

"It sounds as though it's something you've given a lot of thought to."

"Does it?"

I do not reply.

"I am not telling you so you will stop me. I am telling you because you asked me to be honest and I said I would. You called it a contract. I am honouring that contract.

Of course he isn't. It is something even more insidious than honour.

My lover is called Black. Our sex is good. I turn him on when he holds me and the smell of me makes him hard. That is something that can't be faked and without it there is every chance he would be gone in the morning, any morning. It is the smell of me that designs his uncertainty. His cock is sure. It serves to convince. Most of the time the rest of him is screaming for the door.

I understand his honour but I smile at the way it manifests itself. When I was a little girl I heard stories of shining knights on white horses and was struck even then by the absurdity of waiting to be rescued. By the time I was a teenager I understood the fatal flaw. In order to be rescued one needed to design oneself as implicitly needy. What a waste of time. Shining knights are not invented by women. They are in the imaginings of men. Every man wants to be a hero. God alone knows why.

As for Black, he has his limits and they are simple. He will not ejaculate into my mouth until he has told me he loves me. He will never tell me he loves me ergo he will never ejaculate into my mouth. Thus he is a man of honour. Men these days have rules. Sometimes arbitrary, sometimes cosmetic, but rules all the same. He can assume my love. There is no theatre. But he can demonstrate his care for me, his deep and honourable concern, with his cock in my mouth.

I dreamt of him last night. He was in my bed and my head was between his legs. I moved to take him in and found short blonde hairs nestling around his cock. My hair is long and black. His past is short and blonde. Modern convention would have it that I thus remove his cock. I didn't, I picked at his pubic hair like a nit nurse.

"Why June the thirtieth?"
"It's the anniversary of Mum's death."
"Do you believe you are going to see her again."
"Not really." He is looking at me as if I have just said something ridiculous. I have no idea why I asked him that.
"It is a violent death Dennis."
"I want to be sure."
"Do you picture it in your mind."
"Yes."
"What do you see when the train hits you?"
There is a pause. He is looking at the ground and playing with his beard.
"Relief."
His words are disposable but his spirit is not. He may be serious: I have never heard this from him before. I am giving bad head.
"How are you eating?"
"Same as always."
"Sleeping?"
"Same as always."
"Do you imagine your mood changing at all?"
"What mood?"
"The mood you are in now."
"I think my moods are pretty consistent. I'm not depressed."
Probably not.
"Can you say why you want to die?"
"I have considered my options and that is my preferred choice."
Sarcastic. If Dennis were capable of smiling, which he isn't, he would smile now.
The problem with this job is once you have done it, it taints everything you see, everything you do and think. I listen to Dennis, watch his eyes, his body

and I am supposed to know. I must tell the difference between a thousand false screams and the real. I am trained and aware and it is for me to know and invariably I do; I see things that others don't, often ugly things. I can read a lie, a paradox, an unsure eye from a hundred yards. But today it is I who am unsure, an uncertainty compounded perhaps by a lack of concern.

Dennis is no fool. I would expect this type of hysteria from others but it is not quite his style. I think the part of him that cuts and rages and sulks and occasionally shouts bores even him. He has run the gauntlet of psychiatry, and whilst it is proposed that the quality of his life is going to get better (rumour has it he will get his own room soon) he clearly remains unconvinced.

One of the things I like about Dennis is that his posed cynicism and apparent misanthropy is nearly universal. He dislikes everybody equally. I can't be sure but the last time I looked that was not an illness.

He punched an agency nurse once. She told him to get up for breakfast and he said no. After several attempts, in exasperation, she pulled the covers off him. He got out of bed and tried to snatch them back. The stupid bitch kept hold of them and apparently told him that now he was up he might as well stay up. She may have smiled. He punched her straight in the mouth, knocking out two of her teeth and cutting her lip to the tune of four stitches. She threatened to press charges for a while but didn't follow it through. Dennis as a result was poured through the sieve of psychiatry. Consultants, psychologists, nurse specialists and several medical students. He was forced on to occupational therapy programmes. Cajoled, manipulated, insulted and patronised. I would have thrown him out of the hospital that morning and sacked the nurse but such things are easier from a distance.

"You know I will have to talk to the Doctors about what you have told me."

"Yes, but I would rather you didn't."

"That's impossible."

"I know, I'm just saying."

Another silence and then:

"No matter who you tell, nothing will stop me. Eventually I will do it. The only thing that may change is the day, and under the circumstances that would be spiteful."

"I don't want you to kill yourself, Dennis."

"Why not?"

I don't know, I may be tired, but I'm really not sure what of.

Last night Finn was at the gates of the hospital when I left work. The third time in the last five days. When I wonder what makes a mind like that it is not in a professional capacity. It is as a woman. He just stands there in the shadows. Not tall, not speaking, just staring. It has got to the point where I dread leaving work when it is dark. I am afraid of waiting for a bus alone. What's worse is that he is there in my head. I have no space for him but from the time I get here to the time I leave he is there, and that makes me so angry. I did not invite him. Does he imagine I am going to talk to him? Take to him? Shout at him?

"I've seen it in my dreams."
"Seen what in your dreams?"
"My dying."
"Tell me."
"Sometimes I lie awake and think about it. I think very hard and it relaxes me, eases my preoccupations. Puts me to sleep. And then when I am asleep I dream and I have not dreamt for a very long time."
"Can you describe the dreams?"
"It's always the same. A sunny day. People are in summer clothes. Before I go to the bridge I walk in the park and everyone is looking at me. Some children call me names and I think about chasing them but I don't. I go to the station, a perfect summer evening, no people around and the birds are singing. I see the train coming but it is silent. It gets closer and all I can hear is the birds singing. It's fast but in slow motion. There is smoke coming from the train even though it is a modern electric express. The birds get louder. When it is quite close I just lean forward. I don't climb the wall on the bridge, I don't jump. I just lean over and let myself go. I wake up as the train hits me."
"Do you think that is a realistic dream?"
"It's a comforting dream."
He falls silent and I think that there may be something to work on.

Black has nightmares sometimes. He will wake me with a dry monotone mumbling. Little quiet noises like a muffled dog. They get louder and louder and I try to wake him but always fail. Too gentle. He lets out a scream and wakes himself. Wide-eyed and afraid. Unsure momentarily of where he is or who he is with. I put my arms around his head, stroke him, whisper and soothe as if he were a child. He does not speak. Curls up with his head on my breast, goes back to sleep. I lay awake for a long time. I keep guard. I think I could be anybody to him but I would not change places with anyone in the world. Sometimes I talk quietly, about my day, about what I think, anything really. Sometimes I even cry, but of course he doesn't know.

"I don't know what to say."
He glances at me. Catches my eye. Perhaps unimpressed.
"To be honest, I'm not sure how to help and I want to."

I hope he is more convinced than I am.

"I don't need or want any help. I just don't want any interference either."

"That would be wrong."

Another glance. I am really losing it here. This is like trying to run in your dreams. I am getting nowhere. I am tired inside but that is no excuse. I imagine Dennis' dream but instead of Dennis I see Finn. Perhaps he could dedicate his death to me. An act of love or poetry. I close my eyes for a moment and hide from the thought. People keep doing things near me.

"If I said nothing, if I told no-one of your plans, I would be helping you to die. I have a responsibility, Dennis."

I have several. And this I know. This I believe.

Dennis sits with his legs crossed. His right leg tightly twisting back around and up his left calf. From time to time his body rocks gently. Otherwise his position is mostly fixed. There is occasional quick movement, rearrangement of a discomforting body.

If this were theatre I would feel miscast. I may be the paper the play is written on. The door to the playhouse. I would be understudy to Black's heroine. Victim of Finn's decay. Fumbling director of Dennis' soliloquy. But I feel like the audience, and if nothing good happens I'm sure that's my fault. Despite all my gestures of encouragement, my stage setting, I am in the way of the performance. A few acts in and I have lost my lines. Unconvincing actresses are rarely rewarded. However I am more unconvinced than unconvincing.

"What's for dinner?"

"What?"

"What's for dinner?"

"I don't know."

"Who's working this afternoon?"

"I'm not sure."

Another silence. There is a code of practice for all things. This is far from being an exception.

"How do I know what you are saying is not symptomatic of illness?"

"What?"

"How do I know you are not ill?"

He doesn't answer, but shuffles very slightly in his seat.

"If you are ill, if what you show me are symptoms, it is clear I have to act. In fact, to be honest, the mere fact of you telling me suggests an exhibition of symptoms." If in doubt, be callous. Seldom fails.

"I am telling you because you asked. I am not ill, I know the difference. I may have hospital sickness. Not wanting to live is not an illness."

"It is here."

"What?"

253

Mark Radcliffe

I say nothing. My eyes are set on his. Cold. I use what I have, wherever it comes from. His face clenches, unclenches, clenches, unclenches. It crosses my mind that perhaps I should be near the door. Mine appears to be a reckless nature and I am surprised.

"I mean look at it from my point of view. You show me your arm again. We have been talking here for months and now you announce your intention to die. And I listen..."

"Because it's your job." Now who's losing it. Dennis is being petulant!

"Right, because it's my job."

He is quiet.

"Do you want to die?"

"Yes."

"Do you want us to talk about it?"

"There's nothing to say." Such brittle defiance.

"So go ahead and do it."(I can't say that!)

"I will." I am glad no one is listening. I am tapping my foot. My fist is clenched. Fuck this.

I have not told Black about Finn. I wanted to, but I did not want to see him struggle to invent a concern. He would have stumbled toward a role of simple saviour. Out of duty. Guilt and sex and things. I do not want a saviour, a hero. I would have liked him to be a friend — listen, let me know that what I feel is all right even though I already know it. I won't take the risk of telling him. I think I will hold on to the faint possibility that he might just have surprised me.

"If you really want to die, and I say this off the record and in an effort to be honest. To honour our contract, keep it to yourself."

"Oh do you believe that if I talk about it I won't do it?"

"No, certainly not."

He looks at me blankly and speaks again, even quieter than usual.

"My mum isn't dead. I didn't mean to lie, I just exaggerated."

"And what about the rest?"

"The rest is true."

And it occurs to me that he will do it